LOVE NEVER FAILS

CROSSROADS BOOK THREE

JENNY CARLISLE

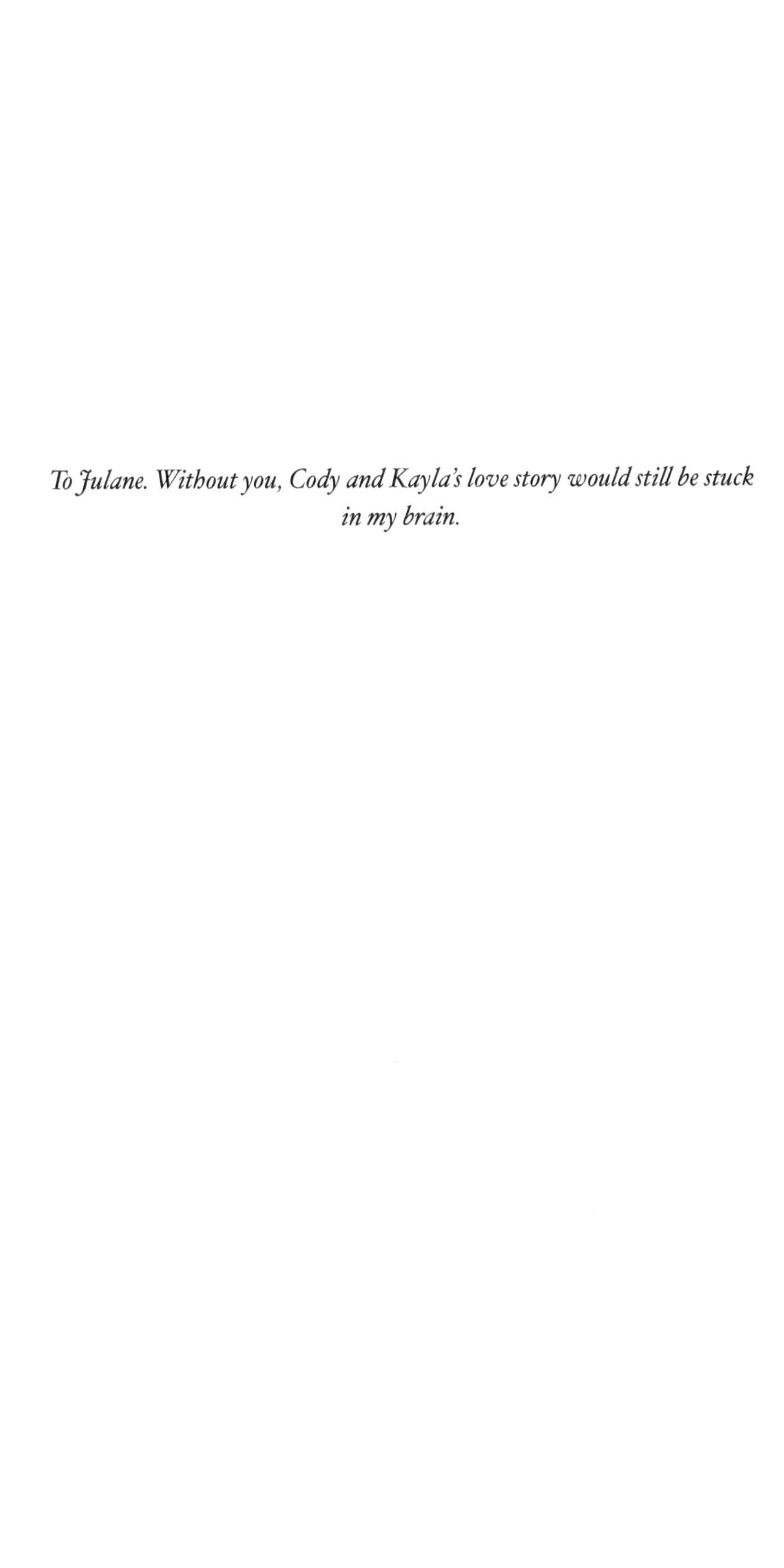

To Julane. Without you, Cody and Kayla's love story would still be stuck in my brain.

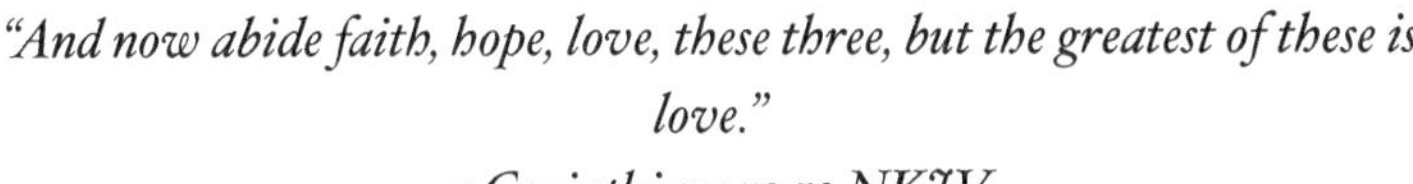

"And now abide faith, hope, love, these three, but the greatest of these is love."
~1 Corinthians 13:13 NKJV

Chapter One

Kayla Caldwell was surrounded by family, but all alone. The soft music playing through the arena's speakers would be easily drowned out if she shouted what she was thinking. *Why, God? Mom and Dad deserved their quick trip to Vegas. I told them I would be fine here on my own. I lied! I'm not fine. That plane was not supposed to crash.*

Granny Caldwell grabbed her left hand, and Zanna Pruitt her right.

Lights dimmed, and a couple mounted on Mom and Dad's horses brought in the American and Arkansas flags. The crowd stood in response until the flags were posted on either side of the stage in the arena's center.

"Please be seated." Her uncle, Smiley Caldwell, stood behind a lectern on the stage. Their neighbor, Felecia Billings's, oil painting sat propped in front of the lectern. The figures of a man and a woman on horseback riding into the sunset were spotlighted.

"I must start with a confession," Uncle Smiley said. "Although I have been preaching funerals for over twenty years, I was not looking forward to this service today. Losing my brother and my sister-in-law seemed so unfair. I felt the Lord was piling misery upon misery. But then, my niece, Kayla, set me straight. She didn't ask too much of me. She just wants me to continue the task God has set before me. That includes helping take over the role of parent and guardian for her and to bring God's comfort to grieving people.

"I can do that, because of the promise Jesus made, recorded in the Gospel of John. He said, 'In my Father's house are many mansions; if it were not so, I would have told you. I go to prepare a place for you. And if I go and prepare a place for you, I will come again, and receive you unto myself; that where I am, there you may be also. And whither I go, you know, and the way you know.' I believe with my whole heart that He has gone ahead to prepare a place for us, for me, for you, for Dub, and for Tina. Now, please join me in prayer."

He could pray—that was his job. Instead, Kayla's mind went back to the conversation he had mentioned. During a late May rainstorm on the way back from Little Rock, Uncle Smiley took her to the site of the awful crash. *To provide closure*, he said. Maybe for him.

Kayla had stared at a pile of debris several yards down the hillside below their truck. She didn't know enough about airplanes to identify what she saw. The remains resembled a metal building after a tornado. Twisted, mangled, unrecognizable. A black stain covered everything. Evidence there had been at least a small fire. She couldn't help shuddering as she thought of what the four bodies must have looked like when the first responders arrived.

"Amen." Uncle Smiley brought his prayer to a close.

Two more speakers stepped forward, adding brief remembrances. Her cousin Junior started a projector in front of the stage. The memorial video Junior and his friend Cody Billings had created filled the large screen.

Kayla looked around at the crowd, mostly dabbing their eyes with tissues. She should be thankful so many people loved her. But, right now, she felt as if she was drifting in the air, like a balloon that had just been accidentally released. Floating aimlessly, with no idea when she'd feel grounded again.

Cody held his breath as the music began. *Please, Lord. Use this video for your glory.*

As the images faded in and out, Cody remembered the pictures he hadn't chosen. So many included a smiling Kayla between her parents. Pictures of Dub and Tina working at the rodeo, or on the ranch. Pictures of holidays with the rest of the Caldwell and Pruitt families. Pictures of each of them as children and young teens before they came together. But Cody had been drawn to the photos of the family of three. He'd gone back more than once to weed out some of those. Today was not just about Kayla, but he could see how much they all meant to each other.

Comments from kids at school haunted him. Had he done enough to dispel the image they held of the "spoiled" rich kid? Yes, Kayla's parents had plenty of money. Since she was an only child, there had been no reason to withhold material things from her. But she hadn't acted like a total brat. Many others with multiple siblings were more guilty of that.

Instead, he had nursed an impossible crush on her for a couple of years now. Since she was a year older, he'd never gathered enough courage to follow through. Then, his bull wreck brought everything to a halt.

He turned around just before the last few frames to see how she was reacting. Thankfully, instead of making her dissolve in tears, the video brought a smile to her face. Others might appreciate his efforts, too, but more than anything he wanted to reach out to Kayla with this production.

She caught his glance and smiled. His cheeks warmed before he faced the front for the final slide. *Okay, Lord. Thanks for the help. I think this was a success.*

Kayla returned handshakes and hugs as well-wishers filed past. The faces were nothing more than blurs. Words all sounded so hollow. As the last person in the line greeted Granny Caldwell on her left, she stepped forward to stand next to her Grandpa Pruitt, called Coach. Since he had graduated from a wheelchair to a walker, he would need a good break in the traffic before venturing to the ramp leading to the exit.

"Hey, Kayla." Cody's deep voice rang out as he rolled up in his wheelchair. "You makin' it okay?"

"Yeah. I think so. Just glad this is over with." She stepped to Coach's left and patted Cody's shoulder. "That video was perfect. How did you get the songs to fit so well with the pictures?"

"I enjoy that sort of thing." He moved closer as Coach walked toward the exit. "One of my high school teachers showed a video I did to the journalism teacher at Crossroads, and he told me I should take television production classes in college."

"I agree. Or maybe even movies," Kayla said. "You have a real talent."

"I just don't think I'd want to be still that long every day, staring at a screen." Cody moved forward behind Coach.

A hug from behind spun her around.

"I think we're headed home, sweetie."

"Okay." Kayla gestured toward Cody. "This is my grandmother, Suzanna Pruitt. All of us kids call her Zanna. Zanna, this is Cody Billings."

Zanna stepped up beside Cody's wheelchair. "Are you the young man who created that video? It was marvelous."

"Yes, ma'am. I am so sorry for your loss." Cody shook Zanna's hand.

"I wish there was a way to show it at the burial service tomorrow," Zanna said. "But I don't think it would work at the cemetery."

"I could make a copy for y'all," Cody said. "Then, you can watch it again anytime."

"Great idea." Kayla walked behind the two of them. "If you email it to me, I'll download it for Zanna and Coach while I'm at their house. I'm staying with them for a few days after the service tomorrow."

"Will do! See you soon." Cody headed down the ramp.

Kayla stood alone at the bottom of the bleachers. If only she could skip the burial service tomorrow. Today's service had been the perfect way to remember Mom and Dad. Tomorrow would be more of the same, with Zanna and Coach's church friends. Other than cousins, few people her own age would attend. She sighed.

The video Cody produced had been impressive. How could someone she barely talked to understand her family so well? It would be wonderful if he came to the next service. Why would he travel so far to attend services for people who were not part of his family? A depressing day now seemed even drearier.

Uncle Smiley waited at the bottom of the ramp with her cousin Faith. Kayla's stomach churned as she pictured the spread of casseroles that waited for them back at his house. Why was it hard to be grateful for the people caring for her? Right now, she just wanted to retreat to the barn, maybe take Sissy for a ride. *Lord, help me paste that smile on for just a little longer. Amen.*

"Thanks for riding with me to Coach and Zanna's." Kayla checked her right mirror before exiting the freeway the next morning. "I want to have my truck at their house this week."

"No problem." Faith replaced her bottle of water in the cup holder. "Be sure to text me if you've forgotten anything you wanted to take to Fort Smith. I probably have most anything you would want to borrow."

"You're the best. I guess it was a little crazy to try to go straight to the pageant without going back home. I would just go today, if I could."

"I know." Faith patted her leg. "Funerals are tough. I think it helps other people more than it helps the family. But it's good to get them over with."

Kayla passed familiar landmarks—neighbor's mailboxes, signs advertising insurance agencies and farm implements. Finally, the dirt road she was looking for. "You've never been up here, have you?"

"What is that?" Faith peered up through the truck's windshield.

"A shoe tree." Kayla stopped the truck under the sprawling oak with old tennis shoes hanging from its limbs. "I don't even think about it anymore. When I see it, I know where to turn."

Faith stepped out of the passenger side and stared upward.

"I have never in my life ..."

"Well then, you haven't lived." Kayla shouted from the open driver's side. "Those are my worn-out high-tops, way up there." She pointed. "I tried tossing them three times, so my oldest cousin Jeremy did it for me."

"Why?" Faith was still giggling as she seated herself in the truck and closed the door.

"I asked Coach that question once. All he would say is 'Why not?'" Kayla continued driving down the dirt road.

"I guess that's the best answer."

Kayla took a deep breath and blew it out. Mom's childhood canvas shoes still swung from a top branch of that tree. If she pointed them out to Faith, she would undoubtedly break down.

Her hair tickled her forehead as the breeze from the open window blew it in all directions. On childhood trips to 'Zanna Camp' without her parents, she'd escaped the rules and just enjoyed being herself. Maybe this dusty back road would ease her heart.

"Here we are." She turned next to the mailbox labeled Pruitt and approached the house from behind. Paved walkways between the outbuildings marked the adjustments made since Coach's accident that happened when she was just a small girl. The paths were perfect when he used a wheelchair, and now his walker.

"What a great house," Faith said as they stopped near the double garage.

"Come around front. You can see the freeway." Kayla's boots hit the blacktop before she led the way to the front porch.

"You know, I think I've noticed this house. So pretty, sitting up here in the trees, far away from the traffic." Faith stood with her back to the porch. "I always wondered where the driveway was hidden."

"Now you know." Kayla ran toward the front porch.

"Hi, sweetheart!" Zanna walked down the ramp to meet them. "Glad y'all made it a little early. The ladies at church have covered me up with cinnamon rolls. Can you two help me out?"

"Of course." Kayla wrapped Zanna in a hug, then stepped out of the way so Faith could collect her greeting.

"Where's Coach?" Kayla started up the ramp.

"Right behind her, as usual." The screen door slapped closed as Coach emerged onto the porch with the aid of his cane.

Kayla bent to hug him. She inhaled the scent of butterscotch and aftershave that was distinctly Coach.

Inside, subdued chatter from the kitchen greeted her as Pruitt uncles, aunts, and cousins finished their breakfast.

"Hi, Kayla!" The chorus of voices fit perfectly in this place.

"Hi, guys. This is Faith, one of my Caldwell cousins." She turned, waving her arm toward the front door.

Her aunt brought a freshly warmed cinnamon roll on a plate and hugged Kayla's shoulders. "I don't want to rush you, but we're expected at the cemetery in thirty minutes." Her calm whisper held a touch of urgency.

"I know. Thanks." She sank her teeth into the delicate sweetness. Hopefully, this wouldn't be the wrong thing to eat with a nervous stomach.

"I think I'll skip the cinnamon roll." Faith stopped behind her. "Kayla, can you show me where to freshen up? I'm sure my makeup is a pure disaster."

Cody added his own "Amen" to the minister's prayer. Those who had been sitting in the family tent stood to form a line and walked past the closed caskets.

A gravel path led from where he sat to the back row of chairs. He could most likely navigate that. Someone would probably give him a push to the front so he could shake hands. Under the canopy, there was room next to the folding chairs. He hesitated. Back-fence neighbors weren't really family.

When Junior had suggested they go to a local sporting goods store after the service, Cody offered to drive. His buddy probably needed him to add some diversion from the sadness. That's what friends did.

Kayla stood and left the front row even before the last mourner. She took two quick steps across the grass.

"Hi." She stopped just to Cody's left. "I just couldn't take it anymore. I know it's rude, but I've had enough." She folded her hands across her stomach.

"Hey. You don't have to sit there any longer than you want to. Today is about you, not them." He wasn't sure where those exact words had come from, but he certainly meant every one of them. "If you want to go for a walk, I'll go with you." He turned his chair around, facing away from the people gathered under the canopy.

"Thanks." She walked beside him as they passed behind the vehicles parked in the paved lot. "I don't know why I'm uncomfortable. It was nice and shady under the canopy. I appreciated what the minister said, the songs were great. I needed the prayers. But ... I just didn't want to hear one more 'I'm so sorry.' Does that make sense?"

"Of course, it does." Cody stopped and turned toward her. "I've heard it an awful lot myself after my accident. You just have to realize that people don't know what to say. 'I'm sorry' is a lot better than some other things. In my case, the one that didn't work was 'look on the bright side.'"

"What? Why would anyone say that?" Kayla held her hand over her mouth.

"I guess they meant, 'at least you're not dead' or 'at least you can move your arms.'" Cody shrugged. "I had a lot of forgiving to do when folks struggled to find something to say."

"Yeah. I'm glad so many are here. Mom and Dad would be impressed and pleased with the services, both yesterday and today." She took a few halting steps before stopping. "Thanks for being here, Cody."

"No problem. I'll miss your mom and dad too." He rolled along, staying a half step ahead of her.

"Are you in a rush to go home?" Kayla stopped just before the pavement ran out.

"Not really." He and Junior could go to that sporting goods store anytime.

"I'd love for you to come out to Coach and Zanna's. I know he'd like to show you his gardens. When we leave, just follow that black car over there. You'll love their place." She walked toward the tent, where outstretched arms greeted her with more 'I'm sorries.' Cody hoped she could handle them a little better now.

"You ready to go?" Junior approached from his other side.

"Actually, Kayla invited me to her grandparents' house." Cody sat beside his own truck. "You want to come out there?"

"Nah. I'll just ride with Hope and O.D. Dad's got Granny and Grandpa with him." Junior waved at his sister, signaling her to wait. "I guess Kayla's glad you came today."

Cody blushed.

Junior smiled. "I'm glad too. You're good to have around now and then. I'll see you back at home, buddy."

Cody hadn't expected to be invited home with Kayla's family after this service. Would he feel out of place?

He hoisted himself into his truck. Dad's suggestion for a smaller pickup made sense now. After learning to use the hand controls, this model suited him just as well as the monster he'd driven before.

After the loading device in the truck bed retrieved his chair and secured it, he waited to follow the family car. Wouldn't Kayla be tired and ready to rest after the past two days? Maybe he wouldn't stay long. It was nice to be asked, though. Hopefully, he'd remember not to say "I'm sorry."

Chapter Two

Kayla hit "send" on a quick text to Cody before the family limousine left the cemetery.

> I'm not sure what the GPS will say. Turn between Phillips 66 and Toot and Moo. Follow the dirt road and turn left at the shoe tree.

She watched as he looked down at his phone, then waved. Even from here she could see the smile on his face. Why was she not ready for him to go home? Inviting him to join the family after the service just seemed natural. Would he be uncomfortable and embarrassed?

Everyone in the car stared out a window as they traveled the rough road to Coach and Zanna's house. Kayla was not surprised at the lack of conversation. There wasn't much left to say.

"Everyone's coming inside, right?" Coach turned around from the seat next to the driver. "The ladies of our church have been cooking for a couple of days."

"We wouldn't want to turn down their hospitality." Uncle Smiley squeezed her hand.

"I can't stay long." Faith spoke up from Kayla's other side. "John K. will be leaving for work soon, and I won't see him again until Saturday night at the rodeo."

"That's right. Our two princesses are making an appearance this weekend." Granny leaned forward to touch her shoulder.

"Kayla is the only one with any official duties. I'm just a tagalong." Faith winked.

"Couldn't do it without you." Kayla leaned against Faith's shoulder.

The driver stopped near the end of the ramp leading to the front porch and jumped out to open the limo doors.

"We made it through, Kayla Grace." Uncle Smiley whispered in her ear as they exited the car.

"One step at a time." Kayla hugged him and noticed Cody's truck pulling up nearby. "I invited Cody Billings to join us. I hope that's okay."

"I'm sure it's fine. Your grandpa said there would be plenty of food." He walked with her to the driver's side of Cody's truck. "Good to see you, young man." He reached to shake Cody's hand.

"You, too, sir."

"Come on in. We'll grab a plate of food and come back outside." Kayla pointed at the large tables overlooking the front yard.

Several vehicles filled the small parking area, and family members surrounded them, greeting each other quietly.

Zanna followed Coach up the ramp.

"Your directions were perfect." Cody waited at the bottom of the ramp. "The GPS didn't say anything about Toot and Moo or a shoe tree."

"I guess that did sound kind of strange. I don't give them a second thought." Kayla fidgeted with the clutch bag she'd brought to hold tissues. "I'm more at home here than at my own house."

"It's a great place." Cody turned toward the long hillside leading down to the freeway. "Terrific view."

"You should see the back side of the property." She pointed behind the barn. "That actually looks down to the river."

"I love being close to the water. I'd love to see that sometime." He moved ahead up the ramp, and she followed.

"Come on, Kayla." Her cousin Jeremy held the screen door open as they entered the house. "Ms. Ellen brought her chocolate pie. It may already be gone."

"An older version of Junior Caldwell." Cody laughed.

"Yep. It's always all about dessert." Kayla found each of them a plate. "But that pie really is special. Ms. Ellen is Zanna's best friend. You'll meet her, I'm sure."

In no time, their plates were full. Kayla followed Cody past Uncle Smiley, who seated himself in a living room chair next to Coach. "Kayla has inherited one of the biggest operations in Big River county. I'm super grateful that Rod and Nancy Hernandez are there to keep things running."

Kayla balanced both her and Cody's plates as they headed down the ramp to the picnic table. Luckily, the trees in the yard protected them from the Arkansas sun.

She'd never thought about how big her parents' ranch was. Especially since Dad had stopped supplying stock for the Crossroads rodeo and sold several acres. Would Rod and Nancy start coming to her for decisions about the business now? How involved would Uncle Smiley be?

"You okay?" Cody's nose wrinkled with concern as she set their plates on the table.

"Yeah." She tried to paste on her smile again. "Thanks again for being here."

"No problem." He handed her a rolled napkin that contained her silverware. "Your mom's side of the family is big, but they all seem nice."

"Between these cousins and my Caldwell cousins, I had lots

of fun, even as an only child." Kayla left the bundle of silverware beside her plate. "I know one thing, though. If I ever have kids, there will be more than one."

"There are pluses and minuses. I've been the only one since my two brothers got married." He picked up a yeast roll. "Sometimes, I get too much attention at home." His face dropped. "That probably sounds like a stupid thing to say."

"No, I understand." Kayla fiddled with her napkin. "I'm sure there will be lonely times, but I haven't had much time to miss the attention from my parents yet."

"What are you two drinking?" Zanna's friend Ellen walked up with a tray full of glasses, a pitcher of tea and one of lemonade.

"Lemonade for me." Kayla stood to help steady the tray as Ellen poured. "Ellen Withers, this is my friend Cody from Crossroads."

"Pleased to meet you, ma'am. And Lemonade sounds great." Cody held his hand out. Ellen placed a cold glass in it.

"You're very welcome." Ellen nodded at Cody, and then whispered in Kayla's ear. "I sent your Zanna to her room. She is awfully tired. You might go check on her in a minute."

Kayla nodded. She hoped that staying here for a few days wouldn't be a strain on Zanna. She had enough to do keeping this place running.

Before they'd finished eating, her grandpa and Cody were locked in conversation. She collected Cody's plate and carried it inside with hers as the two men traveled down the paved pathways leading to each of Coach's current projects.

The dim light of the living area caused her to blink. Now that the memorial services were over, a new set of problems loomed. Would she be expected to take on the running of a ranch along with checking on her grandparents? What would happen when it was time to go back to Fayetteville for school? Maybe, instead of traveling to Fort Smith and other rodeos in the next few weeks, she should stick closer to home. It was all too much to think about. She blinked back tears. If only she could ask Mom and Dad what to do.

Kayla pushed the bedroom door open. "How you doing, Zanna?" Zanna sat on the side of the chenille-covered bed, slipping off her shoes.

"Oh, I'm okay. Come sit with me, sweetie." Zanna patted the bedspread next to her. "I guess Ms. Ellen sent you to check on me."

"She's a good friend." Kayla linked elbows with her grandma.

"Yes ma'am. We're fortunate to have her." Zanna turned to face her. "And it looks like you're making a new friend too. Young Mr. Billings, isn't it?"

"I've known him I guess my whole life. He and his brothers live behind Uncle Smiley, on the other side of the hill, but he was a grade behind me in school, so we didn't spend much time together." Kayla's cheeks warmed. She hadn't stopped to think about how things seemed to be changing between her and Cody. Apparently, other people were noticing.

"You need to go back and make him feel welcome. You and Ms. Ellen both know it only takes me a few minutes of being still to recharge my batteries." Zanna moved over on the bed, stretching her stockinged feet out while she reclined on the pile of throw pillows.

"I think Coach is showing him around his gardens." Kayla tucked a light blanket over her grandma. "I'll see you soon." She leaned over to kiss Zanna's forehead.

From the front porch, she saw Coach and Cody buzzing around the paved pathways in the side yard. Helping Coach plan his garden had inspired her to make things easier for folks who needed help walking.

"Did you tell me your new fella was a rancher?" Coach asked as they stopped in front of her.

Cody blinked.

"Uh ..." Cody hesitated.

"Cody's a friend from the ranch behind ours." Kayla blushed. Just like Coach to jump to conclusions.

"And certainly not the rancher Kayla's dad was," Cody said.

"That's more animals than I want to put up with," Coach said. "I'll stick with my vegetables any day."

"Thanks for showing me around, Mr. Pruitt." Cody reached to shake Coach's hand. "I guess it's time for me to head back to Big River County."

"It was a pleasure, son. Come back and see us again." Coach patted Cody's shoulder.

"I'll walk you to your truck." Kayla followed as Cody headed to the other side of the driveway. It would take him a while to reach his home, but she wasn't excited about saying goodbye.

"Thanks for inviting me over." Cody stopped behind his truck. "I'm sure your family wants to spend more time with you tonight."

"Yeah, I guess." Kayla stood with her hands folded in front of her. "Sorry about Coach's comment."

"Hey. I've been called worse than 'new fella.'" Cody reached up to grab the loader in the bed of his truck. "I'll see you at the rodeo in Fort Smith, this weekend."

"You'll be there to watch your brother in the tie-down competition, right?" She moved closer to him.

"Yep. I hope he and his horse are ready for this. They've been to a few smaller rodeos, but this is a pretty big deal."

"I'll be busy at the pageant. Hopefully, I won't have a lot to do at the rodeo after the grand entry. I'll try to find you." Kayla bit her lip. She would have to start giving the pageant more thought soon. Getting these two memorial services behind her had occupied all her time for days. She could have easily opted out of crowning the new queen for Rodeo Arkansas Teen, but participating might bring her closer to normal.

"This year's winner will have some big boots to fill," Cody said.

"Not that big ..." Kayla lifted one of her feet in front of her.

"You know what I mean. We were all proud when you won last year." His cheeks turned a funny shade of pink.

"Thanks. I've enjoyed it. I'm just glad Faith is still around to help me with this pageant and the summer appearances. I don't know what I'll do when she gets busy with nurse's training this fall." It was hard to think beyond a few days out.

"And you'll be back in Fayetteville then, too, right?" Cody ran his hands through his hair.

"Yes. I don't think there will be as much to do for Rodeo Arkansas Teen after school starts. Then, the new queen will take over at the first of the year." She caught a bead of perspiration as it ran down the side of her face.

"If there's anything I've learned, it's not to get too far ahead of yourself." He rolled back and forth in front of her. "One day at a time is enough."

"For real. Thanks for coming today." She smiled. "I appreciate you being here."

"You're welcome. I'll see you again soon."

In just a matter of a minute or so, Cody was seated behind the wheel of his pickup truck.

A warm breeze toyed with the hem of her dress. She held it with one hand and waved with the other. Time to get out of this funeral outfit and into something more relaxing. The few days of peace she planned to share with Coach and Zanna would pass all too quickly.

Cody watched Kayla's reflection grow smaller as he traveled down the long road behind her grandparents' house. Sneakers of every description waved in the breeze as he approached the 'shoe tree' that marked his next turn. He chuckled. Growing up, that tree had probably never pictured itself looking like this. But it had become an important part of the landscape around here.

What had Kayla said about the view from the back side of

her grandparents' property? He turned left instead of heading back to the freeway. He was always up for a view of the river.

Mailboxes were less frequent, and the road became narrower. A sign reading "Overlook" popped up on his left just before another one announcing a "Dead End." He slowed and turned to find a wide paved area marked with a few parking spaces. One was marked for handicap access, so he pulled in and stopped.

Ahead, the trees had been cleared out, so he could tell there would be a nice view. He opened his door and operated the controls to bring his wheelchair to his side. There wasn't much time before dark, but he sensed this stop might be worth it.

After he was securely seated and his truck was locked, he motored around the back of the pickup, facing a rocky hillside leading down to the river. He shielded his eyes from the bright sunlight coming from the west. The wide channel of the river below him marked it as the Arkansas. Birds sailed gracefully on the wind currents, and a few called up at him from trees below.

A shiny white object caught his eye, and the faint chugging of a barge reached his ears. From behind several rows of massive steel bars, a white tugboat bravely pushed the tremendous load down the river toward Little Rock. He'd need to check out a map to see how near they were to the lock and dam. Watching these monsters navigate through that channel had fascinated him since he was small. He'd even thought about working on one of these boats someday.

His pocket buzzed with a phone notification. Mom.

"Hi." He was glad she hadn't tried to reach him while he was driving.

"How was the service?"

Always hard to answer a question like that.

"Fine. Kayla's folks had lots of friends and family up here."

"Are you and Junior headed back? I want to have plenty for supper." She knew Junior. That would require more than one extra helping of whatever she was fixing.

"Junior went home with his sister. I stayed to visit with Kayla's other grandparents for a minute."

"Okay. I just checked the forecast. Looks like the rain will hold off until tomorrow. Be careful, sweetheart. See you when you get home."

"Bye, Mom."

He stowed his phone in his jacket pocket and headed back to the pickup. Mom was always concerned about him, but maybe a little more since his accident. She had acted the same way when John K. came home from the Middle East.

Middle brother O.D. was the only one who usually avoided being coddled. Good old O.D. had always been the one his parents depended on. Cody was grateful for the support his parents had provided after his bull wreck. Would they ever let him grow up?

Back on the main road, the miles clipped by. The exit that led to the family's hunting cabin was next up. Why not? He flipped on the right turn signal and glided off the interstate toward the two-lane road. This wouldn't add too many minutes.

By the time he reached his next turn, he had met only a few cars. The sun was lower in the sky to the west, and he left his window down, hoping for a breeze. The pine trees crowded both sides of the road, forming a canopy over the truck.

He took a deep breath as he turned off the pavement. The mailbox he'd helped Dad install marked the wide driveway. The cabin itself had changed since his growing up days. John K. had done a great job supervising the remodel that had been necessary after a freak hot water heater explosion.

Cody stopped his truck in its regular spot, and he unloaded his chair. Might as well run in and look around, maybe even use the bathroom. He'd been so pleased about the new ramp on the front porch. Another indication of how much his family cared for him.

Inside, he spun around in the big open living area. John K. had lived here for a while and had done fine. Was that a possibility for Cody too? He poked his head into the bedroom and bathroom. Everything looked ready for a new resident.

With the front door relocked, he headed back to his truck. There was really no reason for him to leave home. But this would be the perfect place to prove he could manage on his own. It was worth considering.

Chapter Three

Kayla slid into a folding chair next to Cody as the first tie-down contestant broke his barrier.

"Hey" Cody sipped his soft drink. "How's the recently deposed queen?"

"Stop." She turned toward him, hands on hips. "I won't be finished with my reign until the end of the year."

"*Aww.*" The crowd reacted as the calf jumped free of the lariat looped around its head.

"Well, that one was slippery calf." The announcer picked up his accustomed patter.

"Just to let you know, I saw the newly selected queen riding behind you during the opening tonight." Cody leaned close to her. "She's probably sweet and all, but I'm afraid she doesn't measure up to last year's winner."

"Good thing you weren't one of the judges. Physical appearance is not the most important thing." Kayla wagged a finger in front of his face.

"Yeah. I'm not cut out to be a judge. That's for sure." He drained the cup and placed it next to his chair on the floor.

"Is O.D. next?" Kayla asked.

"Not sure. I think there may be one more before him. He

and Buck should be in position, getting ready to come into the gate." Cody pointed toward the entryway.

"There's Hope and Faith." Kayla waved at her cousins.

"Hi, Kayla." Junior stood behind Cody when she turned back around.

"Do I have your seat?" She leaned forward.

"No. Stay seated." Junior handed Cody a box of popcorn. "I'll go sit with my rotten sisters. This guy has been looking for you all evening."

Her cheeks warmed. She resumed her place between Cody and another man sitting in a wheelchair in front of the stands.

"Here they come." Cody rolled up to the railing.

The black calf busted out of the gate, followed quickly by O.D. and his buckskin. O.D. twirled his lariat overhead once, twice. The loop grew bigger and still bigger, then wrapped around the calf's neck. O.D. pulled back, tightening the loop, and Buck stepped backward.

"Yeah." Cody clapped, watching intently as O.D. jumped down, ran to the calf, grabbed its flank, flopped it to the ground, and grabbed a back leg. Collecting two more legs, he tied them together with the smaller rope he held in his teeth. He jumped up, holding his hands in the air.

"Okay, Buck, do your stuff." Cody gripped the railing in front of him.

The horse moved forward one step to allow some slack in the rope. O.D. mounted easily, watching to be sure the calf stayed tied.

"That's it." Cody glanced up at the clock above the announcer's head. "Eleven point seventy-five. Not half bad."

"Looks like he enjoys being here." Kayla loosened the lid of her water bottle.

"O.D. or Buck?" Cody waved at his brother as the judges unwrapped the calf.

"Both!" She'd always liked this event. It demonstrated the teamwork of the cowboy and his horse. Unlike Cody's event of bull-riding, where the man and the animal were competing against each other.

Cody took a deep breath and turned toward Kayla again. "Sorry I was sort of pre-occupied. It's a whole different thing when your family's out there."

"Hey, I get it." Kayla nodded. "I've stood next to your brothers when they're watching you." She'd been told O.D. had almost come to blows with the men who held him back when a bull sent Cody flying.

"Family ties. Tighter than any pigging string." He turned to his left as a young man tapped him on the shoulder.

"Hey," Cody greeted the lanky cowboy. "You remember Kayla Caldwell? Kayla, this is the bull rider who won the last Thanks for Hanging On prize from the Billings Boys."

"Sure, I remember. You're Junior's cousin, right?" The young man shook Kayla's hand.

"Don't remind me." Kayla pretended to grimace. "Here, you can have my chair."

"No, that's okay. Keep your seat. I can't stay long." The cowboy crouched down on Cody's left side. "Hey, man. I need to ask you something. If it's too personal, I'll understand."

"Sure. Fire away."

"Well, I don't know how to ask this." He cleared his throat. "That night." He paused again. "Did you have a bad feeling before you got on your bull? I am normally not nervous, but I'm kind of spooked for some reason tonight ... and ..."

"You know, I didn't. Everything seemed normal." Cody did not lower his voice, so Kayla didn't feel guilty for overhearing.

"Looking back, though, I may have lost focus. There was a lot going on. I'm not blaming anyone, you understand. I just don't think my mind was completely right." Cody continued. "Listen, man." He leaned forward, looking the cowboy in the eyes. "It's all about you and that bull. Don't think about anything else. You just tell him who's in charge. Communicate through the pressure of your knees in his sides. Make him move like you want him to move."

"Yeah." The young man nodded.

"Just you and that bull. Block everything else out." Cody patted his shoulder. "You'll be great."

"Okay. I appreciate that." The cowboy rose back to full height. "I'll head down to get ready, then." He tipped his hat in Kayla's direction. "Ma'am."

Kayla nodded. That awful night had changed Cody's life forever. He didn't seem to have any problem talking about it. Could she answer questions about her mom and dad's crash that confidently? It was hard to think about that day, let alone try to talk about it. Cody's courage was amazing.

"Ladies and gents, we want to thank you again for being here tonight." The announcer was filling time before the bronc riding started. "We also want to remind you that tonight's performance is dedicated to the memory of Dub and Tina Caldwell, huge supporters of our rodeo events here for many years. You met their daughter Kayla earlier. She's the reigning queen for Rodeo Arkansas Teen. I think she's still in the arena, so let's show her some love with another round of applause for the angels watching over all of us tonight. Here's to you, Miss Kayla Grace."

The crowd cheered and applauded. If only her hat with its attached tiara didn't make her so obvious. She blinked back tears, raising her hand in appreciation. Cody faced her and winked. Riding in the grand entry had been so much easier than sitting here right now.

Loud rock music filled the arena as the riders milled around behind the gates.

"We're ready to get our saddle bronc competition going. Here's our first rider, Shane Butler, aboard Twister. Encourage this young cowboy, if you please." A huge cheer rang out as the horse and rider paced behind the metal gate.

The crowd groaned as the cowboy took an early exit from the bucking horse.

"Want to go get something to drink?" Cody backed up and headed toward the exit ramp.

"Sounds good."

Would Cody want to stay in the lobby until after the bull-riding event was over? She certainly couldn't blame him. She followed him toward the concession stand.

"I'm not going to miss the bronc riding that much. Watched plenty of it when John K. was competing." He waited for her at the bottom of the ramp.

"Not as exciting as bull-riding?" She stopped next to him.

"I don't know. A horse is a horse, you know." He maneuvered into the end of the line for soda. "They don't seem as menacing as a snorting, fuming hunk of walking dynamite."

"Yeah. I would say you prefer the bulls, for sure." She tried to read the menu above the concession stand.

"Don't pretend you're not a thrill seeker yourself." He pointed at her. "So, here's your mission, if you choose to accept it. You brave the drink line, I'll go get some nachos, and we can meet up in time for the barrel races." He stopped beside her. "Oh, yeah. Do you want anything from the hot dog, pretzel, and nacho booth?"

"No. But what are you drinking?"

"Anything cold and non-alcoholic. You make the call." He shoved a wad of cash in her hand and rolled to the end of a line that wrapped past the T-shirt booth.

Kayla shifted from one foot to another. She'd spent many nights on the other side of one of these concession counters with her mom. Waiting in line was not her comfort zone. She swallowed hard as the lady serving customers handed a small boy his change. So patient and kind, just like Mom.

Shouts from the arena sent people running to get a glimpse of what was happening inside.

"He's all right!" The announcer's voice prompted cheers. "But that was a nasty fall. Let's give him one more round of applause as he dusts himself off."

The night Cody was almost destroyed by a bull, she'd been peddling popcorn. What struck her that night was the quiet. She had gone about her duties mechanically, taking money, dispensing orders with none of her usual polite banter.

When the cheers had resumed in the arena that night, they had been subdued. Many more whispers than shouts reached her ears. How she had wished to be able to see what was happening on the dusty arena floor. Now, she was grateful she hadn't. Did Cody's family relive that horror every time they attended a rodeo? How could Cody sit through a bull-riding competition tonight?

"Ma'am?" The teen behind the counter broke through her daydream. "What can I get for you?"

She ordered a lemonade. "Make it two."

After paying, she balanced the two cold plastic cups. Cody approached her with a dish of chips covered with chili and cheese in his lap.

'It's just you and the bull.' The advice he offered to his bull-riding buddy echoed in her head. Just concentrate on the task at hand. She realized that's how Cody lived his life. Whether that was watching a bull-riding competition, or just making it back to his seat with a lap full of hot, messy food.

"You ready to go back up?" Cody asked.

"Sure." She followed as folks stepped out of his way. Just carry these two drinks without spilling them. *Just you and the bull.*

Cody imitated Kayla's movements as she watched the barrel races. Lean to the left, then the right while the human-equine team rounded the first two barrels. Sit up straight after they navigated the third one. Clap vigorously and cheer as horse and rider made their final dash.

Looking to her left, she caught him watching on the third run.

"Yeah, I guess I do sort of get into it." She poked his shoulder.

"Hey, don't let me interfere. I'm just admiring your technique." He'd never had this much fun watching a barrel race.

The next rider waited in the entryway. Cody resisted the impulse to reach around her shoulders and pull her closer. How would she take that?

"I'm so glad you are here." She leaned closer.

"You read my mind. I was thinking the exact same thing. So, who's going to win this?" *Good job, Cody, let her be the one to move closer.*

"The first girl set the bar pretty high, but they usually save the best for last." She checked the leader's score, displayed above the announcer.

"Well, we'd better get ready to help her." He placed his hands firmly on his thighs, gluing his eyes to the barrel racing team getting ready to compete.

"Are you sure Junior was the clown? Or did you teach him everything he knows?" She laughed.

"*Shh.* We need to concentrate." He gritted his teeth and stared straight ahead.

As the last rider's time was recorded, Kayla raised her fist in victory. Evidently, a family connection was not required for her to find a winner to cheer for.

"Okay, ladies and gents. That concludes the barrel racing for tonight." The announcer's voice became deeper, more serious. "Next up, the event everyone's waiting for. Ten men will battle ten rank bulls in a classic struggle. These athletes have traveled from all over the country to show us what they can do. I know this is why you bought a ticket tonight."

The crowd applauded and cheered.

"I have it on good authority we have a special guest tonight." The announcer's patter continued.

Cody looked up at the digital scoreboard, where a camera panned the crowd.

"A brave young man named Cody Billings completed his eight second ride, earning a very high score at the Caldwell family Rodeo in Crossroads. But that autumn night, the bull was not finished with him." Cody's cheeks flamed. Who was this guy? Why did he feel the need to mention Cody's injury tonight?

"The rodeo family was stunned that night, and we want to let him know we were praying for him every day. We're so glad to see him here tonight, sitting next to last year's Rodeo Arkansas Teen queen. Let's let him hear our support." The crowd cheered wildly, with Junior Caldwell providing a shrill whistle from a few rows behind him. Yeah, this announcement had his buddy's fingerprints all over it. He already felt awkward, in this chair, instead of waiting behind the pens. At least he had a beauty queen beside him to deflect some of the crowd's attention.

He removed his hat, raised his hand, and waved as his face appeared on the huge screen.

"Okay." He whispered through his teeth. "Let's get on with the show."

Somewhere during the third bull ride, Kayla grasped his right hand in her left. His eyes stayed focused on each cowboy. The fourth one actually stayed seated until the eight-second buzzer sounded.

He squeezed Kayla's hand, as the young man celebrated his victory.

"That was a good one," he said when the bull was safely behind bars.

The cowboy who had talked to him earlier took an extra second to rewrap the rope before nodding at the gateman. Hopefully, his jitters had passed. *Remember, just you and the bull.* He tried to send a telepathic message to the arena floor.

Five seconds, six, seven. When the youngster reached eight, Cody held his breath. Now, if the bull would just be polite to this cowboy.

"He did it!" Kayla jumped up, clapping. Cody exhaled, nodding when she turned to face him. Had she realized she was holding his hand? Was it all about the tension of the bull ride? No matter. He didn't regret it one bit.

"Yep. That's a winner." He, the cowboy, and the bull had all survived, and Kayla had shared the moment. All in all, this had been a pretty good night.

Chapter Four

"Text received from ... Faith." Kayla increased the speed of her windshield wipers as the mechanical voice read a message.

She laughed. The robot certainly didn't sound anything like Faith.

With the pageant behind her, project 'keep Kayla busy' was now kicking into high gear. Hope had arranged the Arkansas rodeo queen clinic to be held at Cedar Ridge arena, but Faith wanted to support her as well. Kayla would give both of them a call when she got home.

The rain picked up. Squinting improved her view. Was it worth the delay when she'd decided to spend last night at the motel instead of driving home? Only two more exits before she would be out of the traffic, headed down a more familiar two-lane road.

Somewhere on her left was Coach and Zanna's house. If she took the next exit, she could ride out the storm there. No. This was the perfect time to face up to being on her own.

'Just you and the bull.' Funny how that phrase Cody used kept coming back into her head. Today, her bull was this drive through the pouring rain. Did he realize how much his conversation with a nervous cowboy had encouraged her?

Rubber stuttering against wet glass signaled her to decrease the speed of her wipers as the rain slacked up a bit. She'd been driving since before she was in high school. This particular challenge was one she could easily conquer.

Uncle Smiley had invited her to stay with him and Junior, now that Granny and Grandpa were back home in Texas. Another chance to accept help. She'd lived in a dorm room at college and spent time by herself when her roommate was gone. Mom and Dad's business trips had left her alone in the house overnight several times. Would this be any different?

She sped up to pass a slow-moving tractor-trailer truck.

Being alone this time *would* be different. Because it was permanent. Always before, she'd known Mom and Dad would be home soon. She'd spent the hours before they arrived cleaning up any messes she'd made. Would anyone care what the house looked like now?

She took the exit toward her house making a mental list of the texts she'd have to send when she got home. Faith would be first, since she'd just texted. Uncle Smiley, Coach, and Grandpa, would want to know she arrived safely. Then, she'd call Hope to talk about the upcoming clinic and see what still needed to be done.

Crossing a bridge, she noticed the recent rain had filled this creek to just below flood stage. She longed to hear what Dad would have to say about that. He'd be deciding if it was safe to launch his boat for his next fishing trip. Would she ever have a chance to go fishing again? What it would be like without him? Hollowness filled her insides.

The rearview mirror reflected the rain puddling up on the vinyl bedcover protecting her suitcases. Unloading and unpacking would occupy another hour or so once she pulled into the driveway. But what then? Once her clothes were either dumped in the dirty clothes hamper or rehung in her closet, her footsteps would echo in the much-too-large house.

"Don't be a big baby." She was talking to herself out loud more and more these days. With the music in her truck cranked up, she searched for familiar landmarks.

Just before the road to her house, a narrow street led to the city park. If the rain would just stop, maybe she could sit on a bench for a minute. She parked in the empty lot, turning off her engine. Tears filled her eyes. This park usually brought her peace, especially after a busy day at the rodeo. Tonight, she was totally alone.

Cody stopped at the end of the driveway coming out of the local taco drive-thru. It had been good to spend some time with Grandpa Dee. The staff at the nursing home offered to fix Cody a plate, but nothing they were cooking smelled very good. The only problem with this menu choice was the messiness factor. Not easily eaten while driving.

As he pulled out onto the highway again, Cody headed for the city park. At least the rain had finally stopped. It wasn't dark yet, but before long, he'd have trouble distinguishing what he was squeezing hot sauce on. No use making a huge mess.

He parked under one of the lights and unwrapped a taco. A midnight blue four-door pickup sat in the space next to him and a driver much too small for the vehicle stepped out, locking the door. Definitely Kayla.

Cody watched as Kayla pulled her long denim duster tightly around her and walked down the paved pathway away from their trucks. Why was she here all alone?

She continued to a bench with a view of the river and sat staring straight ahead.

He finished his take-out supper. Should he just drive away

and leave her to her thoughts? What would she think if he drove off without speaking? This was a very well-lit space, but there weren't a lot of other people around. Her dad wouldn't have been comfortable with her being here all alone after dark. His own dad wouldn't like that, even though he had sons instead of daughters.

His made up his mind. He'd use the bag of trash as an excuse to unload his chair and travel past her. Just to see if she was okay. Yeah. That was the plan.

He sighed as he gathered up wrappers and used the controls on the dashboard to retrieve his chair.

Kayla's head turned his way just as the chair came close enough for him to climb into. No turning back now. He placed the trash bag into the pouch at his side and navigated up the short ramp to the sidewalk.

Crickets and tree-frogs rehearsed for their nightly concert as the sky dimmed.

"Hey, Kayla," Cody greeted her as he passed.

"Hi." She waved, then replaced her hand in her lap.

He dropped the paper bag into the trash can and turned to pass her again.

"You okay?" How stupid. Of course, she wasn't okay. She'd just lost her parents. Oh well, anything he said would have probably sounded lame.

"Yeah. I'm fine." She smiled at him. "I'm just not quite ready to go home yet."

"It's a good night for staying outside a little longer. The rain cooled things off." He stopped in front of her.

"My dad and I used to come to this park sometimes when we were in town. Best view of the river. Especially at sundown." She pointed to the colorful sky behind him.

"Yeah. That's pretty cool." Cody followed her gaze. "We have good sunsets at home, but there are way more trees blocking the way."

"Only thing better is actually being on the water." She sighed.

"Dad always had trouble getting home before dark when we were fishing. Mom got so irritated."

"Moms can be like that." Oh, no. How would she take that remark? What were you supposed to say to someone who'd had such a terrible shock?

"Yeah."

So far, so good.

"So, what are you doing out here all alone?" She turned toward his empty truck.

"I went to see my grandpa at the nursing home. Not sure he knew who I was." Funny he mentioned this to Kayla. They'd run into each other now and then growing up, but he didn't remember a lot of conversations.

"I love your grandpa. I remember how much fun he was when the other kids and I came to see you while you were his roommate at the nursing home." She leaned toward him.

"He's a real corker. At least, he used to be." Cody rubbed his arms. He should have grabbed a jacket.

That day when she'd visited with some of his friends had been great. She'd been a pretty good encourager. Now was his chance to return the favor.

They sat in silence for a few seconds. The colors in the sky changed from reds and oranges to pinks and purples.

"Looks like the show's almost over." Cody nodded toward the view.

"Yeah. We'd better head home. I'm glad you were here." Kayla took a step toward her truck.

"Me too. Talk to you tomorrow?" He waited before following her.

"I hope so." She turned back toward him.

He followed at a respectful distance. First step after the school-boy crush stage was successful. Just being around to listen when she needed to talk might be the best plan.

Cody crossed the front of the sanctuary as the evening worship ended. Kayla stood to follow Hope and O.D. toward the exit.

"Hey!" He waved to get Kayla's attention.

Kayla stopped. "Hi. How are you?"

"If you're not in a hurry to get home, how about going to Amy Lou's with me? I could use a good thick milkshake." Besides, talking to her for a few minutes sounded much better than staring at the walls of his room at home.

"Sounds great. Just let me catch Uncle Smiley to let him know I won't need a ride."

She shuffled past the row of folding chairs toward Smiley, who was deep in conversation with one of the members.

"Hey, Cody. You coming over to the arena?" A middle-school-aged boy shouted from behind him. "We're going to practice on the mechanical bull."

"Not tonight." He spun around to face the youngster. "Wear your helmet. Falling from a fake bull can hurt just as bad as a real one."

"Yeah. See ya!" The boy ran to catch up with his friends.

He remembered those Sunday nights after cowboy church. The arena next to the sanctuary was probably a bigger draw than the worship itself, at least for the kids. There would be plenty of adults to help keep them safe, so he didn't feel obligated to stay.

"Okay, let's go." Kayla waited for him near the door.

"Lead on." He followed her out to his truck.

The conversation on the way to the diner was dominated by a discussion of their favorite menu items. Cody couldn't remember anyone else who was so easy to talk to.

Rain resumed as they drove down Main Street. He circled the block, finding the parking place with the widest unloading area to the left of his truck. Kayla waited at the diner's door and held it open as he approached.

"Okay. You've talked me into nachos. Are you sure they won't be too spicy?" She asked as they settled next to Cody's favorite table in the back of the noisy building.

"I told you, it's the jalapeños that make it spicy. If there are too many, just pitch them over to me."

"But I thought you were having a milkshake." She laughed.

"All that talk on the way here made me hungry. I'm getting loaded fries. Extra peppers will *not* be a problem."

Aunt Candace brought two lemonades and placed them on the table.

"Did I get that part right?"

Cody smiled at her. "Do you know everybody's drink order?"

"Just my favorites." She jotted down their food orders and bustled off toward the kitchen.

"Your aunt's a pretty great lady." Kayla slipped a straaw into her lemonade.

"Your uncle is spending lots of time with her, right?" Cody picked up his glass. No time to waste on a straw.

"Yes. I'm glad he has someone in his life. Losing Aunt Catherine was so hard." She leaned back in the booth.

Maybe this was a good time to change the subject. He reviewed the calendar in his phone, searching for events to talk about.

"So, next up is the rodeo queen clinic and then the parade. I guess you have official duties at both, right?" Summer in Crossroads wouldn't officially start until after that parade.

"Well ..." Kayla watched the front door of the café as the entry bell jingled.

"Speaking of your uncle, did he follow you here?" Cody nodded toward Smiley, who chose a table in the front.

"I don't know. He usually sits at the counter when your aunt's working. Tonight, it looks like he's waiting on someone else."

A dark-haired man seated himself across from Smiley.

"Isn't that Mr. Hernandez from your ranch?" Cody faced Kayla. No need to snoop on her uncle.

"Yep. Why is he here without Nancy?" Kayla waited as Candace put their food down on the table.

"Thanks, Auntie." He winked as Aunt Candace walked away.

Why was Kayla so concerned about her uncle meeting with Mr. Hernandez?

"I guess they're talking ranch business," Kayla explained before he asked. "The lawyer said I don't inherit anything until I'm twenty-one. I wonder how the place is doing financially, especially now that Mom and Dad are gone."

Cody picked up a cheesy French fry with his fork.

"Don't you trust your uncle?"

"Of course. I'm worried about what happens in the next couple of years. What kind of problems will I have to deal with?" She picked up a tortilla chip, dipping it in a mound of guacamole on the side of the plate. "Maybe I need to be listening when they're talking about financial stuff."

"I guess your parents wanted you to concentrate on college, at least for a little while." All he had heard from Hope and Faith was how excited Kayla was about studying architecture. She'd probably never pictured herself as the owner of a ranch or a stock contractor.

"Yeah. I'm having trouble thinking much about moving back to college right now." She took another bite of her nachos.

Cody's phone buzzed in his pocket. Mom was calling.

"I guess I'd better get this." Mom was headed to the nursing home to see Grandpa Dee tonight. "Hi, Mom."

"I'm sorry to bother you." Mom was speaking very quietly. "I'm here with your grandpa, and I'm kind of worried."

"What's up?" Cody sat up straighter.

"He doesn't want to eat."

"Maybe he's just not hungry." Grandpa Dee usually had a very good appetite.

"Do you think you could come by? Lately, you are the only one he relates to." Mom sounded more than a little worried.

"Well ..." He never minded visiting with Grandpa Dee. Even when he didn't think he was recognized. But, what about Kayla? "I'll try to go over there in a bit."

"Thanks, son. He needs to eat something before he goes to

bed tonight. Otherwise, he'll wake up hungry in the middle of the night."

"Okay. Yeah. I'll come by." He disconnected and put his phone back in his pocket.

"Everything okay?" Kayla leaned across the table.

"Nothing too serious." Cody used his fork to pick up some fries. "Mom wants me to go by and check on Grandpa Dee. I was thinking of visiting in the morning, but she wants me to come tonight." He shook his head.

"You should go. I can ride with Uncle Smiley." She picked up her plate.

"No." He touched her wrist. "Let's finish our food."

Kayla stared at him. She took a drink of lemonade before speaking.

"You should be grateful. I'd give anything for my mom to ask me to do her a favor." Her voice trembled.

"I know, but ..."

"I'll just go and sit with Uncle Smiley and Rod." Kayla pushed past him, carrying her plate of nachos in one hand, and her lemonade in the other.

Cody finished his food quickly. Was Kayla so concerned about the ranch business? He needed to be more worried about Grandpa Dee. It wasn't any trouble to help his family. Had his annoyance with his mom caused Kayla to leave? One step forward, two steps back.

Chapter Five

"Here. You love cobbler." Cody picked up a spoonful of sweetness and held it near Grandpa Dee's nose. "You can eat dessert first. If anyone gives you a problem, send them to me."

The famous crooked smile made its way across his grandpa's face as he took the spoon from Cody and cut a peach slice in half before taking another bite.

Cody wished for the twinkle in Grandpa Dee's eyes that always came next but didn't expect to see it. He moved the larger plate close to Grandpa Dee's right hand. Even though the roast beef and mashed potatoes were probably cold by now, he might eat some of it.

"So glad you're here, son," Mom whispered in his ear as she hugged his shoulders.

"No problem." He backed away from the table. "Hey, Grandpa. I'll talk to you when you're finished eating."

"The nurse said eating isn't important to him anymore," Mom said as they moved from the dining room to the larger living area out front. "Pretty soon, he may forget how, and someone will have to feed him."

"That won't be easy if he doesn't want to eat." Cody found a spot near the front window. "He can be sort of stubborn."

"I guess it runs in the family." Mom stood beside him. "I was sorry to interrupt your dinner. I thought about calling your dad or O.D., but lately, you're the one he wants most."

"We spent a lot of time together when I was his roommate." Cody rubbed his hands along the armrests of his wheelchair. "I'm not sure he knows I'm his grandson, but he knows he knows me, if that makes sense."

"As much as anything does right now." Mom took a step toward the dining room. "I guess I'll go kiss him goodnight. Oh, wait ..." She stopped and faced him. "Have you talked to Kayla? How is she holding up?"

"Okay, I guess. It's still hard to know what to say to her." That was an understatement. He said something that set Kayla off so much she left their table at Amy Lou's.

"Well, just keep trying. You remember how much you needed friends your age after your accident. She needs the same kind of support right now." Mom kissed his cheek. "You're one of the best encouragers I know." She walked to Grandpa Dee's chair in the dining room, helping him use the cloth napkin in his lap to wipe his chin.

A good encourager? If that were true, he'd learned from the best.

Should he send Kayla a text? Maybe it was too soon. She might still be catching up on ranch finances with her uncle and Mr. Hernandez. Why did she want to take on another burden? Anything he said to her right now would just add to the pressure. He'd keep trying to make her feel better, but not tonight. No way would he give up. That pretty auburn-haired cowgirl was worth all the effort.

Kayla watched the dark shadows of pine trees passing her window as Uncle Smiley drove home. She might have been better off sitting by herself at Amy Lou's tonight. She'd had trouble sitting still when Rod told Uncle Smiley he was "missing a mama cow."

How did someone lose a whole cow? She remembered times when coyotes had raided their ranch, stirring things up and even killing cattle now and then. There had been a storm today. What if the cow had been struck by lightning? Rod didn't seem concerned enough. He'd told Uncle Smiley he sent a couple of guys out to look. How trustworthy were their hands? Why didn't Rod go out himself?

"I thought you were riding with Cody tonight."

Not anymore. She didn't want to hear him complain about his family. "I decided to ride with you, if that's okay."

"I'm perfectly fine with that. It's good to spend time with my favorite niece." Smiley patted her hand. "I hope all of that ranch talk with Rod didn't bore you too much."

"No. I guess I need to stay up on that stuff." She had so much to learn.

"Seems like things are running pretty smoothly. We are blessed to have Rod and Nancy." He switched his headlights on bright as they left the main highway. "I'm busy with the church, so I just asked him to let me know when he needs something."

"Maybe I should be more involved." Kayla twisted her hands in her lap. "Mom and I always just left that stuff to Dad."

"You just need to concentrate on being Miss Rodeo Arkansas Teen and then on your college classes."

"Until I'm twenty-one, right?" Kayla blinked as bright lights from a truck they were meeting blinded her.

"Yes, officially. But I plan on still being around after that, Kayla Grace. Families help each other." He flipped on his right turn signal as they reached Kayla's driveway.

"I know." Outdoor lights illuminated the front of her house.

"We'll just trust in the Lord." Uncle Smiley parked the truck. "Goodnight, sweet girl."

"Goodnight. Thanks for bringing me home." Kayla jogged to

the back door of the house and used her key to open it.

What about the missing cow? Nothing more she could do about that tonight.

The light inside the refrigerator illuminated a piece of apple pie Nancy must have left for her. Her mom and dad had trusted Rod and Nancy. She'd just have to do the same.

She walked through the house, switching on lights. That helped with the dark shadows, but what about the silence? Maybe she'd sleep with the television on.

"I still wish there was a way I could launch this and take it out by myself." Cody commented as he rolled from the concrete ramp onto the metal deck of the boat.

"Maybe somebody will come up with a solution." Dad stepped aside to let Cody take the controls. "But for now, you can indulge your old man a bit. This graduation gift was a little selfish, if you want the truth. Over all those years of selling pickup trucks, I didn't get to fish nearly often enough."

"Best gift ever. I don't know if I've seen one with a built-in-ramp." Cody peeked into the bucket of minnows he'd brought with him. Today, maybe they'd actually catch something.

Cody motored out of the inlet into the main part of the lake. "Nice and cloudy, but Mom shoved a bottle of sunscreen in my side pouch anyway."

"I hope the clouds aren't just teasing. The bass always bite better when the rain's moving in." Dad leaned back in the boat seat and adjusted his cap.

"Maybe it will hold off a while. We've got to go home if there's a real storm. If the lightning doesn't kill us, Mom will." Cody revved up the engine.

Motor noise eliminated any chance of conversation as they headed to Junior's favorite spot. Cody was grateful to have some time with Dad anyway. Could he bring up the idea of looking for a job? Or would Dad suggest hanging out at their family dealership again?

The wake behind the boat dwindled as they slowed and glided into the cove. Shade along the banks would be the best place to cast their bait. He cut the engine and allowed gentle waves to wash against the shiny sides of the boat as they stopped.

"Okay. Here you go, Captain." Dad handed him a rod and reel and reached into the bucket for his bait. "Maybe we'll be lucky today. Whoever catches the biggest fish cleans them, right?"

"Sounds fair." Cody pulled out his phone to check for any new texts. Did he expect Kayla to reach out? It was totally his place to do that if he wanted their friendship to grow, but what to say?

"Everything okay?" Dad baited his hook and sent the wiggling minnow to its destination.

"Yeah, yeah." Cody's cast landed under a large tree several feet away from where Dad was fishing.

"You know, I'm a little surprised you like fishing so much." Dad slowly reeled his line toward the boat. "You used to have trouble sitting still this long."

Sitting still. Well, what choice did he have? Cody hesitated. *Think before you speak.*

"I did like going bank fishing with Grandpa Dee sometimes. I guess I needed a little bit of quiet after being whipped around on a bull." He didn't call Dad on his choice of words.

"I remember that. O.D. and John K. would be out taking target practice, or riding horses, and when you weren't riding the electric bull, you'd sneak off to the creek with Grandpa Dee." Dad checked his bait and gave it another toss.

"Junior and his Uncle Dub sometimes took me along on the Caldwell's boat too." Cody sat motionless for a moment. "But you know, doing nothing is starting to wear on me." He tightened his line. "I'm serious about finding a job, Dad. I know there's a lot I can't do, but I've got to keep my hands busy with something."

Dad's jaw worked back and forth as he reeled his line in again.

Cody's fishing rod jerked in his hand. The tension in his line increased. This must be a good-sized fish.

"Hey!" Dad shouted as Cody reeled the line closer and closer to the boat.

"Yeah. He's on there." His heart pumped in rhythm with the reel as he wound it faster. The tip of the pole pointed down toward the splashing water.

"I'll grab the net." Dad jumped up.

"I don't think he's that big, Dad."

"He's four pounds if he's an ounce!" Dad opened the live well as Cody removed the hook from the fish's mouth.

"Keep or release?" Cody held his prize aloft.

"*Aww*, let's keep a couple before we start releasing. Especially a nice one like that." Dad cast his line near where Cody's fish had been snagged.

A trio of fish later, the sun emerged from behind a cloud. Cody reeled his line in to move it.

"You know, I stayed in touch with the guy who built this boat when I bought it." Dad retrieved a new minnow from the bucket.

"Yeah. I guess that was a good idea." Where was Dad going with this conversation?

"His plant is not too far from our cabin, up by the lake." Dad sent his bait back to a new spot.

"I think I remember seeing that." Cody tried to picture the boat factory.

"He had an ad the other day looking for new employees."

"Seriously?" Cody almost dropped his fishing rod. "I wonder what that would require?"

"Won't know until you ask." Dad's jaw started working again. He pulled his empty hook back to the boat and opened an ice chest near his right foot. "Let's get into these sandwiches your mom packed us."

"Sandwiches for lunch, fish fry for supper. All in all, a great day, right?" Cody smiled. Was there a job he could do from his chair and even get paid for it? He could hardly wait to tell Kayla. Kayla? Not one of his brothers, or Junior? When had this happened?

Oh, wait. First, she'd have to be talking to him.

Kayla read the text from Rod again. All was well with the mama cow he'd been looking for last night. Kayla's time would be better spent finding something to wear for the rodeo queen clinic coming up.

She took another look at the outfits hanging in her closet. Maybe she should move the dressier stuff to Mom and Dad's room. That would make organizing much easier. The big problem with that plan was that her parents' clothes were still there, right where they'd left them. Was she ready to sort through their things to decide what should be kept, what should be donated? Her heart lurched at the thought of opening their bedroom door.

She walked through the hallway with a double armful of sequined jackets and squeaky-clean skinny jeans, headed toward the guest room. Her phone buzzed in her pocket.

"Hey." She dumped the clothes on the queen-sized bed to answer the call from Cody.

"You okay?" His voice held a measure of concern.

"Sure. I just had my hands full. What's up?" She must have sounded breathless.

"Nothing, Just got back from a fishing trip."

Kayla sat on the foot of the bed.

"Did you have a good time?" Hopefully, she wouldn't hear complaints about getting too much attention.

"Excellent," he answered. "But it made me realize I need to apologize for last night."

"Well ..." She wasn't all that upset anymore.

"No, listen. Spending time out there with my dad made me realize how blessed I am. I know you'd give anything to go fishing with your dad again."

She stayed silent, allowing him to continue.

"I'll try to stop being so childish when my parents irritate me. I'm grateful to have them around."

That sounded more like the Cody she knew.

"Did you catch anything?" The number and size of his fish were just a bonus, but she knew how competitive he was. A good catch would add to his experience.

"Yeah. I caught a pretty good one, but Dad's biggest was over four pounds. Our deal was, the one with the biggest fish cleaned them." He chuckled. "So, Dad's doing that now. Mom promised to fry them up for us. You want to come over?"

His apology was great. But she wasn't sure she wanted to be a guest for their fish fry tonight. She'd probably just have a salad for supper. And Nancy's apple pie.

"Thanks, but I think I'll stay home." Maybe he wouldn't feel too disappointed. "I need to get ready for the rodeo queen clinic on Friday."

"That's cool. Are you riding in the parade Saturday?"

"Yeah. All of the girls at the clinic are invited to ride with us. Should be fun." She picked up a blue jacket from the bed. Maybe she'd wear this.

"Sounds like 'princess overload.'" He laughed. "I think they want me to pull a float of some kind. I guess I'll see you there."

"Sounds good." She paused. "Thanks for calling, Cody."

"No problem. See you soon."

She laid back on the bed. The rest of the week would be more fun than worrying about a missing cow. Funny how just that short talk with Cody lifted a burden she didn't know she carried.

Chapter Six

"Okay, ladies. That's it for the horsemanship practice today." Kayla stood next to Sissy in the middle of the arena. "You have all done very well. Remember, the judges are looking for poise while riding. It won't matter if you aren't a champion barrel rider." Even though Faith couldn't be here today, she had this speech memorized. "It's all about accomplishing the list of skills and looking beautiful while you do it."

A dozen very eager teens and preteens smiled at her as she spoke. That is, until her last line about being beautiful. Those words obviously caused distress to the tallest of the group, who stood a few feet to the right of the other girls.

"Now, have a seat in this section." Kayla dropped Sissy's reins, using both hands to point out the area in the grandstand directly in front of her. "We are honored to have someone very special today who will give you tips on looking your best for every pageant."

The girls tripped over each other as they tried to find a seat while looking over their shoulders for a glimpse of the mystery guest.

"Please give a Crossroads welcome to Alex Landry, our current Miss Rodeo Arkansas."

Applause was almost drowned out by squeals. Alex rode through the entryway on her jet-black horse.

"Oh, my. You'd think someone introduced the President of the United States." Alex laughed through her wireless microphone. "I'm so happy to be here today. It's amazing to be in the hometown of Miss Rodeo Arkansas Teen. Kayla, you weren't lying when you told me this town was full of beautiful future princesses." She dismounted and stood next to Kayla.

The young lady who had seemed uncomfortable a moment ago stood at the top of the ramp leading to the lobby. Why wasn't she sitting with the others?

"We're so blessed to have you here," Kayla said, prompting applause from the girls. "I'll be back to talk to you ladies about more pageant opportunities coming up."

"Perfect." Alex touched Kayla's arm. "Now, as Kayla leaves the arena, please watch how she gracefully mounts her horse. Remember, it's all about poise and confidence. Kayla, if you please ..."

Kayla stretched the stirrup down and placed her left foot in, while grabbing the reins in her left hand.

"If your horse is tall, and you're not, some places may have a mounting block to help you get aboard." Kayla paused. "But if not, you might want to bounce a couple of times to get some momentum." She hopped up and threw her right leg over Sissy's back. "You all know how to do this. Just remember to be as graceful as possible." She settled into the saddle and placed her right foot in the stirrup. "Take a good breath and smile when you get seated. We all love riding, so let's sell that to the judges."

She waved at Alex and prompted Sissy toward the exit. The group of girls applauded and cheered. Not a bad reception for mounting a horse.

Outside the arena, she dismounted and tied Sissy to the side of the trailer. As she turned to re-enter the arena, the tall girl sat on a bench outside the exit. They'd introduced themselves earlier. What was her name? Lyndsey? Yes. That was it. "Hey, you're missing Alex's tips and tricks." Kayla stopped near her. "Everything okay?"

"I'll never be as pretty as you and Miss Rodeo Arkansas." Lyndsey kicked the dust at her feet.

"You don't look like either of us, but you are already pretty." Kayla propped her hands on her hips and looked the girl in the eye.

"My mom says my hair is dishwater blonde. Not black like Alex's or dark red like yours. And I have pimples." Lyndsey twisted the end of one of her braids.

"Hey. Remember, beauty comes from the inside." Kayla sat beside her. "You don't need a lot of makeup or fancy clothes. We're trying to help you feel confident. Then, everyone you meet will agree."

"I'll go back in and listen, I guess." She was a little taller than Kayla when she stood.

"I'm glad you're here. When you did your intro, you flashed the prettiest smile. Just bring it out of hiding a little more often." She winked and waved as Lyndsey walked inside.

"Great speech." A familiar deep voice startled her. She turned to see Cody smiling from under his cowboy hat.

"What are you doing here?" She stepped closer to him.

"I saw your truck and trailer on my way by. I had to stop. I've got some exciting news." He rolled forward and back.

"I've got to go in to make some announcements. Then we're done." Her cheeks felt warm. This arena was not on anyone's way from anywhere. He wanted to share his news with her? Anticipation stirred in her belly. "You want to come in?"

"No. I'd be out of place. Like a possum in a room full of Persian cats." He laughed. "I'll just wait out here."

"Okay, see you soon." She almost skipped as she re-entered the arena. Reassuring Lyndsey satisfied. Seeing Cody so excited might be even better.

Cody moved a little closer to the arena's entrance. Cars and trucks lined up like the afternoon pickup line at middle school. Kayla had been in her element talking to that cowgirl. At the rodeo, she'd complimented him on being an encourager. She excelled at the same thing today.

His only purpose was to share his own excitement. The first phone call after the man at Walking Eagle Boats shook his hand had been to Mom. But all he'd said to her was, "I got the job. I'll tell you all about it when I get home."

The details would be much more fun to share with Kayla. After so many quiet, restrained discussions, this one would be a pleasure.

Giggling girls emerged by twos and threes from the arena to head for waiting vehicles. Finally, Hope Caldwell walked through the front glass door.

"Hi, Cody! I didn't expect to see you until the parade tomorrow." Hope stopped in front of him.

"I just came by to tell Kayla something." He looked to her right, hoping to see a turquoise shirt under a gray hat.

"She's coming right out." Hope smiled. "I'm just waiting around to lock up. See you in the morning."

"Are you riding with Kayla?"

"No. I'll be on the Billings Boys float, throwing candy."

"Well, I'll be pulling it. If you accidentally get some candy in my truck window, it won't be the end of the world." He moved closer to the arena entrance.

"We'll see." Hope pushed the glass door open, and Kayla walked through it.

"So, what's the big news?" She stood next to him.

"Well, hello to you too." Cody pretended to be hurt.

"We already said 'hello.'" She punched his shoulder. "Now what's going on?"

"I got a job!"

"What? Where? When?" Kayla took a step backward.

"It's called a finishing prep specialist at a boat factory. The place that built my boat."

"Wow. What will you be doing exactly?"

"I guess I'll find out. Mostly I'll be using a power sander/grinder thing to get the surface of the boat ready so they can paint it. That, and sweeping up the place." He still had problems believing this himself.

"Sweeping?" Kayla looked puzzled.

"Yeah. I might have to have my power chair for that. I might take both chairs. I don't know. I'll just have to work it out. But it's a real job. They'll pay me and everything. I start this Monday."

"That's so awesome. I'm happy for you." She wrapped him in an enthusiastic hug.

"Hey, let's celebrate. How about a burger?" Cody headed toward his truck.

"Yeah. Sounds good." Kayla took a couple steps and stopped. "I need to take Sissy home. Can you come get me in, say, thirty?"

"Sure. That gives me time to go fill my parents in." He gave her a thumbs-up. "If my mom starts asking me a lot of questions about how I'm going to handle this from a wheelchair and how much driving it will involve, I'll do my best not to complain to you about it, okay?"

"Deal." She shook his hand and ran toward the back of her horse trailer.

He drove out of Cedar Ridge's parking lot onto the main road. Better come up with some answers to those 'how will you do it' questions. Mom and Dad would both be full of them. At this point, his answer was 'I'll figure it out.' That might not satisfy them.

A policeman running radar on the side of the road reminded him he'd best keep himself reined in. A speeding ticket would ruin the vibe of this great day. But a new job and a date with Kayla on the same day? Pretty awesome.

"Hey, I have an idea." Kayla bounced into the passenger side of Cody's pickup and closed the door.

"Shoot." He put the truck in gear as she fastened her seatbelt.

"Instead of Amy Lou's, how 'bout we head to Russellville to get one of their burgers?" Would he be up to even more driving this evening?

"Yeah. Sounds good. I guess I'd better stop and get some gas, then." He turned left at the end of Kayla's driveway.

"I'll buy you some gas." How long would it take him to get out and pump gas? "'Cause I remembered I promised to show you the back side of Coach and Zanna's land."

"Cool. I drove to the overlook at the end of that road the other day. It was unbelievable."

She tucked her foot under her. "I think their view might even be better."

"I'll buy the gas. I need to fill up anyway." He navigated into the gas station.

"Then, I'll pump." Kayla stepped out of the passenger side.

She took his credit card and began pumping gas. Taking care of this chore was the least she could do after adding several miles to his dinner plans. Why had she suggested this? Was this celebration for getting a job too important for the neighborhood hangout? Or did she just want more time to talk to Cody? Probably more of the latter.

"All done." She snapped the gas tank cover in place and hung up the nozzle.

"Okay. As my Grandpa Dee always says, 'Daylight's a'wastin'.'" Cody started the truck as she ran around to her door.

The miles to Russellville passed quickly as Cody told her about his trip to the Walking Eagle Boat Company. The details involved—and how he would navigate them—seemed to tone down some of his earlier joy.

"You're gonna be great." She touched his arm. "They'll be so glad they hired you."

"I hope so." Cody flipped on his right blinker. "Well, next exit is Russellville."

"Why don't we drive up past Coach and Zanna's before we eat?" Kayla suggested. "It won't take long. You remember how to get there?"

"Turn between Phillips 66 and Toot and Moo. Then, left at the shoe tree." Cody faked a robot voice.

"Yep. Except, we won't turn at the shoe tree. We'll drive on down a bit farther." Kayla moved her foot back to where it belonged on the floor and leaned forward, watching for landmarks.

Cody's left turn signal started just before she was able to point at the road he should take. An orange sign reading 'Work Area Ahead' greeted them. They passed a tree service truck, parked with its emergency blinkers flashing.

"I guess they're doing some trimming along here. Maybe the utility company." Cody slowed down.

"What?" She gasped, and her hand flew to her mouth. A truck with a cherry picker sat near the turn-off to Coach and Zanna's house. "The shoe tree!"

Just beyond the gnarled old tree, a mobile unit from the local television station was parked next to Coach's fence line. A blonde reporter talked to her cameraman, who was checking his lighting equipment.

"Take it easy. We'll find a place to park." Cody performed a quick u-turn and parked nose to nose with the television truck.

"Go ahead. I can unload on the road here. I'll catch up." He waved toward the passenger door.

Kayla jumped out, landing with both feet in the ditch.

"The work has paused for a minute on a county road just outside of Russellville, where a local landmark will soon be part of history." The reporter stood with the shoe tree to her back. Kayla pulled out her cellphone and found Coach's number. She stepped back toward Cody's truck so she wouldn't interfere with the news report.

"Coach, it's me." She took a deep breath before she continued talking. "I'm fine. But you'd better come meet me."

"Where are you, Kayla? Just give me the bottom line, sweetie. What's happening?" How did he always sound so calm?

"I'm here. At the shoe tree. It looks like they're going to cut it down." She spit the words out.

Cody had unloaded his chair. She waited, and they approached the television crew together.

"Do you live here?" The reporter walked toward them.

"No, ma'am. But my grandparents do." Kayla blinked. Was she on television right now? The reporter drew her hand across her neck in a signal to the cameraman to stop filming.

"What's happening?" Kayla leaned around to see what the tree removal crew was doing.

"I'm Tara Williams." The girl reached out to shake her hand.

"Kayla Caldwell."

"Cody Billings." He patted Kayla's back after shaking Tara's hand.

"We got a call from someone driving by. Do you mind if we interview you about your memories of the shoe tree?"

Coach and Zanna pulled up on his four-wheel farm vehicle.

"Yeah. In just a minute." She walked over to get a hug from Zanna. "Zanna, they can't do this, right? Don't you own the shoe tree?"

"No, honey. It's on the county right of way." Coach stepped down from the four-wheeler. "We knew they were trimming trees, and that they might be widening the road, but we had no clue."

Zanna's friend Ellen slid to a stop in her Jeep on the other side of the road. Zanna ran across to meet her.

"Hi, Mr. Pruitt." Cody moved closer to the utility vehicle.

"Cody, right?" Coach shook Cody's hand. "This will be a huge change for us, but I don't know that there's anything we can do about it." Coach walked toward Kayla. "I'm sorry, Kayla Grace."

Kayla was stunned. Would this old tree really be in the way? Why couldn't they just leave it where it had grown for years? She walked over to follow Ellen and Zanna, who were talking to the tree crew.

"At least, let us save the shoes." Ellen held both hands out toward the man in the hard hat and orange vest.

The shoes. Kayla swallowed back tears. Mom had thrown at least one pair of her of sneakers over these branches. She shielded the sun from her eyes trying to spot the dirty white sneakers with the red ball on the heel. Losing a community tradition was one thing. But this crew didn't realize they were taking away one more connection to Kayla's childhood. One more piece of her mom. Of course, they had to save the shoes.

"I don't know how we can do that, lady." The worker took off his hard hat and scratched his head.

"Okay. How about this?" Ellen paced in front of him. "Let me take some pictures, and we'll let you get back to work. Then, when she's on the ground, we'll get some help to retrieve as many of the shoes as we can."

The man threw his hands up. "All right. But everybody has to stay out of the way. Move those vehicles past where my flagman is standing." He pointed toward the next turnoff.

"Can we get that interview after we move our vehicles?" Tara yelled as she passed Kayla.

"Yes. You can park down that next road." Kayla pointed. "We'll be there too."

"You okay?" Cody squeezed and released her hand.

"I think so. I guess we have to move your truck." She walked over to hug Coach and waved at Zanna, who was already on her cellphone.

"Good to see you anyway, sweetie." Coach drove his utility vehicle down the road leading to their house.

"I'll call you." Kayla kissed his cheek and trudged toward Cody's truck.

Chainsaws and truck motors competed for their spot on the decibel meter as she sat motionless in Cody's truck. This was supposed to be a quick little scenic drive before supper. Would her world ever calm down again?

"Wow, right?" Cody turned his truck around to head toward the next road.

"Unreal." Would she be able to find words when Tara interviewed her?

"We won't keep you long." Tara patted her shoulder as they stood at the end of the road, in view of the activity happening next to the shoe tree. "I hope we can be heard over the chainsaws. So, do you know the history of this tree?"

"You'll probably get more of that from folks who live up and down this road. I can only tell you about the last few years." Tears threatened to leak out of her eyes. "Let me take this hat off. I don't want this to be about me." She handed her cowboy hat to Cody. He winked as he placed it in his lap.

"Okay, just take a quick breath. And we're on in three, two, one." Tara pointed at the camera. "We're here with Kayla Caldwell, who was as surprised as all of us were to find out today marks the end of a famous River Valley landmark. Tell us what you remember about the shoe tree, Kayla." Tara held the microphone in front of her.

"It's been here as long as I can remember. My grandparents live nearby, so I saw it several times a year." What else could she say?

"Are any of those shoes up there yours?" Tara pointed toward the tree.

"Yeah. One of my cousins threw an old pair of my high-top tennis shoes up there. He had to try three times before they stayed." A smile almost broke through as she remembered that day.

"What will it be like to drive this way after it's gone?" Tara pushed the mic toward her again.

"I don't know." What would it be like? Like nothing in her world would ever be the same. But then, she should be used to that. Blinking might not stop the tears this time.

Thankfully, Tara communicated the 'cut' signal to the cameraman.

"Thanks." Tara looked at her watch. "We've probably missed the six-o-clock broadcast, but watch at ten." She patted Kayla's shoulder. "See ya." She jogged toward the television truck.

"They may not be able to get back to the highway anytime soon. That tree crew means business." Cody sat at the end of the road, facing the workers.

"I don't want to watch." Kayla turned toward his pickup. "Do you want to go look at the view from the bluff?"

"Sure." He held both of her hands. "I'm sorry, Kayla."

"Thanks. I shouldn't be so upset. It's not a person, or even a pet. It's just a tree with shoes on it." She sighed.

"But it's the *shoe tree*!" His over-dramatic pronouncement sent her into peals of laughter.

Startled, he released her hands and laughed along with her.

She cackled, she snorted. Tears streamed down her face. She doubled over to get a better breath.

"*Phew*." She held her aching sides." I haven't laughed like that in a long time."

"I've known you for a while, and I don't remember you laughing like that *ever*!" He started loading his chair into the back of the truck. "Is there a place to park down there?"

"Yes." She cleared her throat, trying to regain her composure. "Let me run ahead and open the gate."

Kayla jogged down the right side of the short road. Cody stopped on the level spot and opened his door.

"Wow. You weren't kidding." He pointed through the windshield.

"You can get a little closer if you want to." Kayla walked to his window. "This flat spot extends for several feet, and Coach hires a guy to come and keep it mowed."

"I'll give it a try."

She walked away to allow him space to unload. The view from this spot still amazed her. If it wasn't for the faint traffic noise, no one would believe the freeway was so near. The most noticeable sight was the green canopy of treetops. A large bird sailed on air currents, and a puffy cloud of steam rose from the power plant in the distance. Sunlight reflected on the surface of the river as it wound its way through the landscape.

"This is even better than the official overlook I visited." Cody stopped to her left.

"Isn't it great? Before his accident, Coach and Zanna wanted to live up here." She stood behind him. "I think that's what got me interested in architecture. I drew up some rough plans for an accessible house. I still think it could work. But they're content where they are, I guess."

"They've got a pretty good place down there." Cody rolled forward. "But this is amazing."

"I thought you'd like it. I've watched barges go up and down the river from here. If you have binoculars, you can see so much more."

A breeze rippled through the trees nearby, and a couple of birds practiced their best calls. Chainsaws interrupted the peaceful moment. Cody heaved a big sigh, then sat completely still.

"So, your grandparents own all the land between here and their house?" He pointed.

"Yes. It's mostly filled with boulders, except for this wide spot and the acreage around their house. Not a good place for a ranch like Mom and Dad's, that's for sure." She smiled. "Mom said it was a good place to be 'from.'"

"With the right tent, and a way to make coffee, you'd have a hard time making me leave." Cody closed his eyes and took a deep breath.

"But you promised me a burger!" She poked him in the arm.

"Okay, okay." He turned around to head back to the truck. "Can you behave yourself in the restaurant? No more hilarious outbursts?"

"That felt so good!" She giggled. "Why did it take something sad like cutting down the shoe tree to make me laugh like that?"

"I have no clue how your mind works." He shook his head. "I guess you'll have to ask a psychology professor when you go back to school."

A notification buzzed on her cellphone. Message from Uncle Smiley.

> Give me a call when you have service. No
> emergency.

There was not enough signal up here. She'd have to try when they were driving back to Russellville.

"Okay, burgers it is." Cody moved slowly across the grassy area near his truck.

Back on the road to Coach and Zanna's house, the buzz of chainsaws was joined by the whirring of the huge chipper that ground the smaller branches and leaves into mulch.

"They're making progress." Cody commented. "Do you want to stop again?"

"I don't want to stay and watch, that's for sure." She sat back against the truck seat. "But if you see Zanna standing there, we can stop to talk to her for a second."

"You got it." Cody parked on the other side of the work area. Zanna waved from her spot next to her friend Ellen.

"We talked to the museum downtown." Zanna leaned into the passenger side window. "We're going to take the shoes and send Ellen's pictures to them. They'll make sure the shoe tree is not forgotten."

"Good idea." Kayla patted Zanna's hand. "I guess we'll have to learn to move on, right?"

"We're never ready for changes like this, but they're part of life." Zanna reached past Kayla to wave her fingers in Cody's direction. "Y'all be careful going home. And come back, both of you."

"Yes ma'am. I hope to." Cody caught Kayla's eye and winked.

Kayla checked the cellphone signal when they reached the main highway.

"Hey, Uncle Smiley." She moved the phone to her right hand, hoping not to disturb Cody's driving.

"I thought you might want an update on ranch business."

He sounded a little out of breath.

"What's up?" Did she want to know, or should she let Uncle Smiley and Rod do all the worrying?

"Rod says there are a couple more cows missing."

Her eyes widened as she waited for him to continue.

"The last time, it was just a mama cow who had gone to an out-of-the-way place to calve. But, today, he says there are four, maybe five that didn't appear when he made his evening rounds."

"Does he have any idea what happened to them?" Were the coyotes back?

"Not really. I'm out riding the fence line right now. I just thought it would be easier to keep you posted than to bring you up to date later. Don't worry too much, sweetie."

He must be calling while on horseback. Thank goodness it wasn't raining tonight.

"I'm so glad you're helping out, Uncle Smiley. Cody and I are eating in Russellville, but we'll be home soon." She raised her left hand to let Cody know nothing too serious was happening.

"You two sure are spending a lot of time together lately." A tease filled her uncle's voice, bringing a heat to her cheeks. "Okay. Y'all be careful. Talk to you soon."

"So?" Cody followed the curvy main street through the college town. "Do we need to get you home?"

"No. Uncle Smiley's on top of things. It is sort of strange, though. Cattle don't often go missing like this. I hope he and Rod get it figured out soon."

"Maybe we should form a posse to go look for them no-good rustlers." Cody deadpanned.

"Hopefully not. But you'll be the first one I'll deputize if we do." First the shoe tree, and now missing cattle. "Actually, you can be in charge of the posse."

"Good way to live up to my name." He grinned.

"What?" She was confused.

"My grandpa in Montana is a retired U.S. Marshal. That's why I'm Marshal Cody."

"If I knew that, I forgot." She grinned while he puffed out his chest. "Well, then. I feel much safer now."

"Those ornery cowpokes don't stand a chance." Cody winked.

Chapter Seven

"Come on, Grandpa Dee. Eat just a little bit of this meatloaf." Cody skewered one of the small pieces of meat with a fork and held it toward his grandpa's tightly closed lips.

"Well, how about some mashed potatoes and gravy?" This spoonful met with more success. Cody released the spoon as Grandpa Dee took it from him.

"I just don't know." Mom walked behind Cody and talked softly. "The nurse said he can only have soft food now. It's getting harder to persuade him to eat."

"Yeah. He's probably tired of mashed potatoes. I know he'd rather have a juicy steak than chopped-up meatloaf." Cody didn't like talking about Grandpa Dee like this. He wasn't even out of earshot. So disrespectful. "We'll be right back, Grandpa."

He rolled toward the dining room doorway, hoping Mom would follow.

"Why only soft food?" He watched as Grandpa Dee drug a spoon through his potatoes.

"The nurse said he is at the point now where he's forgetting how important it is to chew everything. He could easily get choked." Mom tucked both of her hands into her blue-jean pockets. "This is hard, son. Instead of asking for something that sounds more appetizing, he refuses to eat what he doesn't like. Sort of like a baby."

Cody nodded.

"Okay. We'll just keep trying to get him to eat, I guess. Maybe tomorrow, I'll bring him his favorite chocolate ice cream for dessert. That would be better than nothing." He moved closer to the table, where Grandpa Dee sat back in his chair, his fork and spoon discarded.

"You finished, Dad?" Mom wiped Grandpa Dee's chin with a napkin. "We can go back to your room now."

"I'll race you Grandpa Dee." Cody headed down the hallway as his mom pushed the other wheelchair. He passed other men snacking on treats their families had brought in. Yep. Tomorrow, he'd bring ice cream.

"Okay, ladies. If we stay a few car lengths behind this float, we'll have a wonderful day." From her saddle, Kayla looked over her left shoulder at the mounted princesses waiting behind her.

"You are so nailing this job of Miss Rodeo Arkansas Teen." Alex and her horse stopped next to her. Her Miss Rodeo Arkansas sash glittered in the morning sunlight. "These girls think you are all that and a bag of chips."

"Wrong. They're awestruck with *you*." Kayla laughed. "Most of them see me too often to think I'm special. But we've had a great time at the events we've done together so far."

"We're about to get even busier. Today is good practice for future parades." Alex relaxed in the saddle. "Your session on horsemanship should help keep everything running smoothly today."

"I hope so." Kayla patted Sissy's neck. "But hey, before we get started, I'd like to say something to the guy who's pulling this float. He needs to know not to make any sudden stops if he can help it."

"Yeah, you'd better tell him that." Alex winked. "Tell Cody I said 'hey.'"

Kayla approached Cody in his truck as it idled in front of the horses.

She pulled Sissy to a stop next to the driver's window. "Are you excited?"

"Oh, yeah. Creeping along a city street towing an overgrown red wagon is a great way to spend a Saturday morning." Cody leaned toward her, tipping his hat back on his head. "You look marvelous, as usual."

"Two days in a row of wearing this official regalia is a little much." She made sure the words on her sash were readable.

"The pains of being a local celebrity." He laughed. "Tell your ladies to hang back a little. Hope and the others will be throwing candy from the float, and there will be crumb snatchers everywhere."

"Yes, sir, marshal, sir." She gave him an exaggerated salute.

"Ready, Cody?" The walkie-talkie beside him in the seat piped up in Hope's voice. "Tell Kayla you'll see her later."

"Ready." He picked up the radio to answer. "See ya afterward?" He smiled at Kayla.

"Sure. I'll have to get Sissy home, but then we can do something if you want."

"Yeah. I need to run by and see if I can get Grandpa Dee to eat an early supper. How about six-thirty-ish?" After checking all three mirrors, he faced her. "*Hasta luego*."

"*Adios*!" She galloped back to join Alex.

"I told Cody we'd hang back." The flat-bed trailer packed with Billings Boys employees and their kids moved slowly forward. "One, Mississippi, two Mississippi, three Mississippi. Let's Go!" Kayla prompted her horse to take the first official steps on the parade route.

Cody braked again to keep the truck from creeping up behind the Crossroads Coyote marching band. This was a nerve-wracking drive. A barrage of dropping pebble noises behind the trailer was followed by shrill screams.

In the rear-view mirror, kids of all sizes and shapes scrambled for the candy being tossed off the float. Kayla and Alex reined in their horses as a roly-poly boy picked up one more all-day sucker before running back to the side of the road.

He'd actually been one of those guys dodging vehicles and horses for a bag of his favorite candy. Today, though, Kayla was in charge of a bunch of inexperienced girls on skittish horses.

Nope. This was not going to happen. Not for the remainder of the parade route. Surely, these kids had picked up enough candy today.

"Hope." He steered with one hand and pressed the button on the walkie-talkie with the other.

"Yeah," She shouted over the excited din.

"Stop throwing candy. If these kids don't get under the wheels of the trailer, they'll get trampled by horses." He couldn't stand it if Kayla or one of her young protegees got hurt in the bargain.

"You got it."

Hope signaled the kids on the float to hold their fire.

Okay. Maybe now he could continue the route without losing his mind.

As he continued his mirror-checking routine, Kayla and Alex waved at the youngsters standing along the route. Hopefully, the absence of kids scrambling on the ground in their path would make this ride more enjoyable for them as well. Those two were real pros at this regal wave bit. The redhead in particular caught his eye. There had been plenty of rodeo entries, parades and barrel races before. Now that he had spent some time with her, she was prettier than ever.

The procession approached the nursing home where he and Grandpa Dee had watched the parade from the front porch last year.

A jarring "Whoop-whoop" called his attention to an ambulance that waited at the edge of the facility's parking lot. A policeman stood in front of his truck with his hand raised.

He stopped and sent up a quick prayer as the ambulance nosed its way through the parade crowd to the next side street, where the siren started up in earnest.

Lord, thank you for the experts who are taking such good care of whomever is in the back of that ambulance. Be with their family through this crisis. And please don't let it be Grandpa Dee. Amen.

He accelerated just enough to catch up to the marching band again without throwing Dad's employees off the float. No wonder he'd been the only one to volunteer to drive today. Pulling parade floats was not for the faint of heart.

Kayla checked the time on her phone after stowing the fancy tack she'd used in the parade. Five-fifteen. Plenty of time to change clothes before Cody arrived. She waved at Nancy, who was serving a tall glass of lemonade to Rod on their patio. Might as well go say *hello.*

"How was the parade?" Nancy walked to the edge of the patio.

"Slow and steady." Kayla laughed. "All of the future princesses seemed to enjoy it. Hey, Rod."

The dark-eyed foreman turned to face her.

"Kayla." He nodded, but quickly turned to face the pasture behind their house.

She sat in a patio chair, following his glance. "Uncle Smiley said we're possibly missing some cattle?"

Was that what had him pre-occupied?

"Sometimes I think I'm going crazy. The guys all give me a

heads-up before they go home in the afternoon, but I've been riding the pasture where the mama cows and young steers stay since one of them had a problem calving last week. There's only thirty total over there, and two days in a row, I've come up with twenty-six." He moved the brim of his hat back to scratch his head. "It's not like we have thousands of acres. There are only a few places to hide. But we have one cow that is pretty distinctive, and I haven't seen her."

"The billboard cow." Nancy sat beside Kayla. "Can I bring you some lemonade?"

"The billboard?" Kayla squinched her nose up. "And, no thanks. I'm good."

"Your Mom and Dad bought a few black and white cows to crossbreed with the Angus. One of them has this big band of white around her middle. I used to tell Dub he should rent her out to someone who wanted to advertise their business. They could paint a logo on her flank with no problem." Nancy smiled.

"Yeah. She's hard to miss." Rod agreed. "She didn't show up for afternoon feeding. She and her new calf are missing, and the other two are steers."

"That is strange, all right. I guess the fences all look solid?" Kayla didn't want to tell him how to keep up with the cattle. He'd been doing it for years.

"As far as I can tell. I plan to take a closer look in the morning. They have to be getting out somewhere." Rod walked to the edge of the patio.

"I know you'll figure this out." Kayla winked at Nancy. "You know how grateful I am for the two of you, right?"

"The life of a rancher." Nancy said. "We try not to burden you too much."

"Hey, I'm a big girl now. I'll do my share. How 'bout I ride the edges of that pasture in the morning? Would that help?" She stepped back toward her own house.

"Sure." Rod nodded. "Let me know if you see anything out of the ordinary."

Kayla waved as she trotted past the barn. Cody's comment about rustlers echoed in her head. He'd been joking. Should she be looking for tire tracks tomorrow? Cows didn't disappear into thin air.

A notification buzzed on her phone.

> Sorry. Have to cancel. Grandpa Dee in hospital.

She typed her response.

> Oh, no. Sending prayers.

She stopped walking and closed her eyes. *Lord, take care of this precious man. He's so special to Cody and his family. Show me how to help. Amen.*

Chapter Eight

"Come on, son." Dad pushed open the gleaming silver door and led the way to the ER exam room.

Inside, Grandpa Dee wore a peaceful expression, as the lone IV pole dripped beside him.

"Just the one machine?" Cody asked the nurse who was removing a blood pressure cuff.

"He has a Do Not Resuscitate order." The young man explained. "The nursing home said he got choked while eating lunch. The staff wanted us to check him out."

Cody nodded, rolling closer to touch Grandpa Dee's hand.

"You gave us a scare, Grandpa Dee." If only those eyes would open, even for a moment.

"Everyone's concerned, Dewayne. I hope we can get you a little more comfortable soon." Dad stood at the foot of the bed.

Cody took a deep breath. He'd be content to just sit here and watch his oldest buddy breathe for the few minutes that were allowed.

Kayla settled into a wicker chair on the patio just as her cellphone rang. Cody.

"So, what's happening in your world? Did you get Sissy settled after the parade?"

"She's running around with Caesar and Breezy, living her best life." Kayla watched the horses make another lap around the corral. "I don't know if she'll want to come inside tonight. It's so nice outside. Unusual for June."

"Yeah. The breeze feels great." The wind whistled through his end of the phone as if to emphasize his point. "But I can't see any stars here at the hospital with all the parking lot lights."

"They're still out there. I hope you get back to where you can see them soon." These days, hearing his voice wasn't quite enough. "How's your grandpa?"

"He's stable. He got choked while trying to eat at the nursing home. They just sent him here to get him checked out."

"I'm glad he's better." She sighed in relief.

"Thanks. Me too. I guess I need to go back inside. Hopefully, Dad will be ready to go home soon. I can't drive his truck," he said.

"I know you'll both be glad to leave that place." Hospitals were certainly not her favorite place, either.

"For sure. Good night, Miss Kayla. Talk to you soon." She could hear a little bit of teasing when he used that Western accent.

"Good night, Marshal Cody, sir." She smiled. "Pleasant dreams."

Lights snapped on at Nancy and Rod's house. Kayla had promised to ride along the edge of the pasture where the 'billboard cow' and the others were missing this morning. Did she have any idea what to look for?

Too bad she hadn't helped her dad more often when he was

working with the cattle. She half expected to see him out there, riding Caesar. Maybe it wasn't too late to learn how to help Rod a little more. But what about her college classes in the fall? Registration time opened in a couple of weeks. She couldn't even recall which classes were important for her degree plan. Too many things to think about.

She walked to the barn. Better make sure the three amigos were set for the night. *Lord, be with Cody's grandpa and the whole family. Help all of us trust in You. Amen.*

Sissy picked up her pace as Kayla guided her out of a wooded area at the north edge of the pasture. Kayla settled into the saddle and allowed the horse to gallop toward the house.

Should she have dismounted and examined the fence? Nothing had appeared out of place. There were no gaps in the barrier that she could see. Especially nothing big enough for several head of cattle to get through.

She passed a group of mama cows feeding their calves. That would add six to her head count. Twenty-six, just like Rod said. If the missing cow and steers were injured or sick, surely she would have seen them. There were some brushy places on the land, but nowhere was it wooded enough for animals to hide for long.

Surely Rod had just miscounted. The missing cattle must be in another section of the pasture with the bulls or the weaned calves. But what about the billboard cow? Her thoughts kept coming back to what Nancy had said about the most distinctive cow in the pasture. If she was in the wrong place, someone would have noticed.

She approached the barn, where Uncle Smiley's truck sat idling in the driveway.

"Just let me unsaddle Sissy. I'll be right along." One more time, she was grateful they attended cowboy church. Most

Sundays, she dressed up a little, but on the days when chores happened just before time to leave, she didn't have to worry about her appearance.

When the tack was hung in the barn, she dashed for Uncle Smiley's truck. If she was going to ride the fence line on Sunday morning, she should get out of bed earlier. It would have been nice to at least brush her hair.

Cody caught up with Kayla as she walked out of church.

"What's up?" He tilted his hat back.

"Not a lot. Hope and I are going grocery shopping this afternoon. I'm out of just about everything at home. She said I could eat meals with her and O.D., but I've got that big kitchen. I should be able to cook for myself." She waved at her cousin, signaling her to wait. "How about you?"

"O.D. and I are driving through to get a burger, then going to check on Grandpa Dee. Then, when we get home, I've got a training video to watch before my first day at work tomorrow."

"That's so exciting. Do you think watching a video will help as much as actually doing the work?"

"I hope so. They said I'll have cleanup duties too. I'm going to practice with the push broom in the barn this afternoon. I don't want to take the power chair if I don't have to." He rubbed his chin, trying to generate a new idea of some kind.

"If you could hang on to a bull for eight seconds, I know you'll figure this out." She gave him a one-armed hug. "See ya later."

Cody headed for his truck.

He wanted to work so badly. This job at the boat company sounded good. Why couldn't he shake these doubts?

Chapter Nine

"Thanks, Rod." Kayla waved as the foreman stopped behind his house. "Let's get you home, Sissy. Caesar and Breezy will be wondering where you've been today."

She unsaddled the horse and turned her out to the corral. Kayla's muscles complained after riding around all day, but she couldn't keep turning a blind eye to everything that happened on her ranch. Uncle Smiley had his own property to tend to. It was way past time she learned to pull her own weight.

Dust billowed at the end of the driveway as Cody's truck approached. He slowed to a stop and waved.

"Hey," she greeted him, as she walked closer.

"What's up?" His arm rested on the rolled down window of his truck.

"How was your first day at the new job?" He hadn't texted her all day, and she'd missed him.

"Busy! But great." He smiled, turning off his engine.

"I was about to get a glass of lemonade. Want some?"

"Sure. I very rarely turn down a cool drink. It's starting to feel like summer out here."

"For sure." She hurried into her kitchen and found two tall

glasses. Maybe he wouldn't mind sitting on the patio to talk. Even though she'd been in the heat all day herself, she didn't want to come inside yet. There was usually a good breeze next to the pool.

"You want to sit out here?" She opened the pool gate, pointing to the group of wicker chairs.

"Sounds great."

She held the cold glass while he transferred to a chair.

"So, you think you will get the hang of this new job? What exactly are you doing?" She'd driven past the boat plant, but she'd never been inside.

"Well, after they get the metal boat all welded together, I'll be the one to smooth out the surface before they paint it. I felt like I was going slow today, but I should get better with the big grinder the more I use it." He took a drink of lemonade.

"Are the people friendly?" Would his co-workers have patience with his limitations?

"Sure. As long as I do my job, I guess they'll stay that way. I don't know how long I'll want to keep grinding metal, though. There were a couple of guys welding, wearing those cool visors and leather aprons, and using a torch. That looks like the best job." He used the arms of the wicker chair to stretch his body upward. "Maybe I'll learn that someday. But today, I'm more worn out than I've been in a while."

"I'm glad you like it." Kayla took a long drink. "I've been learning a lot today too."

"What do you need to know about working a ranch?" He leaned toward her.

"Up until now, most of my chores involved the horses and the barn. Working with cattle in the fields is a whole new thing." She scooted to the edge of the chair. "I was trying to help Rod locate cattle. He thinks there are six missing now."

"That's crazy." Cody looked across the pool toward the pasture. "There shouldn't be a lot of places for them to get lost. Have you notified anyone?"

"I'm leaving that up to Rod and Uncle Smiley. I guess they may report it soon. At this point, it just has everyone baffled." Whose job was it to hunt for missing cows? The sheriff?

"Maybe a flying saucer kidnapped them." Cody looked skyward, twirling his finger.

"Be serious." She smiled anyway.

"Oh yeah, I know it's serious. I guess my brain is fried tonight. Tomorrow, I'll take you for a ride on my UTV. We might be able to bring it to your place to look for clues."

"Thanks. I hate sitting around wondering. I'd feel better if I was doing something to help. Maybe you'll notice something I've missed." Kayla took a deep breath. Having Cody's assistance might keep her from being overwhelmed by this problem.

Kayla sipped her lemonade. Why had Cody come straight here after work instead of going home first? She didn't want to ask. Even though the outdoor space of her house was her comfort zone, the quiet and loneliness weighed her down. No one else who'd visited after Mom and Dad died made her so comfortable.

"I'd better be going." He shifted back to his wheelchair and started toward the gate.

"Do you have to go so soon?" She touched his shoulder.

"I want to see how Grandpa Dee looks tonight. I have this feeling my oldest brother is going to have the same questions I had about the care he's getting at the nursing home."

"That's so hard." Kayla hugged him. "I'll keep praying for all of you."

"That's the best anybody can do right now." Cody took both of her hands in his. "I'll talk to you tomorrow, okay?"

"Absolutely." She followed him to his truck. "See you soon."

Kayla stood in the driveway until he turned onto the road. Too bad she couldn't go to work with him tomorrow. The tasks she faced inside loomed ahead of her. Instead of sorting through her mom and dad's things, should she volunteer to ride through the pastures again? Ranch work was fine, but when Cody was here, she felt different. Safer, more confident.

If she insisted on riding the edges of the property, would Rod think she didn't trust him to keep track of the cattle? *Lord, help me decide what my next steps should be. Thanks for sending Cody to keep me focused. Be with his whole family as they tend to his grandpa. Give them all peace in this situation. Amen.*

Cody's phone buzzed in his pocket.

"Hey. Want to meet me in town for supper?" Just the sound of Kayla's voice brought a smile.

"Sure, where?" Supper was next on his list after a long day at the boat factory.

"There's a new barbecue food truck in the grocery store parking lot."

"I need to clean up first." He couldn't look or smell very appealing right now.

"For a food truck?" Kayla laughed. "Besides, I thought you were going to take me for a ride on your UTV."

"Okay. I'll be there in five minutes." Cody sent another quick text to his mom, who was probably looking out the kitchen window right now.

> Running into town to grab something to eat
> with Kayla. Be back soon.

Cody balanced two boxes holding sandwiches and sides on his lap as Kayla took their drinks to a picnic table near the food truck.

"Still like that job?" She sat at the end of the bench.

"Yeah. It's actually okay. Noisy, dirty. My kind of entertainment." He laughed.

"I've been riding around on the ranch my whole life, but spending one-on-one time with noisy, smelly cattle makes me tired." She took a bite of her sandwich.

"Too tired for a spin around my place on the UTV?"

"*Nah*. Bring it on."

They laughed as they finished their meals.

"I'll follow you home." She rose and carried their trash to a nearby barrel.

Cody led the way back to the Billings' ranch, with Kayla close behind.

"Okay, now where's this amazing vehicle?" Kayla rubbed her hands together as she jumped out of her truck. "We've got some time before it gets dark."

"Come on, it's this way." He rolled toward the barn. Was there enough gas in his vehicle to make a quick tour of their pasture?

"That's awesome. And you can drive it with hand controls?" Kayla ran her hand over the passenger seat.

"Yep. Hop in." He left his chair next to the UTV and moved into place. Looked like there was plenty of gas.

"Great!" Kayla climbed in and grabbed the bar in front of her. "Let's go."

Cody drove around the edge of the barn and headed across the pasture.

"Your land doesn't butt up against ours, does it?" He barely heard her question over the motor noise.

"It used to. Back this way, it meets up with the part your dad sold to that Heston, the casino owner guy."

"Oh, yeah, that's right."

He bounced over ruts and rough places in the pasture, taking it a little slower than usual. No need to throw her out.

They reached the fence, and he prepared to make a wide turn.

"Wait. Stop!" She waved her hands wildly.

He braked, keeping the engine idling.

"Look, it's the billboard cow."

She bounded off the vehicle and rushed to the barbed-wire fence.

"The what? What's it doing here?" Had she said 'billboard cow?'

"Exactly. That's *our* cow in Heston's pasture. I have to take a picture." She pulled her phone out of her pocket.

"Are you sure?" He followed her focus to a black-and-white cow with a distinctive blank space between the black head and the black hindquarters. Okay, a billboard cow.

"Yes! That's one of the cows that went missing. We have to tell the sheriff. That man is stealing our cows."

If this was supposed to be a calm ride around the property to settle their emotions, things were not turning out as planned.

"Yeah, by all means, get your picture. But we won't call the sheriff. The county agent watches out for livestock."

Good thing he'd been with her when she made this discovery. He could hear Kayla's phone call now.

"Nine-one-one, what's your emergency?"

"Our neighbor stole our billboard cow."

Nope. Not how he expected this night to go at all.

Chapter Ten

"So, that's when I came straight home." She pushed her phone across Nancy's kitchen table with the picture of the billboard cow displayed.

"It definitely looks like her." Rod picked up the phone. "Did you tell Smiley?"

"Yes. He said he'd be right home." Kayla drummed her fingers on the tabletop. "Shouldn't we call somebody to report this? Cody said it wouldn't be the sheriff—it would be the county agent. But they need to know, right? It looks like Quinton Heston is stealing cattle from us."

Nancy set a cup of coffee in front of Rod.

"Cody's right. It's the county agent, not the sheriff. He'll need daylight to check this out." Rod picked up the steaming mug.

"I would imagine he'll want more proof." Nancy sat next to Kayla.

"I remember watching y'all put ear tags on the cows." Kayla turned her phone face down. "That's how we prove they're ours, right?"

"Right," Rod said. "But if Heston is stealing cattle, he has probably already retagged them. The new calf wasn't tagged yet, but the steers were."

"I didn't think about him retagging them. But the billboard cow is so different looking. We should be able to pick her out from the rest of his herd." Would the county agent take the word of a casino owner over ranchers who dealt with cattle to make their living?

"Your picture will be a big help, Kayla. Can you send it to me? I'll give the agent a call in the morning. Then, we'll see what other clues we can find." Rod walked to the window, parking both hands in his back pockets as he stared into the setting sun.

"Picture!" Nancy pushed back from the table. "I think I have an actual photo of this cow. Dub and Tina said they were going to buy this black and white cow. I guess I was expecting a Holstein. They called this one a Lakenvelder. She was just so unique. I had to have a picture." She hurried to the large roll-top desk in the corner of the living area.

"I'm glad you're helping us with this, Kayla. I have been feeling the weight of the ranch business lately. Your dad and I made a pretty good team." Rod sipped his coffee.

"I don't know how much I can help, but I'll keep trying." Kayla read a text that had popped up from Uncle Smiley.

> You home?

> I'm still at Rod and Nancy's

It felt good to have someone checking on her.

> I'm headed your way for a quick visit. No emergency, just something I need to share.

She'd have plenty to share with him as well.

> OK

"Here it is." Nancy plopped the photo of the black and white cow in front of Kayla. "Rod and Dub thought your mom and I were nuts, making such a big deal over this cow. Might as well have fun, right?"

Kayla smiled through the tears welling up in her eyes. Nancy and her mom were really hamming it up in this picture. They used their best 'Vanna White' poses to point out the distinctive white band around the cow's middle. Hopefully, having the two ladies in the picture wouldn't keep the county agent from identifying the cow.

"I wrote the date from three years ago on the back of the picture." Nancy flipped it over.

"That's great. Thanks for showing me."

"Remember, even if we show the agent these pictures, Heston will just say he has a cow that resembles ours. Without our tag on her ear, I don't know if this will be enough." Rod paced in front of the window. "And it doesn't locate any of the other stock."

"Yeah. I get it." Kayla walked to the front door. "I'll keep looking and keep thinking."

"See you tomorrow, sweetie." Nancy hugged her. "Sleep well."

Kayla took a long deep breath as she began the short walk to her house. The warm air didn't hold the humidity of a typical Arkansas summer, but right now, some moisture would actually feel good. She kicked up a small cloud of dust as she walked across the driveway. Even a little rain would probably help, but that might or might not happen any time soon.

Uncle Smiley's truck stopped next to hers in the driveway. He took a minute to examine her tires before leaning against his own truck to wait for her.

"How are Rod and Nancy?" He rested his arm on the bed of the truck.

"They're good. They were happy to see the picture I took of the billboard cow, but Rod thinks the agent will need more than that before he can talk to Heston."

"Heston." Uncle Smiley shook his head. "Talking to him when we went out of the rodeo business left a bad taste in my mouth. Your dad's words were, 'his money spends just like anyone else's.' So, he made a deal for the rodeo stock and that piece of land. I don't know why Heston would need to steal cattle. Honestly, it wouldn't shock me."

Kayla took a step toward the back door. "You coming inside? I can get you a cup of coffee."

"Why don't we just sit out here by the pool for a minute?" Uncle Smiley opened the iron gate.

Kayla settled in her favorite wicker chair with her feet tucked under her. The lights in the pool grew a little brighter as the sunlight faded. She still felt proud of this outdoor kitchen and patio. Dad had been impressed by the plan she'd drawn up, and mom had loved the way the whole thing turned out. It wasn't as complicated as designing a whole building, but it had whetted her appetite to learn more.

"I spent a lot of time talking to Candace tonight." Uncle Smiley looked down at his folded hands.

"*Mm-hmm*." Kayla smiled. The spark between those two was obviously growing.

"I've been trying to talk her into going on a mission trip to Mexico later this summer."

"You're definitely going?" She'd gotten used to Uncle Smiley filling in for her parents. Would he be leaving her now?

"I'm considering it. Junior will be fine at home by himself. Now that we have an assistant minister at the Cowboy Church, they can do without me there too. We have fifteen members of our youth group signed up. We need one more female chaperone. Candace would be perfect." He turned to look at Kayla. "With all this business about missing cattle, maybe now is not a good time for me to leave."

He was worried more about the cattle than how Kayla would manage alone? She'd take that as a compliment.

"I think Rod has a handle on the missing cattle thing. Don't let ranch business keep you from your mission trip." She remembered Cody's promise to help her check the fences as well. Time to put her big girl boots on. "I plan to do all I can to help."

"I've been so proud of the way you've handled yourself, Kayla Grace." He smiled at her.

"It hasn't been easy. I think I'm adjusting." She didn't add the thought that flashed through her mind, 'with Cody's help.'

"You are. Continue to trust in the Lord and let me know when I can help." He tapped the end of her nose, the way he'd done since she was small. "I love you, Kayla Grace."

"I love you too." She stood and gave him a hug. With two or three long strides, he reached his truck, and headed for home.

Kayla walked inside, down the hall to her bedroom. What a strange evening. She thought riding around Cody's ranch would clear her head. Instead, they had new evidence that their neighbor might be stealing cattle. Why was this not important enough to get action from the proper authorities?

Now, Uncle Smiley might be leaving. She'd heard so many people talk about "moving on" after a loss. How could she do that when she didn't know what direction to move?

Kayla opened her computer and scrolled down the list of courses she had selected to take this fall. There were still a couple of basic required classes, but for the most part, they looked interesting. This would be the beginning of her degree work on her way to becoming a real architect.

Registration started in two weeks. She could handle most of the process from home.

If Mom were here, tomorrow would be spent shopping for updated items Kayla might need in her dorm room. Instead, she would be grooming horses and checking with Rod and Nancy to see what else she could help with on the ranch. The thought of spending time here didn't sound so bad after all.

She pulled up the picture of the billboard cow again. Should she try to get a better picture showing the cow's ear tag? She'd have to be on the Billings' land or maybe even cross through the fence to get a closer look. Would that be considered trespassing?

She closed her pictures and saw a quick post from Cody.

Thanks for talking to me. I've got to try to get
some sleep so I can work tomorrow.

Sleep tight.

She answered with a thumbs-up emoji, though she considered replacing it with a heart. That wouldn't be right, would it? Didn't he still see her as a friendly listening ear? She wasn't completely sure how she felt about him, either. There certainly wasn't anyone else she'd rather talk to or text with at this time of night. Maybe soon, the heart emoji wouldn't feel wrong.

One thing was becoming clear. Moving to Fayetteville to start her next semester of college was not exciting anymore. Uncle Smiley wanted to be more 'hands off' with the ranch business, so he could concentrate on church work. Until this missing cattle case was resolved, she was needed right here. Then, there was Cody. Could their friendship turn into something more if she lived more than an hour away? Maybe the home she'd grown up in was where she belonged. She switched off the light and pulled back the covers on her bed. If that decision was made, why was it so difficult to close her eyes and go to sleep?

Chapter Eleven

Kayla waited at the barn door as Cody's truck stopped in her driveway. Was he adding early morning visits to their daily schedule? After a couple of long steps, she leaned into his window, getting a whiff of his musky aftershave.

"Won't you be late to work this morning?"

"*Nah*. It's on my way." He opened his door, allowing her to stand closer. "Are you taking Sissy for a ride?"

"It's Caesar's turn." She stepped toward him. "I'll send the other two out to the pasture. Breezy may run along behind for a ways. Those two don't like to be apart for long."

Was that a blush on his cheek?

"Sounds like they're a sweet couple." He stared at the ground between them.

Yes, definitely a blush.

"I'll bring my UTV over after work tonight if you still want to ride your fence line." He finally met her eyes.

"Yeah. That would be good." She kicked the dust. "I'd love to have something else to report to Rod about the missing cattle."

"Is he calling the county agent today?" Cody tapped the steering wheel.

"I hope so. I wish they would go over and look for the billboard cow, but Rod says it's not that simple."

"No. Accusing your neighbor of stealing is a serious thing. I guess he wants to be sure."

Rod and one of his ranch hands approached on horseback.

"Hey, Kayla," Rod greeted her as they stopped in front of Cody's truck.

"Rod, you remember Cody Billings, right?"

Cody waved from the truck. "Hey. Sorry I don't have time to get out. I'm on my way to work."

"Yeah, sure." Rod gestured toward the other rider. "Kayla, you haven't met Austin. We hired him pretty soon after your mom and dad passed. He's already been a big help."

Kayla didn't remember seeing this thirty-ish guy with the long blond hair before.

"Hi, Austin." She walked forward to meet the man with a handshake after he dismounted. "This is my friend, Cody."

Cody raised a finger.

"We're just passing by. I wanted to introduce Austin because he needs to get to know your horses. He has worked with quarter horses as well as thoroughbreds. He can be a big help especially when you move back to school this fall. Austin, when you come over later, let Kayla walk you through her daily routine. She owns three fine animals. They have learned to be a little particular."

"Translate that to 'spoiled.'" Kayla laughed. "Yeah, I'll fill you in later today." She probably wouldn't need much help from this guy since she'd decided not to go to school this semester. He didn't need to know all of that right now.

"Looking forward to it, ma'am." He tipped his cowboy hat and remounted his horse in one smooth movement.

Impressive. Maybe too impressive.

"See you two later." Rod waved as they galloped back toward his house.

Now it was Kayla who blushed. *You two.* As if she and Cody were a couple. Were they?

"I guess I'd better get moving. I won't have my phone with me until lunch, but I'll text you then." Cody interrupted her daydream.

She backed up, allowing him to close his door.

"Yeah. I do want you to take me for a ride tonight. I can have something ready for supper afterward. What do want to eat?" She couldn't believe her own words. Was she really offering to cook for him?

"Sounds great. Surprise me." He winked as he started his truck. "I can't stay too late. I've got to work tomorrow."

"I'll figure something out. Have a good day."

He patted her hand, which still rested next to him on the car door. She stepped back. Dust followed him up the driveway. If every day started with a visit from Cody, she could learn to love staying on the ranch.

Entering the barn, she prepared to saddle Caesar. Hopefully, time would pass quickly. She enjoyed riding Dad's stallion, but she'd much rather be riding with Cody today. She'd heard of paralyzed people riding. Maybe someday.

Nervous stomping and huffing reminded her that her "particular" horses were tired of waiting. A pit of doubt churned in her stomach at the thought of allowing a stranger to help take care of them. Maybe this Austin guy would find more important things to do on the ranch.

She opened Sissy and Breezy's stalls and guided them out to play in the pasture behind the barn. Caesar paced impatiently. The horses couldn't possibly keep up with whose turn it was to go for a ride, but this black stallion understood he was the one selected today.

"Okay, boy. We'll go for a good long ride before it gets too hot outside. Ready?" She talked to him calmly, patting him often through the saddling and mounting process. Would Austin be as careful with Dad's favorite? If she returned to school, would she eventually sell one or all of these four-legged family members?

She shifted her weight as Caesar galloped across the flat area of the pasture. She'd slow him down when they reached the wooded part near the fence. His mane and her long hair flew freely behind them, and she rocked with each of his movements.

If she was so sure about not registering for college this fall, why had she not shared her thoughts with anyone? Not Uncle Smiley, not Rod and Nancy, not even Cody. He had been a great listener. Wouldn't he support her decision to stay here on the ranch?

Kayla slowed Caesar as they approached a water trough near the gate leading to the cow and calf pasture. She opened the gate and led him through, mounting after closing it behind them. She'd promised to check the fence around this area. If there were no breaks, what explanation was there for seeing the billboard cow on Heston's land, other than he had stolen her?

Caesar took a more leisurely walk along the fence line. Kayla couldn't see anything strange here. There certainly wasn't an opening big enough for a cow or even a small steer to squeeze through. She'd have to take a closer look.

"Hey, Kayla!" Austin shouted from his horse a few hundred feet to her right. Cows followed him as he approached, probably hoping he was there to feed them.

"Hi." She turned Caesar toward him.

"All of this land belongs to you now? And all of the livestock?" He and his horse settled in beside her.

Where had that question come from? It shouldn't matter who owned what around here, as long as he was paid for the work he did each day.

"My grandparents and my uncle are involved too." That was all he really needed to know.

"Well, it's a beautiful place." He turned his horse toward the barn, and they walked side by side. "You're a lucky lady."

"It's home." Would it be impolite to encourage Caesar to run again? There was really no reason for her to be nervous around this guy. Lucky? To suddenly own one of the largest ranches in the county before her nineteenth birthday? Lucky to be living here all alone? That was one way to look at it.

"Let's see what that black stallion can do." Austin kicked his horse in the side, causing the sorrel to run hard.

Was that rough treatment necessary? She'd show him how to properly handle a horse.

"Let's go, Caesar." Gentle pressure and a pat on his neck sent the stallion on a quest to catch up and pass Austin and his mount. Kayla slowed her horse down before he reached the gate again.

"I just don't know this horse that well, yet." Austin waved at her. "We'll take you next time."

That was an understatement. None of their horses required more than a little bit of pressure from a good rider. Surely, this guy had something more important to do than run races around the ranch. She dismounted and led Caesar through the gate to the trough. No way would she turn over any barn responsibilities to this guy.

A text from Faith popped up on her phone as she unsaddled Caesar.

> Don't forget that little rodeo this weekend.

> I remember. Thought I might stay with Coach
> and Zanna afterward.

Wait. She'd just decided not to let Austin help with the horses, and she was already planning to leave for the weekend. Could she ask Nancy to check on them? What would Rod think about that?

"Need help?" Austin appeared in the doorway of the barn.

"Nope. I've got it. Caesar will be ready to join his friends outside in just a minute."

"Are you ready to show me what's what in here?" Austin leaned against an empty stall.

"I've got some rodeo business to handle. Why don't you come around just before you get off work this afternoon?" She couldn't put him off forever.

"Sure. See you about 4:30." He peeked into the other stalls before walking out the door he had entered.

"There you go, big guy." She patted Caesar playfully, sending him outside.

What excuse could she use at 4:30?

Cody's number appeared on her phone as it rang.

"Hi." She stepped out of the door of the barn, hoping to improve reception.

"Hey. We're getting off work early. Air conditioner fail," Cody said.

"Wow. Too hot for that." She took a step toward the paddock.

"We're trying to make it past lunch. Probably leave about 2:00."

"That's a long time with no air." She peered up at the cloudless sky.

"If you still want to ride along your fence, I'll run by my house and bring the UTV over to your place. Should be 3:00-ish."

He still wanted to come, after working in the heat all day?

"Great!" She couldn't wait to see him.

Cody might be here when Austin came back. Maybe he could help her decide why the guy creeped her out so badly.

"Gotta get busy. I'll see you soon."

"Bye. Drink lots of water." Was she turning into her mother? He knew to stay hydrated.

Kayla called Faith on her way inside. She did have some rodeo business. Austin didn't need to know it would only take a quick minute.

"Hi." Kayla stepped into the kitchen. "Yeah. I remember that rodeo. They want me there Friday and Saturday, right?"

"Friday evening and Saturday for a matinee. You'll be helping with award presentations. It should be over well before suppertime," Faith said.

"Thanks for helping me keep all this straight." Kayla checked the calendar Mom had posted next to the refrigerator. She'd have a hard time getting rid of it, even after the end of the year. She loved the silly decorations Mom added when she posted an event.

Saturday's entry was extra special. "Kayla Grace 19" was barely visible with the colorful decorations around the words. How did Mom fit so much in a small square on a calendar?

"So, you're okay with outfits and makeup and all that stuff?" Faith asked.

"Oh, yeah. I've got what I need." She'd be fine for the rodeo. But what about her first birthday as an orphan? Usually, the week before the big day was consumed with her parents teasing her about the items on her wish list. Dad especially loved telling her there was no way they could afford any of them. Right now, the only gifts she wanted were to see the two faces she couldn't have. There had been no mention of a party, and she was fine with that.

"Okay. Take care of yourself, and I'll see you Friday. Love you, Gracie," Faith said.

"Love you more, Lainie." She tucked her phone into her pocket and sank into a chair in the living room. This place was too big. Being outside with the horses felt much more normal. She was even beginning to get used to helping Rod with the cattle. But inside this house, the emptiness overwhelmed her.

"Okay. Just a couple more hours, and Cody will be here." Had she said that out loud?

Cody wiped his forehead with a red bandana. If it was this hot in mid-June, what would happen if the air conditioning went out in July or August?

"Knock it off, Billings." His boss walked past. "The sweeping can wait for tomorrow morning."

"Yes, sir." Cody gathered the rags he had been using. "I'll tend to these and head out."

"All right. Hopefully, the air will be fixed. If not, we'll shut down early again." He patted Cody's shoulder.

In the cab of his truck with the air conditioning going full blast, Cody considered taking a shower before going to Kayla's place. Grimy and sweaty on a normal work day, he was especially repulsive today. Cleaning up before driving around her property in the afternoon heat didn't make a lot of sense, though. Maybe she could put up with him as-is.

With the fancy UTV on a trailer behind him, he headed for the Caldwell ranch. Dad had been happy to help him get the trailer hitched up.

Tomorrow after work, he'd go the opposite way, timing the trip from work to the deer lease. It might not be much shorter than going home each day, but by staying there during the work week, he'd prove to his family he could make it on his own. He'd have to get used to not stopping at Kayla's after work. Part of being a working man. He'd just have to start living for the weekend, like everyone else.

Before turning off the motor in Kayla's driveway, he found an old bottle of cologne in his glove box. Maybe he could disguise his scent a bit.

"Hey." Kayla met him at the truck. "I'm glad you're here."

"Me too." Riding around with her would feel great. Cleaning up could wait.

"You take those bumps a little fast!" Kayla laughed as they bounced over another ditch.

"Where's your sense of adventure?" Cody yelled. "These things might be used for work, but they're built for fun. Don't you ride your horses fast?"

"Yeah. I guess bull-riders are better at hanging on." She tightened her grip on a handle in front of her.

"I guess so." He slowed to a stop near the spot where the western-most fence met the northern one.

"I can't get much closer. Can you go take a look at those posts?" Cody pointed to the corner.

"Sure." She stepped off. Two posts were wrapped together with a piece of barbed wire. "Why would someone do this?"

He tossed her a pair of leather gloves. "See if you can unwrap it and wiggle the post on this side."

Kayla held the barbed wire carefully, untangling the strands. With the piece of wire on the ground she tugged on the post, lifting it out of the ground.

"Look." She held the post and pulled the piece of fence back toward her. "It's like a home-made gate. If you pull this back far enough, it makes a pretty good gap in the fence."

Next to the fence, something bright yellow stood out against the dusty brown dirt near the fenceposts. She pointed. "What's that over there?"

"Looks like a pile of ear tags." Cody leaned out the side for a better look.

"That's what I thought. I'll go get them."

"No!" He shouted. "Don't touch them. Stay on your side of the fence and see if you can get a picture."

"Good idea." Her heart pounded. Good thing someone around here had a level head. If this was evidence, she didn't need to add her fingerprints and footprints to the scene.

"I wish we had taken pictures of the fenceposts before you moved them." Cody straightened up behind the controls again. "We'll put things back like they were for now."

"So, you think someone cut the fence, then repaired it after the cows came through?"

"And retagged them as soon as they got to the other side," Cody said.

"Not too smart to leave the tags here." Holding one of Cody's gloves in her teeth, she snapped several good zoomed-in pictures, as well as a full-distance one. Maybe they'd be able to enhance these to identify the tags were Caldwell tags. With both gloves back in place, she pushed the post back into its spot, and wound the wire around to secure it.

"I guess they weren't counting on anyone looking so closely." Cody pointed. "Is that tight enough to hold the fence up?"

"I think so." Kayla turned to look back toward her house. "I don't ride behind these trees very often. Sissy and I usually turn before we get to this corner."

"Let's take those pictures back and talk to Rod." He started the motor of the machine as she climbed in. Would the county agent have enough evidence to confront Heston now?

The ride back to her barn was much quieter. She would have never noticed those tags or the temporary fence repair on her own. Cody's jaw was set and his eyes darted back and forth as they traveled over the bumpy pasture. Their excursion didn't feel much like a joy ride now.

"Is someone waiting for you?" Cody asked as she opened the gate to the pasture just behind the barn.

"Austin." She had promised to show him how to take care of the horses. She could put him off again, telling him she needed to go talk to Rod.

"Probably best not to say anything to him about this." Did Cody have the same bad vibe from this guy?

"Yeah. I promised to show him how to get our horses settled. Shouldn't take long. Then we can go see Rod." She took a deep breath. Could she hide the fact that she and Cody had discovered something exciting on their ride around the ranch? Time to use her pasted-on pageant smile.

"Cool. I'll go put my UTV on the trailer." He dropped her off at the back door of the barn.

She checked to be sure her phone was still in her pocket. Maybe she was being silly. Austin could be a big help in taking care of Caesar, Breezy, and Sissy.

"Out for an afternoon ride?" Austin walked up with a straw in his mouth.

"Yeah. It's kind of hot, but when you move fast enough, there's a breeze." She pushed her hair back from her forehead.

"That's a cool vehicle your friend has. I guess it's controlled with his hands?" Austin watched as Cody drove the UTV toward the trailer.

"Yeah." Cody was amazing, but right now, she needed to down play everything. "Okay, I guess you want to see what I do for the horses. You know all of this, but these three are kind of picky, like I said."

"I think you used the word 'spoiled.'" He chuckled, following her inside.

She quickened her pace, trying to stay ahead of him as she showed him where the feed was stored, how to fill the troughs.

"Got it? I'll be doing this most evenings, but I'll let you know when we need you to fill in. Will that work?" She backed up against a stall door.

"Yes, ma'am. Happy to oblige."

The exaggerated tipping of his hat did nothing to make her feel more at ease. Anyway, that little task was over with. Now to take the pictures to Rod.

"See ya!" He trotted to his pickup.

Kayla breathed a sigh of relief as she met Cody on the path to Rod and Nancy's house.

Chapter Twelve

"So, you just noticed a doubled fencepost, and stopped to check it?" Rod sat across from Cody as Nancy provided them each with a glass of lemonade.

"Yes, sir." Cody nodded. "My brothers and I have done a temporary fix on our fences that way. It won't last forever, but the extra post helps hold the wound-around wire till we can do a better job."

"The whole section of fence opened up when I pulled it back. Like a new gate." Kayla illustrated with hand motions.

"Let me see those pictures again." Rod took her phone, expanding the pictures. "No question, those are our tags. Text these to me, okay?"

"Sure." Kayla took her phone back.

"You two are pretty good detectives." Nancy held her hand out as Kayla shared her phone.

"And not shabby ranch-hands either. I'll bet your dad is glad to have your help, Cody." Rod scrolled through his contact list.

"I do what I can." Cody's cheeks warmed. He probably could do more around the Billings ranch.

"I'll call the county agent right now. I think we have enough to go talk to Heston about what's happening on his land. I've had cows accidently rub their ear tags off, but they don't land on the other side of the fence." Rod stood and walked toward the living room.

"I guess it's not like the old days when cattle were branded. That would make things a lot easier, right?" Cody took a drink of lemonade.

"Honestly, Rod talked to Dub about that." Nancy stood next to Kayla. "It's not common around here, but some people do brand their stock. Especially when your beef starts having a good reputation at auction. When the Caldwell name gets more desirable, the brand will guarantee that the buyer is getting one of ours. It's like a logo."

"I remember Dad mentioning that to Mom." Kayla turned toward Nancy. "We even played around with designing a brand. He'd been thinking about the rodeo stock for so long, he was still getting used to the idea of raising cattle for market."

"We never had a brand, either," Cody said. "This is making me think. I may suggest it to my dad."

"The agent wants the pictures." Rod walked back to the table. "Thanks again for your help, you two."

"Whatever it takes." Kayla walked toward Rod and Nancy's front door. "Keep me informed, okay?"

Cody followed, wishing he'd gone home to take a shower. She'd said something about cooking for him. What must she think of his habit of showing up smelly like this?

"Well, that was exciting." He lagged behind, as they got closer to her house.

"Yeah. It's been quite a day." Kayla opened her back door. "I planned to cook for you tonight. You showed up a little early, but I can still pull something together."

"Do you mind if we take a rain check? I have to work tomorrow, and there's no guarantee on the temperature at the plant. After spending the whole day in the heat, I don't have much of an appetite. What's up for your weekend?" Could they spend more time together soon?

"I have a rodeo on Friday night and Saturday afternoon near where Coach and Zanna live. I'm going up there tomorrow afternoon. Be home Sunday." She moved closer to him.

"Oh." Sunday was too far away. "I'll see you Sunday, then. I've got to say, I was happy to get this job, but I'm already getting tired of the daily grind."

"Yeah. Adulting is not all it's cracked up to be." Kayla laughed.

"Are you taking Sissy to the rodeo?" He changed the subject to soften the blow.

"No. I'm not competing in any events. They'll have a horse for me to use for the entry ceremony. Oh, that reminds me ..." She looked back toward Rod and Nancy's house. "I don't trust that Austin guy with our horses. I think I'll go ask Nancy to look in on them."

"Probably a good idea. He won't give them the attention you do, I'm sure. Well, I'll be headed home too." He moved toward his truck. "See ya.'"

"I'll text you from the rodeo tomorrow night. Good night, Marshal Cody, sir." She smiled.

"Good night." He reached for her hand, squeezing her fingers. His older brother was the only other one who teased him about his first name. Coming from her lips, he didn't mind the jab nearly as much.

Junior Caldwell's number popped up on his phone just before he started his truck.

"What's up, buddy?" Might as well take a minute to talk now. He waved at Kayla with his other hand.

"Keep forgetting to tell you." No surprise here—Junior was not the best at remembering things.

"Tell me what?" Cody tossed his keys up and caught them.

"Kayla's Pruitt grandparents are throwing her a surprise birthday party Saturday night. "

Kayla had gone inside. Good thing Junior didn't call a few minutes earlier.

"Oh, yeah?" Why had she not mentioned her birthday?

"They asked me to invite you," Junior continued.

"Thanks! I need a few more details." His mind raced. Kayla had mentioned a rodeo near her grandparents. At least she'd be in the right place for a surprise.

"The Pruitt place. 5:30 Saturday evening. Should be quite a shindig."

Shindig? Only Junior would use a word like that.

"Sounds good." Hopefully, this surprise would lift her spirits.

"Great! I'll be driving up through Snowville to get Joy, so you can get there on your own, right?"

"Sure. No problem. See you soon, man."

Cody turned right out of Kayla's driveway. He drove past groves of trees on the neighboring land. If Heston was mixing Caldwell cattle with the rodeo stock he'd bought from Kayla's dad, it hadn't been hard to keep them hidden. Except for the billboard cow. He smiled. Billboard cows? Shoe trees? What else would Kayla come up with?

He rounded the curve in front of his own place. That air conditioner would feel so good. The shower would be even better. After sanding boat hulls and running Kayla's fence line, he was ready to relax a bit. Wonder what Mom had planned for supper?

Should he take a gift to Kayla's party Saturday night? He'd never been good at things like that. This needed to be special. Maybe he'd be able to think of something after his shower.

Kayla zipped the garment bag, securing the outfits she had selected for the rodeo. Her open suitcase on the bed reminded her to pack casual clothes for her visit with Coach and Zanna.

She took three pairs of blue jeans out of her closet and added them to the suitcase.

A light jacket tucked in easily next to her blue jeans. That might have felt good on her ride with Cody earlier. He was confident driving his UTV a little faster than she'd expected. At times, the wind had whipped around her arms, chilling them. Other than that, though, the investigative trip they'd taken had turned out very well. As much as she did not trust Austin, being with Cody, she could breathe easily, no matter the situation. His confidence was contagious.

What would happen when Rod and the county agent confronted Heston? He would probably deny having any of their missing cattle. Could she and Rod prove the livestock had been retagged? What if cattle were still coming up missing when it came time for her to move to school at Fayetteville? Another reason to stay closer to home.

After her clothes were packed, she found a small bag for jewelry. Brushing back tears, she picked up a bracelet from her dresser and perched on the edge of the bed. Silver conchos reflected the lights in her room, emphasizing the natural turquoise stones.

What a treasure, especially because of the way she had found it. Nausea churned her stomach as she stood with Uncle Smiley, looking down on the rocky hillside where Mom and Dad's plane had crashed. Why had she gone out there with him? Yellow tape surrounded the airplane's remains because the NTSA was still investigating. They were only allowed to walk around in the company of a deputy. Even though the rain had stopped, the terrain was uneven and muddy.

That day, the jewelry was still in its packaging, still in the gift bag from Las Vegas, where her parents had purchased it. Layers of bubble wrap protected it from the impact. Why had this gift been thrown so far from the wreckage? When she spotted it, Uncle Smiley told her to ask one of the investigators to document it before she picked it up.

Tears washed her cheeks like the first time she'd unwrapped this gift. Her parents knew how much she loved turquoise. The bag, with her name in Mom's handwriting on the outside, was still here in her room. If Mom hadn't marked it, the sheriff might not have allowed her to keep it. There was no doubt it was meant for her. The last gift from her parents.

The bracelet filled an empty spot in the jewelry bag. Mom would not want it to stay at home on her dresser. Kayla would wear it proudly this weekend.

She closed the suitcase and lugged it next to her bedroom door. Now what? The long empty hours before bedtime loomed in front of her. Should she fix herself something to eat? Maybe she'd drive into town. If she knew she'd run into Cody, that would sound like a better plan. Without seeing him at least once, her days were empty. He was probably tired after working in the heat and driving around her ranch. No, he needed his rest.

She wiped the tears remaining on her cheeks. Tomorrow's trip to Coach and Zanna's would provide some excitement. Maybe soon she could manage to entertain herself for more than a few minutes at a time.

Cody used the long metal pole provided in the sporting goods store to pull down a backpack from a hook on the wall. Hadn't he seen Kayla wear this color? Not blue, not green. Turquoise? It looked like it would hold plenty. There was a padded pocket to keep a laptop safe. He opened another flap and found a place for a water bottle. Yes. This would be a good gift. Since he'd been balancing stuff in his chair for a while, he knew how important it was to have a bag that held plenty of stuff.

He carried the backpack to the checkout counter. Should he have it wrapped? He'd not bought many gifts for a nineteen-year-old girl. Exactly none, to be honest. He'd take it home and see what Mom thought about wrapping.

"Can I get you anything else?" The clerk rang up his purchase.

"That'll do it." He handed her a credit card. On the way to his truck, doubts pestered his mind. Would Kayla think it was strange that he wanted to buy her a birthday present? How would she feel about a backpack?

One thing was certain, he was looking forward to seeing her again. Their investigative trip around her land had been great. She was so easy to talk to. How many other girls would enjoy bouncing along with him in his UTV?

The other girls he'd had known only wanted to talk about bull-riding. "Aren't you scared?" "You're so brave." "Your brothers are pretty cute too." So shallow. But then, before his accident, he was probably pretty empty-headed himself.

When Kayla had led the delegation of visitors to see him at the nursing home, she seemed different. Not more serious, maybe just more concerned. More real. From that day, his heart had focused on what seemed an impossible dream—becoming worthy of her attention.

With her own grief fresh in her mind these days, he loved to try to make her smile. Honestly, he was getting pretty good at it too.

So, maybe this backpack wouldn't be too dumb. She could probably use it when she went back to school.

The music in his truck bolstered his mood as he drove home. He was happy they hadn't fixed the air conditioning at the plant today. Working in the heat wasn't so bad when it meant getting of work earlier. No need to tell the boss, though. He did want to return to a full paycheck at some point.

Kayla was probably getting ready for the rodeo. She'd promised to text him. Maybe they could actually talk on the phone instead. Hearing her voice would be the topper to a pretty good day. He'd have to try not to mention her birthday, though. Junior had said tomorrow's party was a surprise.

He passed his own driveway and turned on the dirt road

leading to the Caldwell's spreads. Had Mr. Hernandez talked to the county agent today? Maybe he could find that out before he talked to Kayla tonight.

Driving up Kayla's driveway, Mrs. Hernandez waved at him from the patio, where she was watering the hanging baskets around the pool.

At the back of the barn, the ranch-hand named Austin was unsaddling Kayla's dad's horse. Had he asked anyone about riding the horse? Would Kayla be upset to find out?

"Kayla's not here," the dark-haired lady shouted, jogging toward his truck.

He rolled the window down. "I know. I thought Mr. Hernandez might have some news from the county agent."

"We're Rod and Nancy." She grinned. "And no. He called the agent, sent him the pictures. I think they are discussing how to approach Heston."

"I don't imagine he'll be too excited about being accused of stealing." Cody rested his elbow on the door.

"Probably not. But hopefully, it won't be long till we hear something." She peered into the plastic watering can she held. "These flowers are thirsty tonight."

"We could use some rain, for sure." Cody nodded. "But summer in Arkansas. What can I say?"

"Feast or famine." Nancy tapped his door. "Hey, good to see you. Thanks for helping yesterday."

"No problem." He put his truck in reverse. "See ya!"

Should he mention Austin to Kayla? No use creating more stress for her. They didn't have a concrete reason not to trust the guy after all.

Dad met him in their driveway when he reached home. "Hey, what's up?"

"I'm off work early again." He opened his door.

"Cool. We haven't been fishing in a while. Want to go tonight or tomorrow?"

"I'm busy tomorrow." Cody blushed. There hadn't been a lot of Saturday night plans lately.

"Well, maybe tonight, then. We'll get Mom to make us some sandwiches. She won't mind not cooking. Too warm in the kitchen." Dad helped get Cody's chair from the back of the truck.

"Sounds good" Cody looked down at his chair. "That boat doesn't do anybody any good sitting on the trailer." Friday night fishing, Saturday night plans with a great girl. Life couldn't be better. "Let me go in and talk to Mom a minute first." He'd turn the gift-wrapping job over to an expert.

The crowd cheered as Kayla led the rodeo princesses out of the arena after the opening ceremony. She was thankful the horse she rode tonight seemed comfortable with all of the noise and hubbub.

"Great job, ladies." She addressed the three other girls as they circled around her on their horses.

"Thanks so much for being here, Kayla." Next year's Arkansas Rodeo Teen pulled up next to her. "You are going to be a tough act to follow."

"*Aww*. You will be fine." She winked at the girl. "As long as you can control your horse, your smile, and the flag you're carrying, openings are a cinch." She remembered the first couple of times she'd participated in one of these spectacles. Maintaining composure was easier to advise than to do.

"Anyway. Glad you could be here. I was so sorry to hear about your mom and dad." The blonde lowered her voice.

"I appreciate that. Mom loved events like this, so I feel she is still with me." Kayla looked down at the silver concho bracelet. It was one of the last things Mom touched. Her presence was real.

"I'll see y'all up in the stands." Kayla dismounted and led her horse into the barn behind the arena. How would someone in a wheelchair manage around here? It was a good thing Cody wasn't coming to watch her. Well, not really. She wished he was here. They could stay outside and listen if he couldn't get in. They'd both attended enough rodeos to know what was happening just by the crowd noise.

She'd better send him the text she'd promised.

What's up?

He answered very quickly.

Fishing with Dad.

I'll call you.

She sent one more text, then called. Much better to hear his voice anyway.

"How was your entrance?" He did know rodeo. That was the main reason rodeo queens appeared at events like this.

"Great. All of the girls and the horses were naturals."

"Super." He paused. "Too bad you're not here. It's a great night for fishing."

"Sounds wonderful. Tell your dad I said *hello*." She swallowed hard. What she wouldn't give to be fishing with her own dad tonight. Watching the sun go down together, gliding in with the running lights on. Frogs and invisible splashes welcoming the night.

"I will. Well ..." He seemed to be searching for words. What was he *not* saying?

"Well?" She prompted.

"That's a deep subject." He forced a laugh. "I was just going to say, have a great time with your grandparents. I'll see you when you get back."

"See you, soon. Bye." She hung up. Well, that was awkward. Hardly worth a phone call. He didn't usually have such a hard time talking to her. Was he embarrassed because his dad was listening?

She swallowed hard. No use getting her feelings hurt. Just because the person she most liked talking to couldn't think of anything to say. She blinked back a tear. These big girl boots were getting a workout.

Chapter Thirteen

Twenty minutes to Walking Eagle Boats and twenty more to their deer lease. Cody turned his truck around in the driveway and headed toward the freeway. Leaving from here every morning wouldn't save time, but showing he could be independent was a big step. Dad had been agreeable last night on the lake. Maybe he should take Mom fishing to break the news to her as well. Besides, this road was much closer to the freeway. Just another hop, skip, and jump, and he could visit Kayla in Fayetteville. The only thing he hadn't nailed down was boat storage. Was there enough room behind the cabin for that? Besides, he still needed Dad's help hooking up the trailer. A worry for another day.

The huge gift bag containing Kayla's birthday present shifted in the front floorboard of the truck. Mom had been happy to help. Good thing, because wrangling tissue paper and curly ribbon were uniquely feminine skills. If left up to him, all presents would be gifted in the bag from point of purchase.

He turned down his music as he approached the freeway entrance ramp. That phone call yesterday had been tough. Their conversations had all been on the up and up so far. He didn't enjoy keeping things from her. In this case, her family knew best.

She would probably have argued that she didn't want a celebration this year. In fact, this surprise might not go down well. He picked up on her need for rest and quiet after the rodeos. Would he be the one to calm her down if there was too much commotion?

Signaling before leaving the freeway, Cody smiled as he turned left behind the Phillips 66 station, remembering that first trip for her parents' memorial services. He reached a wooden, hand-painted sign, and flipped on his turn signal.

"Shoe Tree Road."

He laughed. That was a good idea. Many people expected to see the landmark that was now only a memory. After passing a couple of weekend cabins, he approached a parking area full of cars and pickup trucks behind the Pruitt's house.

"Okay, Miss Kayla. So much for your peaceful weekend." He stopped near the ramp that led to their front porch. Vehicles parked nearby didn't include her white truck or Faith's baby blue one. This would be a surprise. He looped the handles of the enormous gift bag around his right elbow and prepared to unload.

"Hey!" Junior met him at the base of the ramp. "Isn't this a great place? Woods behind us, a long hillside leading down to the freeway in front. Pretty cool."

"Yeah." Cody agreed. "Kayla loves it here, for sure."

"There's a table down there for gifts." Junior pointed. "Didn't anybody tell you the size limit for packages?"

"Trying to make a good impression." Cody balanced the big bag on his lap. "I'll be right back." He headed toward the gift table.

"Oh, I think you've already done that. I've been around my cousin since she was an amateur mutton-buster." Junior cuffed the back of his head. "Her face doesn't light up like that for every smelly bull-rider she meets."

Cody continued without looking back. Junior was the king of over-statement. Just maybe he was right this time.

"So glad you came, young man." Mr. and Mrs. Pruitt stood next to the gift table. He moved his cane to his left side so he could shake Cody's hand. "Kayla has nothing but good things to say about you. I think you might be just what she needs right now."

"Good to hear." Cody smiled. "How are you, Mrs. Pruitt?"

"Might as well join the Zanna club." She winked at him. "Everybody under the age of thirty has called me that for years."

"It's unusual. I don't think I know another Zanna." Cody nodded.

"Short for my first name, Suzanna. I like it, but I don't get many personalized coffee cups." She took the gift bag from him. "Here, let me take care of this. Our girl is going to be overwhelmed by all the attention today."

"Yes, ma'am." Cody spun around, looking back toward his truck. Overwhelmed, but in a good way?

"Not every day you turn nineteen." Coach walked with him. "Her mom and dad always made a big deal out of Kayla's birthday. The big celebration shouldn't stop just because they're not around."

As if on cue, Kayla's oversized white four-door pickup lumbered down the road, parking next to Cody's truck. Faith ran up from her own parking spot on the side of the road.

"Surprise!" The chorus of voices disturbed the quiet of the woods around the house. Dogs barked, and somewhere a goose honked.

"Wow!" Kayla shouted as she stepped down from her truck. "What have y'all been up to?"

Cody moved toward her, waiting his turn in the line of huggers.

"Happy Birthday." He wrapped his arms around her.

"You knew when we talked last night." She whispered in his ear.

"Guilty," he admitted.

"We'll discuss that later." She smiled, turning to hug the next person.

Phew. She'd smiled. Maybe she wasn't upset. He followed the crowd down the gentle hill to a line of tables covered with white paper. Apparently, everyone who loved Kayla knew how much she needed this attention. Everyone who loved her? Did he just include himself in that list? Yeah. Maybe so.

"Thanks for coming." Kayla waved as another group walked to their vehicles after the party. What a day. When she and Faith left the rodeo this afternoon, she had no clue what waited for her at the end of Shoe Tree Road.

Cody and his oldest brother were playing rock-paper-scissors as Faith looked on, laughing.

"I don't care if you win, I'm still not telling Mom for you." John K. crossed his arms.

"Hey, fair is fair." Cody laughed. "All right, two out of three."

"What?" Kayla stepped next to Faith, who was opening the door of her truck.

"I have no idea." Faith shook her head. "Hey Billings. Time to get back to Fayetteville."

"Okay, okay." John K. shoved Cody's shoulder. "Behave, Mr. Marshal."

"Yeah. Whatever. You sure that antique of yours will make it up the mountain?"

"Old Greenie and I are ready to race anytime, anywhere." John K. jogged to his vintage truck.

Kayla sent Faith off with a hug. She stood next to Cody as the two pickups drove away from Coach and Zanna's house.

"So, you were in on this whole thing?" Kayla teased.

"Not really. I was just invited." He reached for her hand. "Was it too much?"

"No. I'm okay. Just tired. I feel like I've worn this pasted-on smile forever." She squeezed his fingers. He was the first to ask if she was okay today. Even Coach and Zanna had just assumed she would want a party. When did Cody become the one who could see behind her emotional mask?

"The smile can officially take a break," Cody ran his fingers up her arm. "I guess I should leave so you can have at least a few hours of the peaceful weekend you came up here for."

"No, no." She almost shouted. "I'm happy it's down to just us. Can you stay a little while?"

"Sure. Ready to go inside?" Cody rolled toward the house.

"Maybe we could go for a ride instead?" She'd like nothing better than spending more time with him.

"How was your party, sweetie?" Zanna passed by, carrying two full bags of trash.

"It was perfect." Kayla took one of the bags, and Cody got the other one. "Let us take care of these." She walked toward the dumpster next to Coach's two-car garage. "Cody and I are going for a little drive, and then I'll be inside. Thanks for going to so much trouble tonight. Y'all are the best."

"We love you, sweetie." Zanna started up the ramp. "See you in a bit. Good night, Cody."

"Good night, Mrs. ... *uh* ... Zanna. Thanks for inviting me." Cody reached the dumpster, tossing his bag over the side before Kayla did the same and headed back toward his truck.

She settled in beside him and wasn't at all surprised when he turned down the next road on Coach and Zanna's land. She hopped out to open the gate and got back in without a word.

"Now, let your peace and quiet begin." Cody turned off the truck's motor and placed his arm around her shoulders.

"Amen." She scooted closer and leaned against him. "I'm glad you came tonight."

"I'm glad I did too." His head rested on hers.

Vapor lights from houses in the valley below twinkled bravely. Red taillights danced like fireflies on the interstate.

Crickets and tree frogs sang through the open windows of his truck.

"Oh." Kayla sat upright. "I forgot to tell you *thanks* for my backpack. I couldn't imagine what was in that package."

"It was kind of big. Mom wrapped it. I thought she might fold it up and make it smaller somehow, but I guess not." He laughed. "Did you like the color?"

"My favorite. It matches my bracelet." She held her arm to let the moonlight reflect on the silver conchos.

"Good. I thought you could use it when your classes start at Fayetteville." He turned with his back pressed against his door. "Backpacks. I remember how Mom thought each of us boys needed a new one when school started. Sometimes we would have been fine lugging the old one, or even going without. She'd hear none of that."

"It probably helped her stay organized. If she packed lunches, she knew what to put in each one. The joys of a big family." Kayla tapped the end of her nose. "That's still a big dream of mine. Lots of backpacks, lots of kids."

Cody sat silently for a moment. "Anyway. Maybe you can use it."

Had talk of a family in her future made him uncomfortable? Was she being pushy?

"I'll use it a lot." She sat back against the seat, staring forward. "But I don't think I'm going to Fayetteville."

"What?" His voice was sharper than normal.

"There's just so much going on at home. I can't leave when we're worried about stolen cattle." She tried to keep the whine out of her voice. She didn't have to make excuses.

"But what about your architecture degree?" He touched her hand. "Isn't that still what you want to do?"

"Yeah. No. I don't know." So much for a peaceful evening. Was he forcing her to make decisions about college tonight?

"You've had a lot to think about. And it's only July. You still have almost a month before classes start." He was quiet again. His thumb made circles in her palm.

"Yeah." They'd talked so easily before. Why was this so hard?

"I've decided to make a change too." His voice broke the silence. "I'm going to move up to our deer hunting cabin."

"Why?" She was staying home, and now he was leaving? What was going on?

"Now that I'm working, I need to live on my own. I can't ask Mom and Dad to take care of me forever." Now he was the one facing forward. He pulled away, and held the steering wheel.

Kayla folded her hands in her lap. She couldn't expect Cody to live at home any more than he could expect her to move off to college. Were they on their way to becoming closer than just neighbors or not? If he moved away, she might only see him on weekends, and maybe not even that much. Maybe that's what he wanted.

"That's what you wanted John K. to tell your mom?" Those two made a game out of everything.

"I was just teasing. I've already talked to Dad, but Mom will not be happy. Especially since I'm the last kid at home."

Kayla's eyes filled with tears. He had a mom and a dad at home, and he wanted to leave them.

"You okay?"

She sniffed back the tears. "Yes. You just can't possibly understand how blessed you are to still have both parents." She tried to control the shaking in her voice.

"I do appreciate them so much." He took a deep breath. "But, it's time to grow up. Don't you want to be on your own too?"

"Want to be on my own?" That was too much. "I *am* on my own. I would give anything *not* to be on my own."

The night noises grew louder. There was suddenly nothing else she could say to Cody.

"I'm sorry, Kayla. Really." He put his arm around her again.

"You're right. I can't understand what you are going through. I still plan to be around to listen. Okay?"

"By moving away? Is that your idea of still being around to listen?"

"The way I was thinking, I would be closer to you, in Fayetteville."

"You had my whole life planned out, I guess." This conversation was going nowhere, fast.

"Well ... no ..." He was evidently out of words too.

"I guess I'm ready to go back to Coach and Zanna's. I'll get the gate." She stepped out and took a few long strides up the road. Now, she needed peace and quiet. The one person she thought she could talk to about anything had just completely shocked her. More than her birthday party had been a total surprise today.

Cody drove for a few miles with his music blaring. How could he have messed up his conversation with Kayla so badly? He had no right to force her to do anything. If this was not the right time for leaving the home she had grown up in, so be it. But why did his announcement that he was moving to the family's cabin upset her so much?

He turned off the music as he passed a long tractor-trailer truck, and quickly moved back into the right lane. Why couldn't Kayla be happy about him living closer to her grandparents, closer to the University? The biggest question of all, why did she suddenly decide she didn't want to continue her studies? Did staying at home make her feel closer to her parents? But wasn't it terribly lonely in that big house by herself?

Kayla was right. He couldn't understand. After his bull riding accident, there was always plenty of help for him. Plenty of people were around to encourage him. But he could identify with that feeling of being lost in a strange new world.

His life and all of his future plans had changed in one terrible moment. The long days and nights in the hospital, the grueling therapy, even living in a full-fledged old folks' home had been survivable. He'd held on to the hope that someday he'd walk again. For a while, he even pictured getting back on a bull. But, none of that happened.

Imagine if the people in his life were not there to help him through. What if he'd been by himself in a big, empty house?

Lord, help me find a way to help Kayla. You know I care about her very much. Please give me an idea that will help her feel safe and ready to move on with her life. Amen.

Gliding off the exit ramp, he slowed to navigate the curvy road that passed the cabin.

Lights on this road were few and far between. He was grateful for the white line along the side of the road that reflected his headlights enough to help him find his way.

His mind drifted back to another dark night when he'd been Grandpa Dee's roommate at the nursing home. All was quiet in their room, just like it was in the cab of his truck tonight. The lights went out so early there, and that night Grandpa Dee was snoring with the television on, so Cody had turned it off.

"You over there, man?" Grandpa Dee's voice had startled him.

"I thought you were asleep," Cody answered.

"Nope. Just thinking." The old man's voice was quiet but very strong.

"Thinking?" Most of their talks until then had been about what would be happening at their next meal or during therapy.

"Just thinking. Mostly about how I messed up when I first got married."

Cody didn't know what to say about that. His grandma died when Cody was very small, so he only knew what his parents and older brothers told him.

"You couldn't have done that badly." He waited for a response.

"Yeah, I did. Were you ever married?"

"No." Okay, obviously Grandpa Dee didn't know who he was talking to. Cody decided to just let him talk.

"You know what they say about marriage being fifty-fifty?" Grandpa Dee continued. "Don't believe it."

"No?" Cody remained quiet.

"If you're not ready to give one hundred percent, it won't work." The words were tinged with tears.

"I'll remember that." Cody swallowed hard.

"Good night." Grandpa Dee was quiet then.

A car dimmed its headlights just before it met and passed Cody's truck. "If you're not ready to give one hundred percent, it won't work."

Did he need to live up here on his own to prove he could be independent? If that meant one change too many to make Kayla comfortable, he would stay with his parents for a little longer. Would it make her happy to hear that he was willing to change his plans for her? Would she ever be willing to talk to him long enough to tell her?

Kayla tucked the crocheted Afghan around her legs, feet tucked in to allow swinging.

"It's peaceful out here." Zanna settled next to her in an Adirondack chair.

"Just what I need." Kayla closed her eyes, enjoying the serenade of hoot owls. Was that a whip-poor-will calling?

She was so grateful that Zanna enjoyed sitting quietly. She couldn't come up with words to explain how she was feeling. What should have been an exciting milestone in her life had been emotionally draining. After all the attention from friends and family, she had looked forward to an honest conversation with Cody. Instead, she was bewildered by his desire to leave and his disappointment in her plans to stay on the ranch.

"Well, it's been a long day." Zanna stood in front of her.

"Yes. Thanks again for the party. It was so good to see everyone dressed in something besides funeral clothes." Kayla unfolded her legs and stood to hug her grandmother.

"Should I get you up for pancakes in the morning or just in time for church?"

"Definitely pancakes." Kayla smiled. She remembered so many special breakfasts, just the three of them.

"Okay, sweetie." Zanna hugged her tightly. "The guest room is ready and waiting. Night, night."

"Good night, Zanna. I won't stay out here much longer." Her legs and feet curled back into position, and she retucked the blanket. The swaying swing slowed as her movement stopped.

Stars above her head sparkled brightly. Out here, they seemed much closer than at home, near her pool. Obviously, all of the lights behind her house made the difference. Cody had mentioned not being able to see the stars from the hospital parking lot. Just one more thing they had in common. Was he looking at the same stars tonight?

She hadn't been fair with him. Of course, he had assumed she would be going to Fayetteville for the fall semester. Before tonight, she hadn't shared her doubts about moving away from home with anyone. Couldn't he understand her concern over the turmoil on the ranch?

His surprise about her college plans was understandable. But, his announcement about moving to the family's cabin in the woods had caught her totally off-guard. Just when they were becoming closer, he was leaving her hanging like the old sneakers in the shoe tree. Was she being selfish? They could still communicate by phone and text. He would probably come home most weekends. She would eventually get used to living in her rambling ranch house by herself. Would it be any better to know he was sleeping at his parents' house just a stone's throw away? She was acting babyish after all.

Placing her bare feet on the wood deck below the swing, she

pushed it to start the swaying motion again. If she stayed here much longer, she'd wake up with a crick in her neck and mosquito bites on her mosquito bites. The guest room was better for sleeping. She'd set an alarm to take a shower before pancakes in the morning.

Thank you, Lord. This spot under Your stars has been the perfect haven for me tonight. Now, please help me figure out what to say to Cody tomorrow. He's been a good friend, and I don't want to lose him. Help me sleep well enough to get my thoughts together. Amen.

Chapter Fourteen

"Want to meet us at Amy Lou's after church?" Mom was headed out the door with her bible.

"Sure." Cody followed her.

"Remember, you're always invited to come to our service." Dad locked the door behind them.

"Yeah. I know. I'm getting used to Smiley's sermons." There was nothing wrong with the more formal and traditional worship his parents attended. "I guess being close to a rodeo arena once a week helps me feel a little more like the old Cody."

"Maybe so. But we love the new Cody too." Mom kissed his cheek. "See you at lunch."

The new Cody. The one who was ready to reorganize his future for the sake of one girl. The former bull-rider who now rode a four-wheeled utility vehicle along fence lines.

Would he be missed at Bible study class this morning? Maybe he could be a little late. A few more minutes of fresh air sounded good.

He rolled past his truck to the trailer that held his UTV. Might as well take advantage of a relatively cool June morning for a quick ride around the perimeter of the Billings place.

Wouldn't want anyone breaking their fence like they had the Caldwell's.

He accelerated and followed the north edge of the property. The last time he'd driven along here, Kayla had been next to him. Someday, maybe that would happen again. Reaching a rise, he stopped and turned off the motor. From here, he could see the part of their land that joined with the acreage Heston had purchased from Kayla's parents.

That last time, Kayla had shocked him with her out-of-left-field announcement. 'The Billboard Cow!' He laughed aloud. She had a way of amazing him at every turn.

The uniquely marked cow at the center of the controversy was nowhere in sight. Larger, already-weaned calves munched on grass close to the fence that served as the dividing line. His dad had been teaching him to rotate the types of cattle into different areas. Today, older calves and steers, next week, mama cows and small calves ... Wait, what was that?

From the left of his field of vision, a black blur came galloping up. It looked a lot like Kayla's dad's horse, Caesar. No, it *was* Caesar. How did he get here? Who was that rider? Long, dirty blond hair covered the side of the cowboy's face until he stopped and patted the side of the horse. *Austin!* The ranch-hand they'd asked to take care of their horses while Kayla was gone was riding Dub's treasured stallion on Heston's land.

Austin ambled farther north. The calves scattered, but he didn't seem to be looking at any of them. Two more riders galloped up from the direction of the outbuildings Cody could see in the distance. If only he were close enough to hear what they discussed when the three horses stood nose to nose a hundred feet or so inside the fence.

Turning on the UTV now would call attention to him. Besides listening to what the men were discussing, he badly needed a picture of Austin riding Caesar. There was no way Kayla would have authorized this young man to ride her dad's horse so hard and so far.

No question, he needed to get closer. Without using his vehicle, there was only one choice.

He lowered himself to the ground and reached forward with one arm, then the other. Trying to lift himself to avoid dragging his belly, he maneuvered several feet closer to the fence. Would the riders look his way? Not unless he made too much noise. After that journey, the only thing they might hear was him gasping for air. He needed to go back to the gym to work on his upper body strength.

"So, what else does he want?" Austin was asking.

"What more have you got?" The other guy responded.

"I mean he's got one of the best breeding and milk cows. That and a few young steers. He already bought the rodeo bulls." Austin paced on Caesar. The horse huffed, looking for water.

Cody was sure his heart was beating loud enough for these guys to hear. None of them had noticed him, partially hidden here in tall grass. If he could just stay quiet.

"Hey, you're getting paid. What do you care? If all of their herd gradually migrates over here, what's your problem? As long as we have red tags to replace the yellow ones, right? And we have plenty of tags." The other guy dismounted.

What if one of the horses spotted him? He'd better snap his picture and start moving back toward his UTV.

Cody rolled over to pull his phone out of his pocket. *Ready, aim, 'say cheese' Austin.* He zoomed in and snapped one, two, three. Hopefully the guy's face was clear. There was no doubt about this one-of-a-kind horse.

"Okay, okay." Austin turned Caesar toward home. "Meet me at 7:30 in the morning at the gap. Have plenty of tags. Tell Heston, the price goes up each time we do this."

"Yeah." The first cowboy laughed. "You tell him that."

"Seven-thirty." The other guy kicked his horse in the flanks and rode away from the fence line.

Cody had never had so much trouble keeping his mouth

shut. He wanted to shout at the three. Even something lame like, "How dare you!"

Now to get back to Kayla's ranch to show Rod the pictures. A small stream of blood trickled down his left arm. When he'd come out here this morning, he knew he'd miss Bible class. Now, he hoped he didn't miss lunch with his parents in town.

Grab a tuft of tall grass, pull, drag himself a few feet. Reach for another clump. Drag again. Wow. He was really out of shape.

Breathing hard, he finally pulled himself up into his vehicle. *Thank you, Lord. I've heard You watch over fools. That's a very good thing. Amen.*

A clean bandana from under his seat helped to stop the bleeding on his left arm. He always kept one of those in the utility vehicle and another one in the truck. It was just a habit of his dad from his Billings grandpa. Dad's explanation had been, 'They come in handy.' Napkins after a quick lunch, a makeshift sack for berries he'd picked, now a temporary bandage. Dad was right more times than he cared to admit.

He checked the time before he started the vehicle. He needed to send the picture of Austin to Kayla, and to Rod. Better wait. They were probably still in church. If only he'd been able to record what the three were plotting. Could they be there tomorrow morning to catch the thieves red-handed? He shook his head as he started the engine and headed back to his house. Was this happening, or was he dreaming about some old western movie?

A bump in the pasture jarred him. Real life. Maybe the key to the whole mystery of the missing cattle. After accelerating to get the UTV back on its trailer, he turned it off and pulled his phone out to send some text messages.

First to Kayla.

Call when you can. Big news

Then to Rod.

> Can we meet up? I have something to
> show you.

He checked the time. The third text had to be to Mom and Dad.

> Running late. Wait for me at Amy Lou's.

He practically jumped from the UTV to his chair and headed inside. He'd have to take the quickest shower in history, but no way could he be seen in town looking like he'd just crawled through a cow pasture. He couldn't help laughing. The life of a cowboy detective was not as glamorous as he imagined.

Kayla walked arm in arm with Zanna as the church service ended.

"Did you ask your minister to preach from the book of Job today?" She squeezed Zanna's arm.

"I don't think Zanna has that kind of influence." Coach laughed from a step behind them.

"The sermon did hit home, didn't it, sweetie?" Zanna used her other hand to pat Kayla's arm.

"Absolutely." Kayla wiped a tear from her cheek. "I've spent so much time wondering why God was being so mean to me. Instead of wondering why, I just need to accept that He is God. He can do what He wants. The key is deciding how I am going to react."

Zanna stopped to look into her face. "Did you just turn nineteen, or forty-five?"

"No use questioning God." Coach opened his car door. "We

just have to wait to see how all of this fits into His plan. We may not know 'til we get to heaven, but we have to believe He knows what He's doing.'"

Kayla sat behind Coach and felt her phone buzz in her skirt pocket as Zanna seated herself in the front.

Cody's message got right to the point.

Call when you can. Big news.

Had she expected an apology of some sort? He didn't owe her one. She realized now that her reaction had been the whole problem. At least this time, she would be prepared. She placed the phone back in her pocket. His news could wait until she had a little more privacy.

"Are leftovers from last night's party okay for lunch?" Zanna turned to look her way.

"Of course. I think the only dessert I ate was birthday cake, but it looked like there were a lot of scrumptious things." She had loved all of the 'home cooking' from Zanna's kitchen. She was enjoying cooking more, but mostly for Cody. When she was alone, there didn't seem to be much point. Maybe that was part of the attitude change she needed to make.

"There's some banana pudding left and maybe some of Coach's white chocolate-covered pretzels." Zanna rolled her passenger side window down just a bit.

"What? How did I miss those?" Kayla patted Coach's shoulder from the back seat.

"You were a little pre-occupied with a special guest from the Billings side of the mountain." Coach winked at her in the rearview mirror.

"Maybe." She bit her lip. There was no need telling them about the tense conversation she'd had with Cody last night.

"Well, that's interesting." Zanna showed Kayla a text on her own phone. "Ellen says the man from the museum would like to come by to pick up the box of shoes we collected from the shoe tree."

"They're doing a display?" Kayla had evidently missed part of this discussion.

"Yes. We're even hoping to get a video copy of the news story from that reporter, Tara Williams, at the television station. Museums aren't just display cases and typed descriptions anymore." Zanna held her phone in front of her to reply to the text.

"That's pretty cool," Kayla said. "I never thought it would be cut down, but I'm glad the townspeople have a place to remember it."

"God uses all things for good." Coach piped up.

"Yes, He does." Kayla pulled her phone out of her pocket. As Coach slowed down and turned on their road, she dialed Cody's number.

"I'll be inside in just a minute." Kayla walked toward the front of the house, hitting "Send" to complete the call.

"Hi," she said when Cody answered.

"Hey. I'm glad you called." He cleared his throat. "I want to …"

"No. Wait." She interrupted him. "I need to apologize for the way I acted last night. It's none of my business where you decide to live. If it works better for you to move away from home so you can get back and forth to your job, then that's what you should do." She breathed a sigh of relief. "Now, what's your news?"

"About that. After I talked to you, I realized I don't need to move anywhere just yet. I couldn't handle my job at the boat factory *and* my part-time gig as ranch security if I lived at the deer lease."

What was he talking about?

"What?"

He kept her so confused.

"I took a ride around my own property this morning and

made a huge discovery." He paused. "Wait a minute. I just came into Amy Lou's Diner. I think I'd better go back outside so everyone doesn't hear."

She waited, stunned.

"Thanks." She heard him say. "Somebody held the door for me." He was quiet for another second. "Anyway, guess who I saw on Heston's side of the fence where our land meets his?"

"Come on. I can't guess."

He was obviously enjoying drawing this news out. "Austin. And he was riding your dad's horse."

"*Caesar?*" No way. Austin had absolutely no business riding Dad's prize stallion.

"Yes. And wait until you hear what I heard."

"Tell me." Why didn't he just spill this news?

"Evidently, he's the one who has been opening the fence and sending cattle through to Heston's men so they can be retagged. They're planning to steal some more stock tomorrow morning." Cody spit these words out in a rush.

"Cody! How did they just tell you all of this?" Could he be mistaken? Did they really admit to stealing the cattle?

"Well. They didn't know I was there. I was sort of hiding." She could hear the excitement in his voice.

"Wow. What did Rod say? I guess he'll say the agent needs more proof." She paced back and forth across Zanna and Coach's porch.

"I took a picture of Austin and Caesar. I don't have any audio of the three guys making plans, though." He stopped talking again. "Well. That's crazy timing. Here come Rod and Nancy now. I guess they're eating at Amy Lou's too."

"I'll let you go, then." Should she jump in her truck and head home?

"Bye." He was gone.

Their conversation last night seemed so insignificant now. Could they pin the thefts on Austin and Heston? She should at least explain to Zanna and Coach before she rushed back to

Crossroads. Hopefully, her quivering stomach would calm down long enough to enjoy some of Zanna's banana pudding.

"Another great job, Cody." Rod patted his shoulder. "But I don't know if the agent will act on this without proof."

"Here." Cody pushed his phone over to Rod. "I got as close as I could. You can see the Down-wind Casino logo on the saddles of the other two guys. That is definitely your guy Austin talking to them."

"Yeah. That is pretty good." Rod expanded the photo. "Is that Dub's horse he's riding?"

"No doubt." Caesar was easily recognizable.

"Cody, how did you ...?" Mom's voice was shrill.

"Didn't they see you and your UTV?" Dad sputtered.

"Well, I sort of left the UTV hidden in the brush. I was on my belly in a little ditch, so I don't think they knew I was there." Cody flinched. He knew someone at this table was about to come unglued.

"Marshal Cody Billings!" Heads turned in the diner as Mom trotted out his full name.

"It's okay." He laughed. "I got a little scratched up, but it all worked out."

Mom heaved a sigh and sat back against the wooden booth.

"I'll give the county agent a call. I think someone should be there when this happens in the morning." Rod pulled up the directory on his phone. "He may want to talk to you about what was said, Cody."

"I'm in. Let me know how I can help."

Cody picked up his phone as a message from Kayla was displayed.

Headed home.

Would either of them be needed when the thieves were confronted in the morning? He couldn't speak for Kayla, but he wanted to witness whatever happened at 7:30 a.m.

Be careful.

He should probably take his own advice.

Chapter Fifteen

"Hi. You want some breakfast?" Kayla opened her back door as Cody approached.

"You cooked?" He stopped, sniffing the air.

"Don't look so shocked." She brought a plate of bacon and scrambled eggs to the dining room table. *Hmm*. There was no lower-level counter at their bar. Not accessible.

"It smells wonderful. Trouble is, I don't know if I can eat." He placed the cloth napkin in his lap.

"Same." She sat across from him. "But Rod said we don't need to rush out there just yet. If we spook Austin, he might call this whole thing off."

"That's why we called in the professionals." Cody picked up his fork. "Maybe today, the mystery of the missing cows gets solved for good."

"Maybe. I went down to Rod and Nancy's when the sheriff came last night. And—"

"The sheriff? Not the agent?" Cody interrupted her.

"Yes. He said this crosses the line to criminal activity. He got here a little bit ago in an unmarked vehicle." She wiped her mouth with a napkin.

"Wow." Cody wadded up the napkin next to his plate. "I'm

glad he believed us. So, now we just wait to hear from him and Rod? I'm no good at waiting."

"I know. Me either." Kayla was beginning to love watching for that excited sparkle in his eyes and the way his mouth twitched when he concentrated on something. "Hey. I haven't thanked you. You went above and beyond yesterday."

"Aww, shucks, ma'am." He grinned.

"No, really. When I shared this problem with you, I didn't dream you'd be so committed. I love your concern." There was joking, and there was being serious. Right now, she wanted to get her point across. "You don't have to care about our ranch business. I'm grateful you do."

"I like feeling useful. I was raised to do what you can when you can. I have to be more creative these days, but I'm still trying." He reached across the table and captured her fingers under his.

"I didn't ask if you wanted coffee." She sat up straighter but didn't pull her hand away.

"You know, I could use some." He nodded. "I never drank it until I spent so much time in the hospital. Their beverage choices were kind of limited, but the nurses always kept a pot of coffee going."

She searched through her parents' stash of individual pods and turned on the machine. Flavored, strong brew, decaffeinated? She took a chance and chose one that said 'Medium Roast.' Another thing to learn about this guy. Maybe she'd develop a taste for coffee too. It would be nice to have one more thing in common.

A message from Nancy popped up on her phone.

> Rod said to stay inside until he waves from in
> front of the barn.

"Cody, Rod said to wait inside the house for a minute." She showed him the message.

"Wait? Why? What's happening?" Cody rolled to the back window for a better view.

A four-door truck rolled into the driveway, with sirens blaring and blue-lights flashing. She hadn't stopped to consider that Rod and the sheriff might be in danger.

Two police officers jumped out of the truck and ran behind the barn with guns drawn. Kayla stood behind Cody, gripping his shoulders.

"Here they come." Kayla pointed out the window.

Austin walked with his hands behind his back, followed closely by the sheriff. Two more men were behind them. Rod rode his horse at the rear of this crew.

As they passed the window of his house, Rod waved at Nancy.

"Should I find a to-go cup for your coffee?"

"Coffee?" Cody was already moving toward the door. "Who needs coffee? Let's go!"

She opened the back door. The patio around the pool was calm and inviting, but they passed the gate and headed toward the barn instead. Nancy met Kayla, linking arms with her as they stood a safe distance from the police car.

"Rod has his rifle," Kayla whispered to Nancy.

"I know. It scared the life out of me when I saw him loading it this morning," Nancy whispered.

"Doesn't scare me. Makes me feel safer." Cody leaned forward.

The officers quickly handcuffed the two men. Austin never looked up as the sheriff opened the back door of his car and shoved him inside.

Rod dismounted and holstered his gun.

"I guess that takes care of that." He walked over and hugged Nancy.

"Were they surprised to see you?" Cody craned his neck to watch the police car's backseat as the officer slid behind the steering wheel.

"You could say that." Rod laughed. "I was glad the sheriff was there before Austin arrived. He found the other guys at the gap, with their tagging tools in hand. They couldn't deny what they were about to do. I just followed Austin out there. He was so flustered to see the sheriff, he couldn't even come up with a good explanation."

"So, what happens now?" Kayla rested her hand on Cody's shoulder.

"They'll be questioned at the sheriff's office. I'm sure Heston will deny any involvement." Rod pushed his cowboy hat back from his forehead.

"I wish I could have recorded that conversation I heard." Cody pulled up the pictures he had taken. "I think a couple of these stills are actually videos, but you can't hear their voices."

"That's okay." Rod took a step toward his patio. "One of these guys will undoubtedly want to share the blame when they hear about the penalties they're facing."

The deputies sped off. Close behind, the sheriff used the blue light in the dash of his unmarked vehicle.

"I'd better call Uncle Smiley." Kayla pulled out her phone. "He wanted to be here this morning, but he couldn't risk making Austin suspicious. He'll be happy to know y'all took care of things. Come with me?" She waved at Cody.

If anyone had tried to tell her all of this would happen so soon after her mom and dad died, she would not have believed it. What if Cody hadn't heard Austin's plans? If Austin had continued stealing cattle, what would have been his next move? Would she have been safe in her own home?

She sat on a wicker chair facing the pool, patting Cody's knee as he stopped in front of her. "Uncle Smiley. It's over. The sheriff took Austin and the other two guys away in police cars."

"That's terrific," Uncle Smiley responded. "Are you okay?"

"Yes, sir." She closed her eyes. "I'm so relieved."

"I'll be over to talk to Rod about the details. I guess they'll want us to come to the courthouse to file charges."

"Probably." Kayla opened her eyes and squeezed Cody's hand. She'd be fine turning the court details over to Rod and Uncle Smiley.

"Okay, Kayla Grace. See you soon."

She released Cody's hand and placed her phone back in her pocket.

"Want to go inside for that coffee now?" She took a step toward the house.

"No. I've got to go to work." Cody finished the text he was sending on his phone. "I told Mr. Dawson I had personal business this morning but would be there when I could. He'll be excited to hear all about this."

"You're a real hero, Mr. Marshal." She grinned.

"Why, thank you, Miss Kayla." He tipped his cowboy hat. "May I call on you later, ma'am?"

"I'd be honored." She walked with him to his truck.

"Looks like I'm leaving at the perfect time." Cody pointed to the end of the driveway, where an SUV painted with the local TV station's logo had just turned in. "You're about to be a star."

"Oh, no." Kayla stepped back as he started the truck. "I'll have to go get Rod. Call me when you get off work."

"You got it." His pickup spun gravel as he turned out on the main road.

Tara Williams stepped out of the SUV, gathering up her microphone before closing the door. How did the TV station hear what was going on so quickly? Maybe she could at least check her makeup before this interview.

Cody used his left hand to feel for burrs in the metal after sanding the side of the new boat. He was getting used to this routine now. Not as much thinking required since his first day here. More time for his thoughts to wander.

The slight panic he'd sensed in Kayla when he drove off this morning had been an improvement. Being able to reassure her was worth all the scratches and bruises on his arms.

Truthfully, those battle scars were refreshing after long months of being careful about every move he made. He would never outgrow the rush of living dangerously.

"Looking good, Billings." His boss walked past. "When this one moves up the line, how 'bout you sweep the shop?"

"You got it." Cody appreciated the confidence that was placed in him at Walking Eagle. Instead of asking 'Do you think you can handle this?' they just expected he could. So far, he'd been able to manage everything thrown his way.

While using his unique sweeping technique, he passed by the welding station. Rather than just smoothing things over, *this* was where the real work happened—in the shop. Without proper welds, these boats wouldn't be seaworthy. Welders were paid much better than he was, their expertise appreciated by the management.

Conversations during breaks fueled his desire to learn more about welding. With the right training, he could overcome any barriers. This was totally do-able.

Daydreaming about another job was not getting the floor swept. He picked up the pace, spinning in a half circle before moving to a different part of the floor. Hadn't one of the guys mentioned training nearby, maybe at Ozark? He'd have to check further when he got home tonight.

There was undoubtedly more money to be made welding than crawling around in cow pastures. That brush with the Wild West had been sort of exciting, though. He'd have to turn on the local news when he got home to see if Kayla's interview did the caper justice.

"Hello," Kayla answered her phone on the way out the back door.

"Seen any more cattle rustlers on your ranch, ma'am?" Cody used his best western accent.

"Nope. They've all turned tail and run off." She stopped walking.

"I'm leaving the shop. Want to go get something to eat tonight, or are you trying out a fancy gourmet recipe?"

"I have no plans." Wasn't it cool that they seemed to be past the formalities when they wanted to eat together? Being with Cody was the important part. The menu was totally optional.

"I think I'll have enough time to take a quick shower before the evening news comes on," he said. "Don't want to miss your debut as a crime solver."

"I could come to your place. We could watch it together before we leave for supper." Kayla opened the barn door. She'd have to get the horses settled quickly if she was going to leave.

"Sure," he said. "See you in a few."

Kayla made sure the three horses had what they needed. No rain in the forecast tonight, so they could stay out and enjoy the slightly cooler twilight if they wanted.

She went inside, ran a brush through her hair, grabbed her keys, and headed for her pickup. After the events of this morning, she was much too excited to sit by herself for an entire evening.

Had she ever been inside the Billings' house? For all the years they had been neighbors, she and Cody hadn't run in the same circles. There was one time, a few months after Aunt Catherine passed away. Cody's mom had thrown a big party for John K. when he came back from the Army. Felecia Billings was great at making folks feel welcome.

Kayla rounded the curve in front of Cody's front gate. The Billings' barn colorfully displayed Felecia's most recent mural. There was Cody in his graduation gown, tossing his mortarboard high in the air above a fishing boat. She'd heard his mom usually painted the whole mural in one night. Somehow, that didn't surprise Kayla. Evidently, Cody had inherited his stubborn determination from his mom.

"Come right on in." Cody's dad opened the back door as she approached. "We're eager to get the whole cattle rustling story. Our son can't seem to sit still long enough to tell us anything."

"He was quite the hero." Kayla walked through the kitchen to the living room.

"Please, make yourself at home." Cody's mom waved at the sectional facing the television. "Can I get you something to drink? Cody says you like lemonade, just like he does."

"No thanks. I don't think we'll stay long after the news report." Kayla perched on the edge of the couch.

"Okay, on with the show." Cody emerged from the hallway. He winked in her direction while running a comb through his wet hair.

"Next up, real live cattle rustlers strike the ranch of a local rodeo princess. Then, is there any good news on the horizon for rain-thirsty farmers in the area? More after these messages." The television news show teased the story with a shot of Kayla talking to Tara.

"*Woo-hoo*. Can I have your autograph, ma'am?" Cody transferred out of his chair to a spot on the couch next to Kayla.

"Oh, you." She punched his shoulder.

"Mom, bring us some popcorn." Cody's dad leaned back in his recliner.

Kayla turned to look at his mom. "Are they always like this?"

"They're starstruck." Felecia perched on the arm of Dave's chair.

"So, it's my understanding that one of your ranch employees will be charged with conspiracy to commit theft?" Tara pushed the microphone in front of Kayla's face.

"We haven't heard the charges yet, but the sheriff did witness some strange behavior this morning," Kayla answered.

"And your ranch hand was detained?" Tara prompted.

"Yes, ma'am, along with two men who were waiting on the other side of the fence."

Kayla flinched as she watched herself focusing on the camera.

"Do you think these guys were acting on their own or was the owner of the other ranch involved?" Tara asked.

"We don't know. That's why the sheriff took them in for questioning."

Cody elbowed her gently. "Good answer," he whispered.

"We think you're very brave to catch these men. I guess you were just protecting your property, right?" Tara asked.

"Yes, ma'am."

Maybe she hadn't looked too nervous, though her insides had turned to quivering jelly during that interview

"Thanks, Tara." The anchor took the report back to the news desk. "Now, we'll go to our weather team to see if there is any relief in sight for the parched River Valley."

"Wait." Kayla jumped up. "She didn't mention Rod and Cody at all."

"That's okay." Cody reached for her hand, pulling her back down. "You can have your little moment of glory. After all, she's right. You were protecting your ranch."

"Whatever." How embarrassing. She had not done anything but ride along with Cody and point out the ear tags. If he hadn't been with her, she probably would have ruined the evidence.

"I hope they put those guys in jail." Felecia patted Kayla's back. "You've been through more than enough without this, Kayla."

"I'll agree with that." Kayla rose from the couch. "But I'm sure it will be long drawn-out process." She was so glad Cody would be nearby. A process that would be much easier with his support.

Chapter Sixteen

Cody found a wide parking space near their favorite pizza place. Kayla had downplayed the news report, but he felt like celebrating tonight.

"I should have called ahead." He opened his door. "They're busy tonight."

"I'm in no rush." Kayla unbuckled her seatbelt.

He was safely on the ground before she exited the truck.

He wasn't in a hurry, either. After years of running from one activity to another, he was beginning to appreciate taking a good deep breath now and then. Especially when he was in such good company.

Inside, he led the way, finding a table near the back of the restaurant. They passed lots of familiar faces and heard more shouts of 'Kayla' than 'Cody.' Small town America at its best. Not only did everyone know everyone, they also noticed who was spending time with whom. His chest puffed out just a bit. He was not embarrassed to be seen with Miss Rodeo Arkansas Teen—not in the least.

They settled in and discussed pizza toppings. No surprise, they agreed quickly on a good mix of meat and veggies. He finally took another one of those deep breaths and smiled at her as the waitress placed their lemonades on the table and promised to bring their meal ASAP.

"So, how does it feel to be a celebrity?" He teased.

"I wish you'd stop. This coming from the champion bull-rider and heart-throb of Crossroads High."

"All in the past, now." He unwrapped a straw and placed it in the frosty glass. "You, on the other hand, are just reaching the peak of your popularity."

"As my Granny Caldwell always says, 'you just won't do,' Cody Billings."

What a joy to see that sparkle in her eyes. If he had to crawl through a cow pasture to catch a cattle thief once a week from now on, moments like this would be worth it.

"Hey, girl!" From behind Cody, a short, dark-haired teen ran up to hug Kayla.

"Hey! Cody, you know Maddie, my roommate at Fayetteville, right?" She pointed to the chair beside her, and the girl sat down, pulling it closer.

"Yeah. How you doin', Maddie?" He greeted the girl. Would this table be big enough for all of Kayla's admirers?

"I'm great. But you two." Maddie pointed at them playfully. "I can't believe you are out there catching crooks together. Are you switching your major to criminal justice, Kayla?"

"Hardly."

Could Maddie see Kayla squirming? She obviously hadn't shared her change of plans with her old roommate.

"Hey. Remember, we don't have to live in that smelly dorm anymore." Maddie elbowed her. "Mom and I went up last week and found a cute apartment within walking distance of campus. It's got four bedrooms and two bathrooms. Now all we need is to find two more people to live there with us."

"Well, I ..."

Cody nodded at the waitress as she brought their pizza.

"Y'all need three plates?" the waitress asked.

"No, I'm leaving." Maddie stood. "We'll talk later." She

leaned down to hug Kayla again, whispering loudly. "Glad to see you looking so good. Love ya,"

"I'll call you," Kayla turned to Cody as Maddie walked away.

"Why does everyone want me to move up there?" Kayla moved a slice of pizza to her plate.

Cody added some parmesan cheese to his slice, trying to avoid her eyes. "I guess they just assume that's what you want."

"I don't know anymore." Kayla spread a napkin in her lap. "There's still so much to do on the ranch. How can I leave?"

"Have you withdrawn from classes?"

"No. I haven't officially registered either. I have until a few days after the semester starts again in August to take care of all that. For now, the school thinks I'm a continuing student."

"Remember, I'm around to help Rod when he needs anything. I go right past your place on my way to work, so I can always leave early and take a lap on my UTV if you want." He actually felt more needed there than on his own ranch. Could he ease her mind enough to allow her to move back to school?

"So, you want me to leave too?" Kayla paused, her slice of pizza in mid-air. "What if I don't want to go back?"

Uh-oh. Where was this conversation headed? Cody cleared his throat.

"No one is trying to tell you what to do." *Tread carefully, Billings.* It actually would be hard, only seeing her on weekends. But, if she didn't go back to school, would she be happy as a full-time rancher?

"I know. I do appreciate you being around to help. You have relieved a lot of stress for me, Marshal Cody." There it was, that little hint of teasing had returned to her voice.

"Pleased to be of service, ma'am." He tipped his non-existent hat, prompting a giggle.

Help her make up her mind, Lord. I appreciate a nudge now and then if I'm about to say the wrong thing. Amen.

Kayla was quiet as Cody's truck left the lighted city streets. Maddie was assuming a lot. Moving back to Fayetteville had seemed impossible before the cattle thieves were caught red-handed. Cody had helped solve that mystery. But what if more problems arose? Could she handle being two hours away? What if the new person Rod hired was even more irresponsible than Austin?

"It's getting cloudy." Cody leaned forward, squinting through the windshield. "Wonder if we'll get some rain after all?"

"You sound like the typical farmer now." Kayla laughed.

"The weather is always a safe subject." He flashed his famous grin her way.

"I'm sorry I haven't been talkative tonight." Kayla moved as close as the seatbelt would allow. "Maddie got me to thinking."

"I thought you were pretty sure about not going back this semester."

The only thing she was sure about was that she was talking to the right person.

"I don't know. I guess I'm worried about what happens if Uncle Smiley goes off on a mission trip." She watched mailboxes and vapor lights pass her window. Cody would be dropping her off at her truck soon.

"Honestly, you haven't had to rely much on him lately." Cody looked ahead.

"True. You and Rod and Nancy have been the biggest help."

"Like I said, I'll be close by. I can be there in no time, except when I'm working."

She was still surprised he'd given up on moving to the cabin so easily. Another reason she didn't want to be in Fayetteville, with him down here.

He turned into his driveway and came to a stop near her pickup. This evening was ending too soon.

"So, what's up for you tomorrow?" He turned toward her, removing his seat belt.

She unlatched hers as well, scooting closer.

"I've got one of those riding clinics. You know, like the one we had at Cedar Ridge?"

His face was very near, and her heart raced.

"With a rodeo afterward?"

What? What was the question?

"No. I'll be home early in the afternoon."

The vapor light behind them blinked as a tree branch waved in front of it.

Cody reached around her and pulled her close. Surely, he could hear her heartbeat.

His warm breath touched her cheek, and then she felt the soft pressure of his lips on hers. She closed her eyes, and he deepened his kiss, locking his fingers in her hair.

He pulled away slightly, and she took a quick breath, waiting for more.

"I guess I'll see you tomorrow, then," he said softly.

"*Uh-huh.*" How stupid. Couldn't she think of anything else to say? At the moment, not really.

"We'd best say *good night*." He straightened.

She sat straighter, folding her hands in front of her.

"Yeah." Say more. Anything more. "To answer your earlier question, I do feel safer now. That's what makes it hard to move to Fayetteville."

He nodded. "I get that." He paused.

She hadn't seen him at a loss for words very often. She waited.

"Sitting here with you feels right. I guess we just have to think past this moment and be careful about what comes next." He wrapped his fingers around hers.

If that didn't sum everything up in a nutshell.

"You're not only brave, you're incredibly smart, too, Mr. Marshal, sir." Using her teasing tone might relieve the tension.

"Pleased to hear your opinion, Miss Kayla." He released her hand, and touched the end of her nose with his finger. "Now, the proper thing for me to do would be to escort you to your door."

"No, that's fine." She smiled. "I can find my way from here. Good night."

"Night."

Outside his truck, she walked the few steps to hers. Safely behind her own steering wheel, she started the engine, turned on the headlights and waved in his direction.

"Oh, my. What happens now?" The sound of her own voice in the empty cab made her jump. She turned at the end of his driveway and headed home.

Instead of going into the house, Cody left his truck running and pulled out of his driveway. What had just happened?

Silly question. He'd acted on the feelings that had been building up for weeks now. But what was Kayla thinking? One shy little kiss. He sensed they both wanted so much more.

He drove past the high school, and thoughts in his head got more confused. Most of his male friends had lots of adventures with the opposite sex during their time in that building. The girls had always seemed to compare him to other guys. His daredevil, bull-riding persona fascinated some of them, but repulsed others. Even a lot of his male friends didn't know what to make of him.

Then, when he was coming into his own before his senior year, his life had taken an abrupt turn. Looking back, during the time he had been rehabbing from that injury, there hadn't been many people outside of his family who came around. With the exception of Junior, who was more like a brother, there was only one—Kayla Caldwell.

Why had they not been closer before now? Probably because she was in college and he wasn't. Now, he was encouraging her to leave again. What was wrong with him?

He was afraid of the answer to that question. The period of recovery after his bull-riding wreck had brought him a long way.

Constant adjustments to his lifestyle had not been easy, but he'd managed. But what if he was not ready for the next step—a physical relationship with a long-term partner—a wife? What if he could never be a father?

He passed the nursing home and resisted the urge to go inside, even though Grandpa Dee might be awake. Mom said he was becoming more agitated every time she visited him. Soon, interruptions to his daily routine would be too stressful. Best to prepare for losing his favorite roommate for good. That wouldn't be easy.

What was he accomplishing by driving around town all night? He laughed. Grandpa Dee would say, 'Because it's too late to go fishing.' He found an open parking lot and navigated a wide turn, heading back in the direction of home. No need to run out of gas.

Help me clear my head, Lord. Thanks in advance. Amen.

Chapter Seventeen

In the middle of a rodeo arena the next Saturday, Kayla was distracted by the problems this facility would pose for someone in a wheelchair. Changes could be made easily and simply. But that was not her reason for being here.

"Thanks again for your participation today." Ten pairs of eyes were pinned on her. She returned her thoughts to the task at hand. "You all have demonstrated your horsemanship skills. Remember to take good care of your horse buddies, and they will take good care of you."

She mounted Sissy and left the center of the arena to cheers and applause.

"Thanks again for being here." The organizer of the event shook her hand as she reached the entryway.

"No problem. Y'all have some awesome girls here. I'm glad to be able to help them."

Sissy paced impatiently. "Sorry, girl. I know you were just getting warmed up in there," she whispered into the horse's mane.

Kayla dismounted and led Sissy to her trailer. A text notification buzzed in her pocket as she began to remove the saddle.

Wish you were here.

She clicked on a selfie of Cody on his boat, with Junior smiling in the background.

Instead of Junior?

Don't let him hear that.

The text was accompanied by a 'laugh so hard I'm crying' emoji.

You two have fun. I'm almost done at this clinic.

Kayla placed the phone back in her pocket. She should have invited him to come along. But he might not have been able to come inside anyway. Back to the building design issues.

As she went through the familiar routine of loading Sissy in the trailer, she thought again about the courses she'd picked for the fall semester. Her arguments for staying on the ranch sounded thinner and thinner. If all she could think about was building design, she might as well be sitting in a classroom, studying it.

"Okay, girl." She finished wrapping Sissy's legs and walked her up the ramp into the trailer. "Let's go home."

She latched the back door and jumped into her truck. One more event checked off her responsibilities to the Arkansas Rodeo Teen pageant. They'd done fine without Faith today. Mom would be proud that she was completing her reign.

What would Dad say if he knew she had considered delaying her degree? She was waffling back and forth on that issue. Dad would tell her to make a decision and stick with it. She blinked back tears, longing to be able to have a sit-down discussion with him.

The tender goodbye from the last time she'd seen Cody

didn't help. While the cattle were missing, he'd come by nearly every day on his way to or from work. If she lived in Fayetteville, she'd only see him on weekends. Would their new relationship be over before it started?

Cody disconnected the boat trailer from his truck and turned to go toward the house. Mom waved at him from the flowerbed.

"Isn't that your iris bed?" He paused as she leaned on her shovel.

"Yep." Mom wiped her forehead with a pale blue bandana she took from her pocket.

"You're digging them up?" He moved next to the wheelbarrow. "Aren't these the bulbs?"

"Rhizomes." She picked up a dusty clump. "And here, you can help."

"What do you want me to do?"

She handed him a pair of scissors. "Just trim the green part down to about an inch and throw the rhizomes with the roots into this bucket. You can leave what you cut off in the wheelbarrow."

"O-kay." He took the scissors and picked up the first iris. "Mind if I ask why we're doing this? I mean your irises are always so pretty. Why dig them up? If they needed trimming, couldn't you do that while they're still planted?"

Mom turned over another shovel full of dirt.

"We could leave them where they are." She tossed another rhizome into the wheelbarrow. "But if they stay buried for too many years, they might stop blooming. I like to dig them up every couple of years, clean them off and replant them. They enjoy the fresh start."

"So, you're planning to put them back where they were?" He was puzzled. "What good does that do, exactly?"

"They won't all go back." She wiped her forehead with the back of her glove. "I'll give some away, and some get culled. When I replant them, they'll have more room to thrive if I don't bury them too deep. Sometimes change makes them shine brighter than ever."

He worked silently for a while. Change made them shine brighter. He understood the concept. Working at the boat factory was giving him confidence. He could have just continued with familiar things, working on the ranch, fishing. But learning something new and mastering new skills had renewed his hope for the future. Change was making him shine.

"You're awfully quiet over there." Mom straightened up, stretching her back.

"Just thinking." About Kayla, but Mom didn't need to know that.

"That's a new concept for you," Mom teased.

"Yeah, maybe it is." He laughed. Could he get his thoughts together enough to talk to Kayla about change?

He trimmed two more irises. Truth was, as much as he encouraged her to go back to school, he liked having her close.

'If they stay buried too long, they might not bloom.' Mom's words echoed in his head. Kayla needed to bloom. If that meant leaving home to continue learning something new, he'd have to let her go. She'd be even more beautiful if she were allowed to shine.

After unloading Sissy from the rodeo, Kayla sat in a wicker chair, staring at the swimming pool. The evening sun warmed her forehead, causing her to turn her baseball cap around and wear it the way it was designed. She shielded her eyes, searching the sky for any hint of a cloud. Sometimes, a summer afternoon included a thundershower, but that didn't seem to be happening today.

She pulled her cellphone out of her pocket and scrolled

through the University's website again. The posts aimed mostly at incoming freshmen counted down the days until classes started.

Maddie's pictures of the apartment she was renting popped up again. Her friend was seeking decorating advice. Which comforter for her bed? Should they hang curtains, or just go with the mini-blinds that were provided? Right now, she had no answer for all of that.

She stood up, walking toward the gardening tools next to the barn. Mom's petunias were hardy, but they wouldn't last much longer in this heat. Would the water hose stretch that far? Might as well just use the watering can. Making a few trips back and forth to the faucet wouldn't kill her.

Water splashed on the toe of her boot as she turned the faucet off. Kayla thought about her mom every time she watered the flowers. She looked back toward the house, where some plants were finished for the season, and others waited their turn to bloom.

Why hadn't she spent more out here with Mom when she had the chance? If she was going to take care of this place, both inside and out, she'd need some help. There were lots of flowerbeds at Cody's house. Maybe his mom could give her some advice.

Her phone rang, and she looked down to see Cody's name.

"What are you up to?" It was good to hear his voice.

"Just watering flowers."

"Want to go get some supper?"

Even though the sun was hot, she was enjoying being outside. Did she want to sit inside a restaurant with Cody? Sunlight glinted off of Dad's barbecue grill.

"Want to come over here? I could cook something on the grill"

"Great. What can I bring?"

"Dessert." That was the response Mom usually gave when a

guest asked to help with the supper menu. What would he come up with?

"You got it. What time?"

That's one thing she liked about this guy. No hesitation. Just get to the point. But how much time did she need?

"Maybe about seven?" That should work.

"See you then."

What had she done now? She didn't know what kind of food she had in the house. Did Cody like hamburgers or hot dogs better?

She finished watering, ran the can over to its storage spot, and headed for the kitchen. Time for a quick inventory and probably a trip to the grocery store.

"Did you and Junior catch our supper for tonight?" Mom popped in through his open bedroom door.

"Nope. Unless you know what to do with tree branches and empty bread wrappers."

She knew catching fish was not the point of those trips.

"Probably not. I'll come up with something." She laughed.

"I've been invited to Kayla's for supper." He spun around to face her.

"Oh." Her short response spoke volumes.

"Yeah. She likes cooking, but needs someone to cook for. I guess I'm a good guinea pig." Mom was obviously a little uncomfortable about him spending so much time with Kayla. Probably most moms went through this with their last "baby."

"She could come over here." Mom leaned against his doorframe.

"Thanks. But she's already made plans. I told her I would bring dessert."

"So, you're cooking too?" Mom wouldn't make much of a

poker player. The expression on her face showed nothing but doubt in his skills.

"Of course not." He laughed. "I thought I'd go find something at the store."

"Good plan." She smiled. "Well, I'll go see what your dad wants, then."

What was he getting into here? On so many levels. Kayla's cooking skills were the least of his worries. He realized there was no one else he'd rather spend a Saturday evening with. But he wondered where they were going from here.

If they became even closer, would that make it hard to continue with her education to do what she wanted with her life? By offering to help at her ranch, was he intruding in her business?

He remembered their goodbye kiss in his truck. Would it become even harder for them to be alone together? He didn't want to make her uncomfortable, but he might be crossing the line to being too comfortable.

Wow. Just think of a dessert, Cody. One step at a time.

He could think better in his truck. First on the agenda, wash the truck and fill it with gas. Then, he'd look for ideas at the grocery store.

Help me, Lord.

Kayla pushed her shopping cart to the meat department. Dad never bought pre-made hamburger patties. But what was the secret to holding them together while they cooked? Hot dogs would be easier.

She selected the brand Mom always got and placed it in the cart. Her quick inventory of the fridge had showed plenty of mustard and ketchup. So, next was buns. Steering around a man in an electric scooter, she was careful not to knock over a display of pickle relish in the aisle. Pickle relish? Would Cody like that? Sweet, or dill?

She reached for a jar of dill. A familiar cowboy hat approached from the end of the row. Well, no need to try to keep the menu a surprise.

"Hi." Cody stopped in front of her, on a scooter just like the one she had passed in the meat department. "I didn't know what kind of dessert you liked. So, I went with something sort of healthy."

"Watermelon?" What a good idea. She smiled.

"I remembered what my Grandpa Dee told me about picking one out." Cody rolled the melon over to show her a large yellow spot on the bottom. "These are supposed to be the best ones."

"Yeah. I think you're right. I hope you like hot dogs." She pointed at her cart.

"Got mustard?" He moved over to look into her cart.

"Yep. Sweet or dill relish?" This was actually fun.

"Do I look like the sweet type?" He tried out a scowl. It didn't work.

"Not a bit." She pointed to the dill relish. "Okay, then. I'll get some buns and chips and we'll be set. No need to wait for seven o'clock. Just come over whenever."

"Fritos." His comment flew over his shoulder as he headed for the checkout.

"Fritos." She steered to the chip aisle. She should have known better than to stress about cooking for this guy.

Cody stacked his plate on top of Kayla's and took the pile of trash to the can.

"Delicious," he commented on the way back.

"I didn't think we'd still be eating at almost dark." Kayla threw a watermelon rind in the can.

"Well, it took us a bit to figure out your dad's space-age grill." Cody laughed.

"I knew it had pellets, but how do you decide what temperature to use for hot dogs? Dad mostly smoked big pieces of meat. He was always saying 'Low and slow.' So how do you do hot dogs low and slow?" Kayla waved her hands in front of her at about waist height.

"You don't." Cody nodded. "I've only used charcoal. The key is just keeping the fire going long enough, and in the right spots."

"I don't think we'll be on any cooking shows any time soon." She shook her head.

There was that sparkle in her eyes again. The reason he couldn't look away for long.

"Bottom line, best hot dogs in Big River County." He came a little closer to her wicker chair. "And look at this outdoor kitchen. Most *houses* don't have a setup like this inside."

"Dad said I did a good job putting things in the right spot. It's all about the 'triangle,' fridge, stove, prep area." Her voice was quieter as she looked toward the rocked-in appliances.

"You *built* this?" What?

"No, no. I designed it. Don't get me around any power tools, or even hand tools, for that matter." She stood, running her hand over the sealed and polished concrete counter-top.

"See there? You're a natural." Cody decided to tread carefully. He already knew she didn't appreciate being told what she should do with her life.

"*Hmph.*" She nodded briefly.

What did that mean? She agreed? She disagreed? Leave it alone.

"What are we going to do with the rest of this watermelon? You brought enough for an army." She lifted the paper-towels that covered the leftovers.

"You can share with Rod and Nancy and the ranch hands." Cody picked up another small piece. "But if you want, I'll help you cut it up and put it away. I happen to be brilliant at that."

"Brilliant? What are you, a British secret agent?" She picked up the melon and walked toward the house.

"No secrets. What you see is what you get." He retrieved the tray with the dishes and silverware. "Do I need to bring our glasses inside?"

"Next trip." Kayla started toward the kitchen.

He followed as quickly as possible, heaving a sigh of relief. Why had he been worried about being alone with Kayla? So far, they had been their normal, relaxed selves tonight. They'd been too busy cooking and laughing about cooking to be anything else.

Should he try to start steering the conversation to her college plans? Somehow, that didn't seem right. He'd just not bother her about it. No stressing.

"Coming in?" She held the back door open. "I'm looking for Mom's biggest Tupperware bowl. Now, finding the lid may be another story."

Kayla plopped the melon in the middle of the kitchen island. He'd never be able to reach it there.

"Now what, Mr. Brilliant?" She stood with her back to the refrigerator, arms crossed.

"You'll need that big knife and a cutting board." He reached for the bowl she offered him. "Cut the slices into fourths and scoot them to the edge of the counter. I'll grab them and fit them into this bowl. Rocket science one-oh-one."

"Why do I put up with you?" She took the knife and large cutting board to the island. "Watch where you're reaching."

The chopping and laughing continued until the island was a mess, and the watermelon was safely sealed in the bowl.

"Okay. Now, I'll wipe this off and we can go outside. Mopping the floor can wait." Kayla placed the sealed bowl in the refrigerator.

Cody headed back out the door. Was Kayla uncomfortable inside her own house? With its open spaces and high ceilings, it could be an intimidating place. There were probably too many echoes, too many memories.

Outside, the sky was turning pink, and the tree frogs warmed up for their nightly chorus. Easy to see why she spent so much time on the patio she'd designed. Now, to convince her she had a duty to do this same sort of thing for other people. Slow and steady, Cody.

Chapter Eighteen

Kayla put away Breezy's tack and turned the mare out to run with Caesar and Sissy. The routine of riding one of them each day was going well. Did she imagine it, or were they aware of whose turn it was? Horses were intelligent, but that might be pushing it.

She left the barn and strolled toward Nancy's house. With Cody working, she was at a loss for someone to chat with. No one else seemed to be concerned with the day-to-day life of a rancher. Maybe Cody wasn't either, but he was good at pretending.

One of Nancy's dogs ran to meet her, and she reached down to scratch his ears.

"Hey, lady!" Nancy greeted her. "How were things around the ranch this morning?"

"Under control." Kayla ambled closer. "Looks like Rod and the guys are taking care of business. Are you busy?"

"Catching up on laundry. Then, I promised Rod I'd help with some painting later. Come on in." Nancy led the way through their kitchen door.

"Painting? I could help with that." Kayla immediately started picturing which old clothes she could wear for the task.

"Sure. I guess it's more properly staining or water treating. Some new cedar fencing out at the edge of our part of the yard. Not too exciting." Nancy brought Kayla a glass of lemonade, joining her at the kitchen table.

"Not quite as exciting as catching cattle thieves, I guess."

"Thankfully." Nancy sipped her iced tea.

"You know, I'm surprised we don't have our stock back yet." Kayla wrapped her fingers around the cold glass.

"Wow. I'm so glad you said that." Nancy popped up, walking to Rod's desk. "I was going to call you today."

"Me? What can I do?" Kayla knew Cody might have to testify since he'd heard the three hands talking, but she'd only witnessed the tags on the Heston side of the fence.

"The agent said we could speed up the process if we have vaccination records for the females." Nancy opened a folded piece of paper. "When the state vaccinates for Bovine Brucellosis, a permanent tattoo is applied, showing ownership."

"And our cows always get their shots. I remember Dad being very proud of that." Kayla scanned the paper.

"Rod said your dad has those records. He can come up and help you find them if you like." Nancy refolded the paper and returned it to the desk.

"No. That sounds like a good project for me. Then, I'll help you paint the fence." Kayla finished her glass of lemonade.

"Call me when you find it. Rod will be happy to get this settled."

"Won't someone have to go testify in court?" Kayla dreaded that.

"Oh, yes. But right now, they're gathering evidence. The court date could be months away. Cattle thefts are not a big priority, I'm sure."

"Unless they're your cattle," Kayla agreed. "Thanks for the lemonade, friend. I'll see you soon."

She rushed out the door, straightening her baseball cap to shield her eyes from the sun. At last, something meaningful to do. Not that taking care of horses wasn't important, but this was much more exciting.

The overhead can lights in Dad's office didn't help much as she opened the top of his four-drawer file cabinet. Another design flaw in this house. A horizontal file with a nearby table lamp would look classier and make the contents easier to see.

She flipped through folders that weren't in any order. First, accounts payable. Uncle Smiley had looked through this and taken care of outstanding bills early on. Accounts receivable was also empty, since everyone who owed the family money had been kind about taking care of debts.

"Plans," she read aloud. *How vague is that, Dad?* She retrieved the folder and opened it to reveal copies of blueprints. A new shed Dad had built for farm equipment. The original plans for the house, dated before Kayla was born. Behind them, a piece of legal-size copy paper with a penciled drawing made Kayla's breath catch.

Pool, patio, and outdoor kitchen was written neatly across the top of the paper in her fourteen-year-old handwriting. On the bottom right, her fanciest cursive writing formed a signature. "Kayla Grace Caldwell."

Tears washed her cheeks. She hadn't realized how important this piece of paper was to her dad. The real contractor had used a more professional drawing. But Dad had kept this one. How long would this random crying last?

The reverse of the drawing had something taped to it. Flipping it over, she found old photos of the completed patio, with brand new furniture. Standing between her proud parents, Kayla wore a broad smile. Why did she not realize Dad kept this? How did it avoid Mom's scrapbook? She placed the drawing carefully back in the folder, with one shuddering breath to prevent an all-out sob.

"I'm glad you liked it, Dad," she whispered.

After a few more folders full of rodeo stock transactions, she opened the second drawer.

Bingo. The first folder was clearly marked 'Vaccinations.' Most showed only dates, or purchases made from the local veterinarian. Dad and Rod handled many of the preventive shots themselves. Inside, a letter-sized folder displayed the word 'Brucellosis.'

"*Woo-hoo!*" She pulled out the folder and sat at Dad's desk. The documents for each year were stapled together, and each cow was identified with a tattoo and a specific number on the ear tag.

Scrolling down to Nancy's contact, she called with one tap.

"I found it!" Hopefully, Nancy would know who was calling.

"You did?" Good. She understood instantly.

"Tell Rod we are on our way to getting our stock identified. At least, the cows." Was this what a detective felt like when he cracked a case? Maybe Maddie's suggestion about changing her major wasn't too far off. This was fun.

She hung up from talking to Nancy and checked the time before calling Cody. He was still at work. Unable to resist, she sent a quick text.

> Can't wait to see you this afternoon. Exciting news to report.

The coolness of Dad's leather chair brushed her arms. Had she really just thought about changing her major? That assumed she was returning to college. The idea wasn't sounding so bad anymore.

Heat rose from the driveway outside the window. If she moved to Fayetteville, she couldn't sit here and watch for Cody's truck every day. That firm resolve to go back to school didn't last long.

Now what? Should she take this folder to Nancy so Rod could use it to call the agent?

"Nancy!" Rolling the chair back from the desk, she jogged a few steps to her bedroom. Time to get into those painting clothes.

"So, what's the big, exciting news?" Cody called Kayla from his hands-free phone in the pickup.

"Well. It's more than I can explain on the phone." She sounded out of breath.

"You okay?" Maybe she was riding.

"Yeah. I just pulled down my mask. I'm helping Nancy paint a fence."

"Oh!" He laughed, picturing this uncommon sight. Somehow, he knew there was not a hair out of place in her dark red braid.

"You're on the way? Can you stay for supper?"

"Sure. But it's my turn to cook. My drive-through skills are spot-on." Of course, there was no one he'd rather share a weekday supper with.

"Thanks. It will take me a minute to clean up."

No need, he thought. But he knew she'd argue.

"I pass a Chinese place, a taco place, and a barbecue place."

"Pulled pork sandwich with slaw. Baked beans and potato salad."

He should have known she'd have her order all figured out.

"My pleasure, ma'am." Was it dangerous to drive while smiling this big?

"No need for drinks. I've got that covered at home," She continued.

"Of course, ma'am. As you wish." He used his left turn signal and waited for traffic at the hole-in-the wall barbecue joint.

A few minutes later, he slid to a stop in her driveway. With the food balanced in his lap, he met her on her way out of the house. Once again, she was more comfortable outside.

"Thanks for bringing supper." Kayla spread a tablecloth across the patio dining table and arranged two place settings. While Cody placed food on the table, she opened the little fridge.

"I'm having water. Do you want a soda?" She turned to face him.

"Water's fine. I haven't been hydrating as much now that they fixed the air conditioner." He unwrapped her sandwich, and then his. "So, enough with the suspense. What's your news?"

"I've been working on getting our cattle returned." She settled at the table across from him.

"Really? Did you go over to Heston's place?" He wasn't sure he liked that idea.

"No, of course not. But Nancy said even pictures wouldn't be positive identification. The agent suggested we find the documentation from brucellosis vaccinations for the cows. The state uses numbered tattoos and a special tag. Each cow has her own unique number, and that is a lot harder to remove than a simple ear tag." She picked up her sandwich. "I was so excited about searching Dad's records that I forgot all about eating lunch."

"Of course!" Cody smacked himself in the forehead. "We had some of our young cows vaccinated a few months ago. Why didn't I think of looking at those records?"

"Hopefully, we'll get the cows back home soon. Rod said we have three missing. We may never get the calves and steers identified, but it's a start." She handed him a fork for his baked beans.

"Good work, there, deputy." Cody laughed.

"So, I have an actual title now?" She smiled at him.

"I think you're up to the task."

Was she enjoying this ranch business too much? Should he try to convince her to continue her architecture studies? This didn't seem like a good time to bring that up. No use nagging her about it, anyway.

"*Hmph.*" She read a text on her phone. "That stinks."

"What?" He set his sandwich down and started on his potato salad.

"Maddie says they canceled the Fourth of July fireworks in Crossroads due to a burn ban." She frowned.

"Not surprising." Cody took a sip of his water. "We haven't had nearly enough rain lately."

"How do you do the Fourth without fireworks?"

"There are other ways to celebrate." He emptied his water bottle with one long swig. "It's hot out here. If I wasn't afraid of getting your pool dirty, I'd just plunge in, clothes and all."

"You're brilliant!" She jumped up and stood at the edge of the pool.

"*Huh?*" She was full of surprises. But what was she talking about?

"If we can't have fireworks, I'll have a pool party for the Fourth of July." She faced him. "You're off work, right? Do you have big plans?"

"Nope. Sounds like a great idea. Want me to bring a watermelon?"

"Yeah. You picked a great one last time." She perched on a wicker chair and pulled out her cellphone. "I'll send out feelers to see if anyone else wants to come."

"Great!" Swimming did sound good with the weather staying so hot and dry. Today, though, his shower at home sounded even better. "I'll leave you to your planning. Let me know if I can do anything else." He took a load of trash to a nearby can.

"Oh, I'm being rude." She caught up with him. "Thanks for bringing supper. I can clean everything up. I'll send you a text when I get the details figured out for the Fourth."

"Sounds like fun." He pulled her down and kissed her tenderly.

She held his hand as she straightened up before allowing him to pass.

As he left the driveway, Kayla was texting furiously. He kept her in his rearview for a bit, enjoying her excitement. First about ranch business, and now about planning a party. Was she so settled in now that she'd give up on going back to college?

The idea didn't make him sad. He'd landed a decent job at Walking Eagle boats. Maybe she could find plenty to do without leaving home.

Having Kayla close by to share a meal and brighten his day after working so hard was growing on him. The word 'content' had always sounded too tame. With Kayla around, contentment didn't seem so bad.

Back at home, he parked next to the empty flowerbed. Mom's comment about her favorite flowers rang in his head. 'If they stay buried too long, they'll eventually stop blooming.' Was there danger in this new routine of theirs?

He headed for the shower. Clean body—clear head. That was the plan.

I think it's a great idea!

Maddie's text was filled with happy emojis.

Call me.

"It's my first party without Mom and Dad," Kayla said as Maddie answered the phone. "I just hope people don't think there will be alcohol or other crazy stuff."

"*Nah*," Maddie said. "You're still the same Kayla. They know that."

"Well, let's see how many people want to come, then. I'll try to have enough snacks. The main thing is to cool off in the pool." She put Maddie's call on speaker and scrolled through her contacts list.

"We can all bring something." Maddie replied.

"Thanks. Cody's bringing a watermelon." Kayla smiled. This might be a lot of fun.

"Oh. Cody's coming?" Maddie paused. "He can still swim?"

"Of course." Kayla's cheeks blazed. Would her friends make Cody uncomfortable? He was probably used to insensitive remarks like that. If they were going to be a couple, she'd have to learn to deal with them too. Wait! Were they officially a couple now?

"Yeah. I'll see you on the Fourth, then," Maddie said.

"Awesome. See you then." Kayla pasted on her rodeo queen smile, hoping it made her voice sound upbeat.

Her first gathering at her house without her parents? A Fourth of July without fireworks? What was she thinking? Having Cody here might be the best thing about the day.

# Chapter Nineteen

Cody's body made a bigger splash than he'd planned when he lowered himself into the cool water of Kayla's pool. Lack of control of his lower limbs made a graceful entry almost impossible. No use being self-conscious. No one else was paying attention.

Kayla waved at him from the diving board, where she prepared to make a much more stylish entry into the deep end of her pool. As far as he could tell, this party she'd planned was a big hit with all in attendance. Her dive was effortless, and the splash minimal as she dropped below the surface and made her way back up.

"Hi." She surfaced just a few feet away from his spot at the edge of the pool.

"Hey there." His heart pounded as he released the concrete side and used his arms to scull closer to her. Of course, he'd known she'd be dressed in the trendiest beach outfit she could find, but being this close to her was proving much harder than he'd anticipated. *Come on, Dude. It's not like you've never seen a girl in a swimsuit before.*

"Having fun?" She placed her arms across his shoulders, locking her hands behind his neck.

"Sure." He moved his arms a little faster, trying to stay afloat.

"I think I'd enjoy swimming more if it was just the two of us," she whispered.

"That's not a good attitude for a hostess." He laughed. "We can make that happen another time, okay? Want to race?"

"Really?" She released his neck.

"Across the pool and back. Go!" He allowed her a small head start, and then used the crawl stroke he'd learned during water therapy. Maybe not as graceful as an Olympian, but it worked. Turning without the special pull buoy he'd trained with was not easy, so she made it back to their starting place ahead of him.

"You're pretty good!" Kayla held the side of the pool as he finished.

"I'm out of practice." Cody rested beside her. "Could you save me a second or two and grab something for me?" He pointed to the foam buoy sticking out of the pocket of his chair, just out of his reach. "That thing helps me float."

"Sure." Kayla scrambled up, grabbed the figure-eight-shaped foam device, and handed it down to Cody.

He placed it between his legs, eliminating the need to constantly move his hands quite as much. "Thanks. I'll be ready for a rematch on that race soon."

"Can't stand to be beaten by a girl?" She sent a tiny splash into his face.

"Kayla!" A chorus of male and female voices beckoned from the diving board.

"Watch this." Maddie ran to the end of the board and executed her own version of Kayla's dive.

"Throw out the top and bottom judges, and she still wouldn't score anywhere close to yours." Cody winked at Kayla.

"Okay. I guess I'd better be hospitable." She moved away from him and swam toward the diving board again, using long, even strokes.

"What's up?" Junior popped up nearby, spouting a stream of water skyward with his clasped hands.

"What's that, your whale imitation?" Cody laughed.

"Nope. It's a challenge. Want to race?" Junior looked behind him. "Last one to the other side of the pool has to cut the watermelon."

"You're on." Cody took off with the buoy in place, using his modified stroke to stay several feet ahead of Junior.

Raising his head out of the water to take a huge breath, he used two more strokes to reach the opposite side of the pool. He pushed up on the concrete with his arms, turning his body around to reach a sitting position.

"Impressive." Junior spluttered from the poolside below Cody.

"I agree." Junior's girlfriend Joy swam to Junior's side.

"Did I hear something about watermelon?" Kayla sat beside Cody on the edge of the pool, locking elbows with him.

"Okay. I'm going." Junior pushed himself up, leaving a dripping trail to the long, green melon resting on one of the patio tables.

"That was amazing." Kayla leaned close to Cody, looking up into his eyes.

"Your rematch might have to wait." Cody took a deep, cleansing breath. Junior's challenge had inspired him, and he had surprised himself. "I just couldn't let that clown win."

"He didn't stand a chance." She leaned against him. "Would it help if I go get your chair? Everybody's been waiting on the melon. I hope there will be a piece left by the time we get there."

"I don't mind swimming back over there." Cody pointed. "I'm getting re-acquainted with some of the muscles in my upper body today."

"*Mm-hmm.*" She sat back, nodding, with her lips pursed together and her eyebrows raised. "Okay, then. I'll make sure to save you a slice."

Cody slid back into the water and used slower strokes to go back across the pool. Kayla's comment about wishing they were alone in the pool played back in his head. He had to admit it was a very good thing that there were other people here.

Kayla couldn't take her eyes off Cody as he pushed himself out of the water and back into his wheelchair. She knew he was athletic, but today, his well-toned muscles were on display.

There hadn't been any ignorant or rude comments since Cody arrived. He'd established a reputation for toughness in his bull-riding days, and now, he was adding to it. Pride bubbled inside her to admit she was "with" this handsome cowboy.

Maddie walked up behind Kayla as the two waited for watermelon.

"Yep. I see how it is." Maddie tapped her shoulder. "I found one more roommate for our apartment. Maybe Cody could be our fourth."

"What?" Was Maddie purposely trying to embarrass her? "No. He's not going to be at Fayetteville this fall."

"Oh. That's tough. It's not that far from here, though. I guess you can still see him most weekends." Maddie took a slice of melon from Junior.

"Give me Cody's, please." Kayla took a slice in each hand. Maddie was still assuming she would be her roommate. She'd have to make a final decision soon. Cody stopped to chat with a couple of her friends on the way back to claim his watermelon.

Now that the cattle-stealing adventure was over, she was more confident about leaving things in Rod and Nancy's hands. Cody had been a big part of that too. She was still amazed how quickly he had changed his plans to move away. Other guys she'd dated hadn't even been willing to change their dinner plans for her.

Would he be disappointed if she decided to attend classes in the fall after all? There was entirely too much commotion around to talk to him about that today. *Pasted-on princess smile, don't fail me now.*

"Looks like the melon was a big hit." He laughed as he took a slice from her. "Junior may not even get a piece. Next time you have a pool party, it may require two of those bad boys."

"You're not only an Olympic swimmer, you're a watermelon connoisseur." She laughed.

"*Whew.* Wouldn't want to order business cards for that job." He took a big bite of the pink fruit, sending a stream of juice down his chin.

"*Uh-oh.*" She watched a seed hit the ground at his feet. "This is going to be a cleaning nightmare. Mom's rule about no food poolside totally slipped my mind today."

"Oops." He leaned down, prying the seed up with his fingernail. "I promise to stick around to help."

"I'll take you up on that." She smiled. *Yes, please do stick around.*

Cody ran his fingers through his wet hair. The guests were gone. They had managed to get the pool area clean. Finally, the alone time they both longed for.

Kayla sank into the wicker chair in front of him.

"Tired?" He moved closer, resting a hand on her shoulder. Thankfully, it was now covered by a lacy coverup shirt.

"Yes." She leaned against his hand, closing her eyes. "Thanks for your help."

"My pleasure." Did she realize how appropriate that little catch phrase was? At this point, very few things would bring him more pleasure.

"It's only a few hours until sundown." She looked toward the horizon. "Now is when we should be finding a good spot to watch fireworks."

"We didn't know how much we enjoyed them until we couldn't have them." Cody agreed.

"So philosophical." She raised a finger to emphasize her point.

"We've both had to make adjustments, right?" He was so close to her face that their noses almost touched.

"I couldn't have done it without you," she whispered.

"I think you could. You're pretty amazing." He reached around her back, and pulled her closer, pressing his lips to hers. What he'd been wishing for all day long. He released her and looked into her eyes.

"I'm amazing? You're even more amazing." She ran a finger up his bicep. "Thanks for being here."

He straightened. "No place I'd rather be."

"I've been thinking about something all day." She leaned back against her own chair. "I've made a decision. I want to thank you for helping me feel secure about leaving the ranch during the week this fall."

"You're going back to school?" He made an effort to keep his voice soft, though his heart thrummed harder against his ribcage.

"I think so. The classes I want to take are more related to my degree this time, instead of just basics." She reached for both of his hands. "But I'm going to miss seeing you on your way home from work."

He swallowed hard. "That's been fun. I don't want to hold you back. I think you're meant to design amazing spaces for other people. Not just here on your own property." That sounded cliché, but it was true. So many others could benefit from her vision for making living spaces accessible.

"I'm not in a hurry to leave. We have about a month before I move away." She squeezed his fingers. "Let's enjoy it."

"My pleasure." He leaned in for another sweet kiss.

A loud 'ping' rang out from the pocket on his chair that held his phone. A similar one followed from wherever Kayla had stowed hers.

"It's my brother, O.D." He scanned the message.

"And?" Kayla walked across the patio.

"It says, 'Can y'all make it to Aunt Candace's house tonight? Everybody will be there.'"

"Mine says 'Do you know where Cody's Aunt Candace lives?' It's from Hope." Kayla turned her phone toward him.

"Those two. They could save some effort if they talked to each other. Does that sound okay?" Cody took a deep breath. An interruption in their alone time was probably a good idea.

"I guess." She shrugged.

"Here's another text. It says 'Try to make it by 8:30.'" He smiled. This family of his, seriously.

"Why 8:30?" She stood next to him.

"Who knows. Try figuring out the inside of my brother's head, I dare you."

"I need about thirty minutes to get dressed." She pressed her hand to his shoulder.

"Let's tell them we're coming." He started his reply. "Then, I'll race you across the pool before we go."

"You're on." She laughed, peeling off the lace cover-up, and tucking her phone into a tote bag next to the picnic table.

He hurried to the edge of the pool and dropped into the water, just as she popped up after diving from the board.

"On your mark, get set, go!" He took off. In no time, he felt splashes as her feet kicked up water near his face. No problem. Winning this race was not a big priority.

Kayla sat as close as her seatbelt would allow as Cody drove up the crooked two-lane road to his aunt's house. Pine trees on either side swayed in the hot summer breeze, and a shimmer of heat rose from the black-top.

"I hope it's okay we brought our leftover chips and drinks from the party." She glanced behind her to make sure the ice chest was riding well.

"Definitely." Cody patted her knee. "Aunt Candace never arrives at a party empty-handed. It's how we roll."

"O.D. said *everybody* would be there. Who do you think that means, exactly?" After entertaining friends all day, she had hoped to relax with just Cody. Not meant to be.

"Probably just Caldwells and Billingses." He turned into a long, paved driveway. "That's plenty, don't you think?"

"Yeah. For sure." She smiled. Had Faith and John K. come down from Fayetteville?

She checked her reflection in Cody's side mirror as he unloaded his chair. Could other people see the glow in her face? Most of it came from today's hot sun, but the excitement left over from her party might be a big part of it too. Not to mention time with a certain Marshal.

It's been a good Fourth, Lord. Thanks for everything.

Cody used his fingers to form a whistle, attracting some help to carry the ice chest down the hill to Aunt Candace's pavilion. Mom had talked about how nice this place looked, but he hadn't visited since all the work was finished. He took the tote bag full of potato chips from Kayla and started down the paved pathway.

"Hey Kayla!" John K. hugged her before picking up the ice chest. "Glad you could work us into your busy schedule, Marshal Cody." He bumped Cody's shoulder as he passed by.

"How will the Northwest make it through the Fourth without their chief firefighter?" Cody moved into position behind his brother.

"I was lucky I was already scheduled to be off." John K. headed down the paved pathway. "Hopefully, with the fireworks ban, things will be pretty quiet."

"It's kind of strange not to have fireworks." Kayla spoke up from behind Cody.

"But smart. One spark could take out acres of land on a day

like this." John K. took long strides to get down the hill quickly. "Faith's going to be glad to see you, Little Bit."

"Little Bit?" Cody laughed.

"You know he has nicknames for everybody. It could be a lot worse, I guess."

"Yeah. He just calls me Marshal. O.D. got stuck with 'Squirt'." Cody checked his phone for the time. 8:15. They'd met the deadline.

Inside the pavilion, hugs and handshakes greeted them. Smiley Caldwell paced nervously, looking out over the water. He turned for a moment to peck Kayla on the cheek, then resumed his contemplation.

"This is a beautiful spot." Kayla pulled a chair up next to Cody.

"We're glad you're here." Mom hugged Kayla, and then Cody. "Do y'all need something to drink?"

"I'm okay for now." Cody reached for Kayla's hand.

"Me too." Kayla squeezed his fingers.

Junior waved from the opposite side of the pavilion, holding onto Joy's hand with his free one.

Aunt Candace walked up to stand next to Smiley. He turned toward the rest of the family as the sun dropped lower, creating a kaleidoscope of colors in the sky, reflecting in the water behind them.

"Well." Smiley took his hands out of his back pocket and removed his cowboy hat. "Happy Fourth of July. Y'all might be wondering why we had a specific time to begin this gathering."

Aunt Candace had a startled look on her face. Had she not expected Smiley to lapse into official host mode? After all, he was a preacher.

"It's because we can't have fireworks, so I'm taking advantage of God's nightly presentation instead. I have something very special to say." He dropped to one knee, placed his hat on the planks next to him, and removed something from his pocket. Aunt Candace covered her mouth with her hand.

"Candace, while we are compassed about by this great cloud of witnesses, I want to know if you'd consider running the rest of our earthly race by my side. Will you please do me the honor of being my wife?"

Only a few frogs dared to break the silence as everyone in the pavilion held their breath.

"I would be delighted." Aunt Candace reached down to place her hands on each side of his face.

Smiley slid the ring on her finger, then stood to pull her close for a kiss. Cheers and whistles shattered the peace of the riverbank.

Chapter Twenty

"Wow." Kayla remained in her chair as the other guests lined up to congratulate Uncle Smiley and Candace.

"Did you know this was happening tonight?" Cody leaned toward her.

"Not a clue." She shook her head. "But then, I haven't talked to Uncle Smiley much lately."

"Yeah. We were kind of preoccupied with the whole missing cattle thing." Cody rolled toward the line of people greeting the happy couple.

Kayla followed behind him.

"So happy for you two!" She hugged Candace and reached for Uncle Smiley's arm.

"I guess I should have shared this news with you, Kayla Grace. But I didn't even tell my three kids. Saying it out loud to anyone but Candace was too scary." He held her hands for a moment.

"Just be happy, Uncle Smiley." She hugged him, breathing in the same scent her dad had worn. What would her parents have thought about this development?

Cody's mom waited on the other side of Uncle Smiley and handed each a plate and steered them toward the snack table.

"Quite a celebration." Cody used tongs to serve some homemade cookies. "Want some?"

Kayla nodded and poured some peanuts from a jar onto her plate and then his. Maybe a little too much celebration. She settled back into her chair as conversations buzzed around her. What would happen now?

Candace had been renting this place out for reunions and parties. Surely she wouldn't move away when it was just getting started. Would Smiley move here? What about Junior? Why did any of that matter to her, anyway? That was their lives. She had enough worries of her own.

"A dollar and a quarter for your thoughts." Cody bumped her arm. "Inflation."

"I don't know. I guess this is a lot to take in." She leaned her head closer to him, hoping the rest of the family wouldn't pick up on her confused emotions.

"Today was a big step for you, right?" He took her hand in his. "Having so much company at your house, then hearing about another big change tonight. I get it."

"Somehow, I knew you would." She returned the comfort she saw in his eyes with a shy smile. "Like I said. It's a lot. Not good, not bad, just a lot."

"Yep." He nodded. "We can leave any time you're ready."

"No, that's okay. I'll try to be sociable for a few more minutes." She leaned into the camping chair she sat in. Night sounds washed over her, calming her nerves.

Cody moved away, talking to his brothers and his parents.

"You okay, sweetheart?" Uncle Smiley stopped next to her, touching her shoulder.

"For sure." She added artificial perkiness to her voice. "I'm a little tired. That swim party at my house was almost too much fun."

"I know what you mean. Keeping this secret all day has me

worn out too." Uncle Smiley's eyes twinkled. "But she said 'Yes,' so I can breathe now."

Kayla laughed out loud. "Breathing is a good thing, Uncle Smiley." She stood up to wrap him in a hug. "I love you."

"I love you too." He walked toward Candace.

"You want to get some snacks to go?" Cody appeared at her elbow.

"I've had plenty. Get whatever you want."

"Okay. I'll be right back." He traveled back to the snack table.

"Hey." Faith walked closer to her. "I'm glad you were here for the big event. You never know what's going to happen when this clan gets together."

"That's for sure." Kayla stood. "Oh, I wanted to tell you something too. I'm going back to college in the fall."

"Was that in question?" Faith tilted her head.

Kayla realized she hadn't shared her doubts with her cousin at all. Cody had become her sounding board. "Well, not anymore. Maddie has an apartment lined up for us. So, hopefully, I'll see more of you and John K. after classes start."

"Sounds great, Gracie." Faith hugged her, then whispered in her ear, "I'm glad to see you and Cody are getting closer too. Those Billings boys are great guys."

"Thanks." She swallowed. How would her relationship with Cody change when she moved away?

"Okay. I've got some of everything now." He held up a paper bag full of snacks. "I'll get John K. to load the ice chest. Are you ready to go?" He beckoned his oldest brother with a crooked finger.

She had to agree with Faith. The Billings boys were great guys. Especially the youngest one.

They chattered all the way back to her house, about everything and nothing.

"Oops." Cody pointed out a bright display of fireworks in the distance. "Those folks think the rules don't apply to them."

"I hope it doesn't cause a fire." She turned her head to watch. Was that happening near Hope's house? Maybe on Heston's land?

"Me too. I guess you can't fix stupid. If they make much more noise, the sheriff will be out here."

"Not a job for the marshal and his deputy, though." She grinned.

"Nope. We're off duty tonight." He laughed.

She sat quietly for a moment as he turned off his motor in her driveway. Her pillow called to her, but she was in no hurry to get out of his truck.

"What a great Fourth this turned out to be." He reached across the seat to touch her hand.

"For sure." She turned to face him. That sparkle in his eye was becoming one of her favorite sights. "Guess we'd better say good night."

His lips touched hers briefly, then moved to her forehead. "Good night." His hands moved from her arms up to her shoulders, and he stared into her eyes for a moment. He kissed her again, reaching behind to press her body against his.

Kayla sank into his arms with her eyes closed, her core quivering, her heart beating against his. She tilted her head up as the kiss ended, waiting.

A tiny groan escaped his lips, and he added some distance between them, his fingers caressing her arms before releasing completely.

They sat silently for a moment. Their eyes met, and his smile was softer, more vulnerable than she'd ever seen.

"I think it's time for me to leave." She barely heard him speak.

"What if I don't want you to?" Was she really saying this?

"Trust me. It's time." He sat up straighter, holding both of her hands in his.

"Okay." She'd have to calm her heart rate down just a bit before she could make it into the house. "Talk to you tomorrow." She opened her door and stepped down to the ground.

"I'm counting on that." He winked and waved.

As he drove away, she took a long deep breath. She'd just have to get used to this pounding in her heart, because it wasn't going to change for a while.

She walked toward the barn, flipping on the switch inside to find all three horses sleeping peacefully. Either Rod or Nancy must have covered for her tonight. What a blessing they were.

"Good night." She switched off the brightness in the barn and walked through the soft glow of the vapor light to her back door.

Cody turned out of Kayla's driveway and took the shortest route home. He'd probably be there before his parents. Tonight, he was grateful he hadn't moved to the cabin. Tomorrow was a workday, and it would start early.

Today had been a good day. He was glad to be able to help Kayla feel comfortable with having guests at her house.

Comfortable. There was that word again. Was he allowing himself to become too comfortable with Kayla? Just a minute ago, he'd wanted to move beyond comfortable to intimate. Not the time or place for that next big step.

Another set of illicit fireworks lit the sky. Was it wrong of him to assume someone on Heston's property was responsible? After recent events, that crew had earned a bad reputation. He understood the need for excitement. A burn ban on the Fourth of July was hard to accept, but things could get out of hand in a hurry. So many important things could get out of hand.

He turned into his driveway. Still, in all, he'd had more excitement than most people his age. Looking back on the life adjustments he'd made, it was no surprise he felt old before his time.

Inside the house, he stopped in the kitchen. He hummed to himself before unwrapping one of Aunt Candace's famous brownies. The perfect bedtime snack.

He scrolled through his email, checking the deposit of his latest paycheck into his bank account. Another good reason for living at home. This salary was not nearly enough to support himself if he moved out on his own.

He chewed a bite of brownie. Comfort food. If he ever wanted to live on his own, he'd have to give up some comfort.

He'd never really gotten all the details about welding training. Ozark's website showed a certificate he could get by the middle of next summer. Could he continue to work at Walking Eagle while he took the classes?

Inside his room, he prepared for bed. Tonight, at Aunt Candace's house, Smiley Caldwell had reminded him what he wanted most in life. The security of a family who loved him, feeling needed and valuable, and having a good woman by his side for the journey.

Would Kayla be that companion? To provide for a family, he'd need to live up to his own potential. Learning a trade that made more money was a start. But what if he couldn't be the husband Kayla needed or the father for her future children?

Mom and Dad were in the kitchen when he got out of the shower. He threw on some clothes and joined them.

"Quite a day son." Mom poured herself a glass of milk. "Want some?"

"No, thanks. I'm good. I guess Aunt Candace is pretty excited."

"I'm so happy for her. And for Smiley." She sipped her milk. "They both deserve happiness."

"God is good." Dad stood just inside the back door.

"Yes sir, He is." Cody needed to be sure about his school plans before bringing his parents up to date. This was not the time to bring up the big question in his mind either. It could all wait. "Good night."

Back in his room, he looked up the information about welding school again. Even if Mr. Dawson allowed him to continue working, could he handle sixteen credit hours of classwork?

Pictures of guys wearing face shields, holding welding torches filled his screen. If he did something like this every day, the hours would pass quickly. Was there a better way for him to see the results of his hard work? Good pay, hard work, an element of danger. In other words, right up his alley.

If Kayla was away in Fayetteville all week, having classes of his own would make the week go by faster. Would she look forward to seeing him on weekends, or would new friends and activities make her forgot all about him?

He closed the computer and climbed into bed. After spending so much time encouraging Kayla to follow her dreams, now he was unsure about doing the same thing. This was harder than getting on the back of a kicking, snorting bull. Probably because the ride he was anticipating would last a lot longer than eight seconds. At least he prayed it would. Maybe for the rest of his life.

Kayla and Sissy galloped across the pasture behind the barn as the sun emerged over the pine trees behind her house. Afternoon heat would make this ride miserable, but right now, it was just what she needed. She reined Sissy in and dismounted to open the gate.

"That felt good, right, girl?" She patted the sorrel's neck and climbed back into the saddle. "Let's go make sure you've got plenty of water." The horse's pace was slower as they approached the trough.

Only a few more of these early morning rides. Last semester, Mom and Dad had made sure all three horses got their exercise.

Would Nancy be able to dedicate enough time to do this each day?

"We'll still have weekends." She reassured Sissy as she lowered her head into the trough. Weekends with the horses, weekends with Cody. Life was about to get complicated. What was it Cody had said? "You're meant to design beautiful spaces for other people, not just on your own property." She smiled. It did feel good to know he understood her dreams.

"Okay. Let's get this tack off so you can enjoy your day." She unsaddled the horse and led her out to join her buddies.

Maddie's text appeared on her phone.

> I think I have two roommates lined up.

She had been too busy to give roommates a second thought.

> Good news

Kayla leaned on the corral fence and watched as Sissy nudged Breezy with her nose.

Maddie stopped texting and called instead. "So, what are you doing today?"

"Nothing that I know of." Kayla looked around. There didn't seem to be any pressing work around the barn.

"Want to run up to Fayetteville to do some shopping? We'll need towels, bedding, all that stuff," Maddie said.

"And we have to go to Fayetteville, why?" Kayla laughed.

"Girl! What's around here besides Walmart?" Maddie asked. "I was thinking we'd go by the apartment to find out about moving in. Classes start in the middle of next month, but I might move early.

"Yeah. I'm in. Should I meet you somewhere?" Kayla looked toward Nancy's house. She'd check in and send a text to Uncle Smiley. And Cody. Of course, Cody.

"That would help. Where?" Maddie asked.

"You know where my cousin Hope works? Cedar Ridge Ranch?"

"Yeah. At the old rodeo arena, right?"

"I'm sure it would be fine to leave my truck there. Unless you want me to drive." Kayla knew Hope would approve of this plan.

"No, I'll drive. My car gets better gas mileage. See you in about thirty minutes? We can get up there in time to eat lunch somewhere on College Avenue." Maddie was talking very quickly now.

"See you in thirty." Kayla sprinted inside to change clothes. No use looking like she just came in from riding a horse.

She sat down on the side of her bed to compose a text to Cody. Make it two.

> Sorry, won't be here when you get off work tonight.

> Maddie and I are going up to check out the new apartment. Call me later?

Cody wiped off his grimy hands with a rag and checked his phone message. Things were changing already. Kayla wouldn't be waiting at her house when he got off work this afternoon.

He sent a quick response.

> No problem. Catch you later.

He picked up his grinder and resumed working. She was doing exactly what was right. Completing her degree would require them to be apart. Any healthy relationship could survive separations, right?

But he had been looking forward to telling her about the welding certification. *Come on, Cody, grow up. You know she'll be as excited as you are about this. You don't need her buy-in.*

At lunchtime, he popped the top of a soda and took the first bite of cold roast beef with horseradish mustard on white bread. Just what he needed.

"Hey, Billings." Mr. Dawson sat in the chair next to him. "Do you need to leave right at quitting time today?"

Was his boss psychic?

"No. No reason I can't stick around. What's up?" He took another sip of his soda.

"We have a customer who ordered a special accessory for the boat we're building. I was hoping you could help me test it before we turn it loose." Mr. Dawson leaned his chair on the back legs, propping himself against the wall.

"Sure." Doing something beyond paint prep? *Yes, please.*

"Okay, meet me at the boat ramp at the end of the road when your cleanup is finished." Mr. Dawson left the breakroom. "I think you'll like this contraption."

"Will do." Maybe there would be time to float the idea of his welding certification too. Cody returned to the boat he was working on. What sort of contraption? Why was he the right guy to test it? Might as well get ready to find out.

Chapter Twenty-One

Kayla carried her plate of food to the table where Maddie and the new roommates waited. She'd ordered banana pudding for dessert, which usually made her very happy. Today, she couldn't stop thinking about a big juicy slice of watermelon.

"Kayla, this is Lydia and Paige. They both remember having a class with you last year." Maddie pushed a paper-wrapped straw across the table to Kayla.

"Western Civilization, I think." Lydia reached across the table to shake Kayla's hand.

"That was a huge class." Kayla couldn't bring their faces to her memory at all.

"Yeah, I remember. You asked some good questions." Paige unwrapped her flatware.

"Usually about the buildings in whatever time period we were discussing." Lydia picked up a napkin. "I loved it because the professor was a big architecture nerd. It always got him off topic. Not nearly as boring as the regular lecture would have been."

"Kayla's majoring in architecture." Maddie pointed at her with her thumb.

"Who'd-a-thought?" Lydia and Paige laughed loudly.

Kayla listened as politely as possible to the chatter at her table. Had Cody been disappointed he wouldn't see her this evening? She regretted riding up here with Maddie. She had no idea how long it would take to finish their lunch, and then the shopping was just beginning. If they were in separate vehicles, she could make some excuse to leave early.

"So what color are you doing your room in?" Maddie was talking to her.

"I love turquoise." Kayla hoped none of the others had mentioned the same idea. She didn't want to be accused of not listening to the conversation.

"Yeah. I remember that. But not just the color, the stone, right? Like that bracelet." Maddie pointed.

"*Uh-huh.*" Kayla nodded.

"Didn't you say your parents got you that, before—" Maddie stammered.

"Maddie told us." Lydia patted Kayla's hand. "I'm so sorry about your mom and dad."

"Thanks." Surely, the next semester of living with these girls wouldn't be this awkward. She didn't remember having so much trouble talking to people as a freshman. "Anybody need a refill?" She picked up her cup and Paige's.

"It's diet." Paige nodded. "Thanks."

"She seems nice," Lydia's whisper as Kayla walked away was not soft enough to keep her from hearing.

"She's okay. Kind of serious most of the time. But I told you she's a rodeo queen, right? So, there is that." Maddie's voice was not any quieter.

Kayla chuckled. What was she getting into? At least this was a four-bedroom apartment. She'd be able to get all the solitary study time she needed.

She returned to the table with the drinks. A few weeks ago, she hadn't wanted to be by herself at all. Now she craved privacy. Well, there was one person she didn't mind talking to, but he was working right now.

"All right, girls. What stores do we need to hit?" Maddie pulled out her phone. "We need to figure out our route."

Cody stopped at the end of the concrete ramp. A gleaming new version of the boat his parents had given him for graduation waited on a boat trailer.

"Hey, Billings." Mr. Dawson shook his hand as Cody rolled up beside him.

"What's up?" Cody couldn't even act patient. He had tried all afternoon to figure out what accessory they were going to test.

"You told me you have one of these, right?" Mr. Dawson pointed at the boat.

"Yes, sir. I love it. I never dreamed I could get in and out so easily and drive it myself." Cody still considered himself blessed to be working for the company that built his boat.

"So far, you've always had someone with you to help you launch it, right?"

"Yeah. I haven't figured out how to do it by myself." He wasn't proud of his limitations, but he wasn't ashamed to talk about them, either.

"Well, I think we have something that should help fishermen in chairs. I don't know of any reason why it won't work with our boats, but I want to be sure." He walked to the front of the boat. "Have you ever seen a remote trolling motor?"

"You know, maybe I have. I don't know of anyone who uses one." Cody took the controls from Mr. Dawson. "I guess this is easy enough to figure out."

"Your generation can operate controls like that in your sleep." He laughed. "With a little practice, I think you can use it to turn the boat around after it's launched. Then, with the boat's ramp sitting here open on the dock, you should be able to get in easily after you park the truck."

"You're totally serious right now?" Cody held the controls

like they were solid gold. What a game-changer this would be if it worked.

"Okay, let's try it." His boss released the tow chain. "It has a magnetic lock to keep the boat from coming off the trailer too soon. My truck doesn't have hand controls, so I'll back it down into the water. When it's floating, use this lever to put the trolling motor in the water. Then see if you can reverse it, turn around, and come back up to the boat ramp."

"Forward, backward, turn it—with this joystick, right?" Cody pointed at each part of the controller.

"You got it. Keep the speed pretty slow until you get the hang of things."

"I thought I'd driven just about everything." Cody laughed nervously. "But a full-sized remote-control boat? Amazing."

The truck and trailer pulled away from the water. Cody used the controller to make sure the free-floating boat didn't stray very far.

"Pinch me," Cody said aloud. "This is really happening." After heading slightly in the wrong direction, he corrected. He used the steering mechanism to turn the boat around with the wheelchair ramp coming up on the bank.

"I knew you could do this." Mr. Dawson slapped his back. "Now, go get in that thing."

Cody moved up to the handle that operated the all-important boarding ramp. When it was safely flat against the concrete, he rolled aboard, still holding the remote control for the trolling motor. He blinked back tears. Did this man realize the value of this fairly simple process? It spelled freedom to so many people in his situation. Amazing.

How many weeks' wages would one of these things cost? Saving up for it might delay him moving out of his parents' house. Totally worth it. He couldn't wait to tell Dad and Junior. And of course, Kayla. He had so much to share with Kayla.

"Great!" Mr. Dawson broke up his daydream. "Now, I'll back

the trailer into the water again. You get out and see if you can load it with the remote too."

"Totally doable." Did he sound confident? This task would be a little more difficult, but at this moment, all things felt possible.

Kayla waved at Maddie as her compact car left the Cedar Ridge parking lot. She tucked the sack containing her massive comforter safely into the back seat of her truck and slammed the door.

Never had she seen so many different fabric patterns. Her princess smile had come in handy as the four of them debated whether or not everything in their rooms should match. Then, decorating the common areas had required serious negotiation.

She started the truck, glancing at her phone messages before putting it in gear.

Cody's message first.

> I have so much to tell you.

She couldn't imagine he'd want to hear much about her day.

> I'll call you when I get home.

Even shopping hadn't been as much fun as it should have been today. The other girls were beyond excited about moving into this apartment. Maybe that was her problem. She had moved past being excited about things like that.

She switched on her headlights, driving the familiar route home at dusk. Cody was working tomorrow, but maybe they'd be able to get together for supper. Today would have been much more fun if she'd been shopping with Cody. She'd dreamed of shopping for a new home but had always pictured it would be with a future husband, not college roommates. Someday, maybe. Did Cody have the same dream?

Because he had become part of hers.

Cody pulled up social media while he waited for Kayla to call. Her friend Maddie had tagged her in pictures of their day.

Kayla smiling as she held up a cute lamp with a western-themed lampshade.

All girls loved shopping. He hadn't minded it when he had picked out her birthday gift. It might be even more fun if they did it together. Maybe someday they'd shop for their own place. Together.

There were more pictures.

Kayla laughing with the other girls in a selfie near the football stadium.

Kayla posing like a fashion model in front of Old Main.

Somehow, his news about the welding school seemed insignificant. Would she care? Oh, and he'd figured out how to operate a boat with a remote trolling motor. That piece of news seemed so lame right now.

The big question—would she include him in all of her future adventures? Would she be a part of his?

He wanted her to pursue her dreams of completing her degree. But now it looked like she was traveling in a totally new circle. Would she care about what was happening in his world?

Maybe he'd talk about the welding certification with his parents first. Then, when he decided if it was doable, he'd tell Kayla.

"Hey." Her voice sounded a little down when he answered her call.

"How are you?"

"Tired. Actually, worn out," she answered. "I think Maddie enjoys shopping a lot more than I do. In fact, I think she enjoys it more than almost anyone. I thought we'd never get home."

"I'm sorry you had a bad day." Was he secretly glad she hadn't enjoyed her day without him? Maybe just a little.

"No, not a bad day, really. It was fun. I think maybe I'm getting old. I was glad to get home." She laughed. "So, what's your big news?"

How to sum it up without boring her?

"My boss asked me to help test some new equipment this afternoon. It's a new accessory for the boats we make." That was totally true.

"Cool. What does it do?" She did sound interested.

"It helps navigate the boat. Makes it easier for guys using a wheelchair." He tried to hold back some of his excitement.

"That's always good, right. So did it work?"

"Yeah. It did. It's so nice to be the guy who can do more than just sand the side of a boat to get it ready for painting." That maybe didn't sound too boring.

"I'm so proud of you."

"Thanks. You know I'm proud of you, too, right?" He raised his voice a little.

"Yes, sir, Mr. Marshal, sir." He could hear the silly smirk in her voice.

"Okay. It's another workday tomorrow."

"Take me to supper tomorrow? Or should I cook?"

"Either is fine. See you then." It didn't matter. As long as they were together.

"Okay. Can't wait to see you. Good night," she said, sleepily.

"Good night."

He laid his phone on the dresser. Those pictures didn't look like she was having a bad day. Was he about to lose his rodeo queen to the excitement of the big city?

Cody joined his parents in the living room, where they were debating which of three houses the couple on television would pick. Why did they enjoy this show so much? They'd lived right here in the same house since before he was born and had never talked about moving. No explanation necessary if it made them happy.

"You're not going to see Kayla tonight?" Dad placed his arm around Mom.

"She's pretty tired after shopping for her new apartment all day." He headed for the kitchen to look for a snack.

"Probably a good thing." Mom leaned into Dad's shoulder.

Did they think he was seeing too much of Kayla? What business was it of theirs? He squeezed chocolate syrup into a glass, then filled it with milk. Best to just leave Mom's comment hanging.

He stopped next to the couch. "I do have something to run by y'all, though."

Mom turned the volume down.

"What's up, son?" Dad faced him.

"Well, you know I like my job at Walking Eagle Boats." He cleared his throat.

"Seems like tough, dirty work, but you've never minded getting dirty." Mom grinned.

"Yeah. I'm getting used to the daily routine." He rolled around in front of them. "Not that it's boring, but I don't know if I want to do that for the rest of my life."

"You haven't been there long. Give it a chance." Dad sat up, leaning toward him.

"Oh, I don't want to quit. I've seen this other guy working there. He's a welder. What he does is so much more important to the whole process. If the welds aren't good, the boat sinks." Cody pulled up the technical college's website. "I think I might like to go for a welding certification."

"Welders make good money. You might not have to stay with the same company either. There are tons of welding jobs out there." Dad nodded.

"Isn't that a dangerous job?" Mom moved away from Dad. "I mean, the fire, the fumes. Couldn't it affect your vision?"

"Danger is this kid's middle name." Dad reached for her hand.

"I'll have to think about all that." Cody refreshed the website. "It seems like a great opportunity to learn a skill that will make more money in the long run. The down-side is that I might not be able to swing full-time working hours and full-time school, and they don't have on-campus housing."

"How far would you have to drive?" Mom wrapped her fingers around Dad's elbow.

"Ozark." Cody handed her his phone. "So, that's doable."

"Son, you know Mom and I are proud of you. You've already accomplished so much. We're here to support you, and you've got a place to live here. That should help." Dad looked at the screen as Mom held it near him.

"Yep." Mom reached for Cody's hand. "I've learned to pray instead of worry. It's worked well so far. If you listen to the Lord's leading, you won't go wrong."

Cody took his phone back from Mom. Maybe this could work. Living here, he could check on Grandpa Dee more easily. Kayla would be in Fayetteville, he'd be here, both pursuing their dreams. If those dreams took them down paths that didn't intersect, was he ready to take that risk?

Chapter Twenty-Two

Kayla stood near Nancy's back porch, a cheesecake she'd picked up at the grocery store in hand. Cody's comment about his aunt never arriving empty handed rang true. Besides, Kayla was about to ask her friends for a very big favor.

"What's that?" Nancy opened the gate to the iron fence that surrounded their deck.

"I didn't know which flavor you liked best, so I bought the assortment." Kayla placed the box on the kitchen island.

"Well, bless you. We'll just sample the sampler. You want coffee?" Nancy brought out two plates and two forks.

"No, thanks. Ice water would be great." Kayla sat at the island, as her friend finished serving. Coffee when it was hot outside? She wasn't there yet.

"What an unexpected treat." Nancy smiled as she savored a bite of cheesecake.

"I have an ulterior motive." Kayla folded her hands on top of the island. "I'm going to need some help with my horses."

"Hey, you know that's not a problem." Nancy picked up a bit of cheesecake. "What's up?"

"I'll be moving to Fayetteville soon. Maybe even before the

first day of classes. I'll be home on weekends. Sissy will still be going to some rodeos, but I want to exercise the other two enough to keep them happy." Kayla sat back in her chair. Would this impose on Nancy and Rod?

"You know I love those three like they were my own." Nancy patted her hand. "Rod's been thinking this might happen, so he mentioned hiring some help. Maybe a high school student who could come over after school every day. I guess you'd like to meet them, right?"

"I need to trust you two with that." What if the new ranch hand decided to "borrow" one of their horses without permission? Rod and Nancy would obviously be more cautious this time.

"We all got burned with Austin." Nancy took a sip of her coffee. "I'll make sure to let this person know what we expect."

Kayla nodded. "Thanks. I guess it's time for me to leave my comfort zone. Being here without Mom and Dad has been tough, but it's also hard to pull up roots and take the next step."

"You're amazing, my young friend." Nancy carried her empty plate to the sink.

"Glad I don't have to do it all alone." Kayla stood to meet Nancy in a hug.

Cody ran his hand across the surface he was sanding. With ear protection, the grinding noise was almost mesmerizing. Plenty of time for thinking.

The disapproving look he'd caught over the top of Mom's readers last night was stuck in his head. He'd known her long enough to understand that body language. She could read what bothered his conscience.

Spending time alone with Kayla was exciting and at the same time, worrisome. The feeling wasn't entirely new, but with the girls he'd admired in school, temptation hadn't been so strong. He cared too much about Kayla to take that risk.

Soon, she'd be gone to school, but until then, stopping at her house every day after work was not a good idea. How would he explain this, without making her feel like he didn't love spending time with her? Since she'd been busy yesterday, she'd expect to see him today.

The solution was easy. Spend more time with other people around. Back to sanding. More time for thinking.

Cody mopped his head with a towel as he drank a soda in the breakroom. What was this message from Junior?

> Hey buddy, call me before you leave work if
> you can.

"Dude," Junior answered quickly.

"What's up?" Cody took another swallow of his soda.

"Are you busy tonight?" Junior asked.

"Not that I know of."

"I'm headed out to Snowville this afternoon to talk to Joy about the old gym we're fixing up. You said you'd like to see it. We could eat at the barbecue place."

Was this guy psychic? The perfect solution to his Kayla dilemma.

"Sounds great. Okay if I bring Kayla?"

"Sure. I'll be there all afternoon. They're having some kind of community meeting to talk about the gym. You can come whenever," Junior said.

"You know it'll take us a minute to get there. I'll let you know if she has other plans." As long as her plans were not to stay at her house all by themselves.

"Awesome. See you soon, baboon."

"Whatever, clown face."

Better ask Kayla now. There wouldn't be much time to waste when he got off work.

"Hey," she answered as quickly as Junior did.

"I can't talk long, I'm on break."

"Everything okay?"

Had he made this sound too urgent?

"Yeah. I have an idea about where to eat supper tonight. It's sort of a long drive. You might need to be ready when I get there." No time to explain the whole thing.

"I can be ready anytime," she said. "Should I dress up?"

"You always look great." Was that a safe answer? "I'll run home to take a quick shower after work, then come right over." Cody paused. "As long as you don't have something else planned."

"Not a thing. Can't wait to see you."

"Me too. I think you'll like this place. See you soon." He tucked the phone back in his pocket and headed back to the production floor. *Thank you, Lord, for Junior Caldwell.*

Kayla read Nancy's text as she pulled on a new pink T-shirt.

> You might want to come over. Rod's got
> something to show you.

> Be right there.

What in the world?

She jumped into her boots and checked the full-length mirror before running out of her bedroom.

Cody would be here soon. Hopefully, he'd wait a minute. She needed to come back in to check her makeup.

Dust rose behind the dual-wheel truck Rod was using to pull a stock trailer to the fence near the barn.

Nancy waited for her in the driveway, and they walked together. Kayla needed to grab a hat too. This sunshine was brutal.

"What's going on?" Kayla knew she wouldn't get an answer.

Nancy pointed toward the back of the trailer.

"Come on," Rod prompted, tugging a lead rope.

With loud grunts and *moos*, a large black head emerged, followed by a lumbering cow's body.

"She's home!" Nancy shrieked.

The billboard cow stumbled down the ramp and moved away from the trailer.

"I think you're happier about it than she is." Kayla laughed.

"Your vaccination records did the trick." Rod stopped nearby. "There are three more females to pick up. The sheriff said it may take longer to identify the calves and steers."

"Great!" Kayla jogged to the fence. The cow found a tiny piece of grass in the corral to munch on. "Looks like she was treated okay."

"She's a valuable asset." Rod rolled up the lead rope. "My theory and fifty cents won't buy a cup of coffee, but I think Heston wanted to build his herd. He has rodeo stock but wants to get in on the beef production business. This was an easy way to start."

"Thanks for all you did to get her home." Kayla shook his hand. "Our ranch is in good hands." The thought crossed Kayla's mind that Rod might need a bonus of some kind. That was something Dad would have done. She'd talk to Uncle Smiley.

"Hey!" Kayla turned to see Cody waving from his truck.

"I'll go fill him in." She ran across the driveway.

"Tell him thanks for his help too." Rod waved at Cody. "You two did some good detective work."

"Is that the billboard cow?" Cody leaned out his window.

"The one and only!" Kayla tapped his arm. "Rod said to thank you for helping bring her home."

"Glad to be of service, ma'am." He tipped his cowboy hat.

"I've got to run inside for a minute, then I'll be ready to go." She waved as she hurried to her back door. Only a couple more weeks until they'd be living for weekends. She planned to enjoy these weeknight visits as much as possible.

"Have you been here with the rest of the Caldwells at Christmas time?" Cody stopped in front of the old high school in Snowville.

"Sure. I remember their live nativity scene. I loved being able to walk right up to the manger. One time, they had a real baby sleeping in there. Mom had to convince me all the way home that it wasn't Jesus." She glanced down the hill to the old church, where the reenactment had happened. "Why are we stopping at the school?"

"Junior wants us to meet him and his girlfriend Joy here." Cody opened his door. "They've been doing a lot of work restoring it. They're excited to show off what they've done."

"I love old buildings. Almost as much as brand new ones." Kayla stood at the back of the truck while he unloaded.

"He said there's a series of ramps that go up this hill." Cody waited for his chair to arrive next to him. "We'll see if we can figure out where we need to go."

Junior came running down the concrete ramp with Joy following behind.

Cody rolled to the bottom of the ramp. "Let's see what you've done."

"We spent most of the community's budget on this ramp," Joy said. "Junior couldn't wait to invite y'all as soon as it was finished."

Cody smiled. His friend had been his major encourager and cheerleader since the day of his bull wreck. The video of that ride showed Junior had sacrificed his safety to protect Cody from the raging animal. Junior, of course, downplayed his role.

"Kayla, we're about to hire an architect to help us improve this place." Joy opened the school's front double doors. "The gym's this way." She led them through the recently waxed hallways to another set of doors.

"The transition could use some work." Kayla helped Cody across a bump.

"See. That's why you're here." Junior raised a finger. "Where's my notebook, Joy?"

Joy handed Junior the yellow legal pad and pen she'd been carrying.

"So, you're the secretary?" Cody laughed.

"I know my place." Junior scribbled furiously.

Inside the doors, Cody gazed far above at the old-fashioned bright lights that illuminated the gym. He backed up to allow a gray-haired lady, followed by a man using a cane, to bustle past them.

"Excuse us." The man nodded as he shuffled past.

"We need to move off the track." Joy pointed. "Let's stand over here, in front of the old concession stand."

"Yeah, right now, the track goes around the outside of the basketball courts. Someday, there will be new bleachers in here, and that will change things." Junior pointed.

Kayla's jaw worked as she scanned the room. "Where do you see the new bleachers going?"

Junior took notes as Kayla and Joy plotted out the best place for seating. A half dozen people made laps in front of them, and Cody tried to stay out of the way.

"Someday, I think we could add a second floor. See those huge iron beams up there?" Junior pointed over their heads. "Kayla, do you think they would support more rooms, maybe even workout equipment?"

"That's a question for an engineer." She leaned against a post. "But from what I can see, this will be a great gym. I hope to have lots of kids someday, and I'll bet by the time they come along, this will be a favorite hangout."

Cody swallowed hard and tried not to let his face go pale. Once again, the talk of kids. Lots of them. Was there any way they could be together if he couldn't be the father of her children?

"We'll have an entire team of experts, I'm sure." Joy led Kayla to the middle of the gym floor. "The first step is to get a rough idea of what we want so we can apply for help. Ironically, even though there are only a few residents in this little town, we may not qualify financially. It will probably take some rich benefactors and sponsors instead of government aid."

He began to lose track of what Joy and Junior were talking about. Grants, loans, private donations.

Where did Cody fit in this picture? He'd been so proud to find out he could launch a boat by himself. What good was that if he would never have a son or daughter to take fishing? Besides, he had just pictured himself as being a part of Kayla's life, and now he wasn't sure he should even try.

"So. Are you hungry or not?" Junior slapped him on the shoulder. "Let's go see if there's anything edible at the little dive next door."

"He's joking." Joy moved closer. "Big Ed's Barbecue is mildly famous. People drive out here from Fayetteville and even Little Rock on weekends. Come on, Kayla. Let's go find a table." The two linked arms and headed back through the gym doors into the main school building.

"I never knew how serious Kayla is about this architecture thing," Junior said when the girls were out of earshot.

"She'll do big things," Cody agreed. With or without a broken-down ex bull rider dragging her down.

"We'll have to hurry to be sure these two don't leave us in the dust." Junior helped push Cody's chair over the bump in the floor.

"You're awfully quiet." Kayla was sure she'd done most of the talking on the way back from Snowville.

"Just listening to you."

"I haven't seen Junior so excited since the rodeo ended." Maybe she could get him to talk about his best buddy. What was wrong anyway?

"Yeah. Joy is good for him."

"It's more than that. This gymnasium idea is so cool." She smiled, remembering Junior flipping the pages of his legal pad as he filled it with notes. "So, what is he majoring in again?"

"Physical education. He wants to be the community's coach, giving everybody in town a way to be active." He checked his rearview mirror. Ending the conversation again?

"He kept using the word accessible. Not just all ages, but all abilities." Her cousin had become a champion for disabled people. Just like she tried to be.

"I'll give him that." Cody nodded. "Not bad for a rodeo clown."

"And supper was great. Snowville is a wonderful little town."

"*Mm-hmm.*"

It was no use. Kayla sat quietly, watching the mailboxes and pine trees glide past the window of the pickup. She and Junior and Joy had carried the conversation during supper too. Whatever had Cody upset had happened earlier.

She sighed so loudly, he glanced her way, but didn't speak.

Why had such a good day turned out so rotten?

Chapter Twenty-Three

"You want to watch Family Feud?" Cody switched Grandpa Dee's television channel. The familiar music didn't rouse the old man's attention. He waved his hand feebly in Cody's direction but said nothing.

Mom had warned him of the change in his grandpa's behavior. Instead of responding to a select few people, these days almost no one had success.

Maybe he shouldn't let the television do all the talking.

"My new job is going pretty great." He turned the volume down. "I'm helping build boats. You like fishing, right?"

"Fishing," Grandpa repeated.

Okay. He was paying attention.

"I'm hoping maybe Dad can go fishing with me this weekend. Or maybe Junior Caldwell. Or even Kayla."

Kayla. She'd sounded a little disappointed when he called to tell her where he'd be tonight. Disappointed, but maybe not surprised. After all, the quick goodbye kiss on her cheek last night hadn't been too exciting for either one of them. The burden of the conversation they needed to have weighed him down. How could he summon the courage to bring up a guaranteed deal-breaker?

"Fishing." Now, even Grandpa Dee was trying to get the conversation back on track. Time to snap out of this funk.

"Yeah. I caught a pretty good bass when I went with Dad." He pulled his phone out to display a picture.

A nurse peeked in from the hallway. "How are you tonight, Mr. Tolliver?"

"Fishing," Grandpa Dee replied.

"You've been fishing?" She laughed. "Well, I hope you catch enough for all of us." She winked at Cody. "We're moving to a new room tomorrow."

"New room?" Cody switched the television channel again.

"I told your mom this afternoon." The nurse stepped closer. "Mr. Tolliver needs more conversation when y'all are not here. We have a man down the hall who could use company, so they're going to be roommates.

"Right, Mr. T? You and Joe should get along just fine." She walked over to check his blood pressure. "Come back and see us, young man. Y'all are so good about visiting. He's a lucky guy."

"Sure." Cody rolled out of her way. It was good to see the nurses hadn't given up completely.

"Y'all enjoy your visit. I'll be back" The nurse waved as she stepped into the hallway.

"Want to watch the news?" Cody stopped channel surfing when Tara William's image appeared onscreen.

"An update on the cattle rustling story we brought you several days ago." He turned up the volume.

"There is new evidence that points to prominent Crossroads businessman Quinton Heston's involvement in this incident. What seemed to be a minor theft may turn out to be much more. Tune in to our nightside report for the latest details."

Kayla's text popped onto his screen.

> Candace said to tell you and Grandpa Dee
> hello.

Can I call you?

Sure.

She picked up immediately. "I told Candace to come back to get my order."

"Make sure you watch the late news tonight." He laid his hand on Grandpa Dee's arm to prevent him standing up without help.

"Really?"

"Yeah. Evidently Heston may not be able to deny he's involved with stealing your cows."

Grandpa Dee was determined to stand. There might have been a better time to call Kayla.

"Thanks for letting me know. I'll be sure to watch. Tara's channel, right?"

"Yeah. Gotta go." He reached for Grandpa Dee's hands, steadying him.

Abrupt again. If he was trying to have a conversation with Kayla, this was not the best way.

"Yeah. A cheeseburger sounds great. Oh, and add bacon." Kayla smiled at Candace as she jotted down her order.

"Bacon makes everything better." Candace added to her note. "And lemonade, right?"

"You've got it."

Kayla twirled the wrapper from her straw absently. Why had Cody hung up so quickly? Didn't he want to talk to her? She'd have to get used to not seeing him every day when school started, but at least he could pretend to miss her.

What had he said about Heston? It would be hard to wait for the ten-o'clock news.

"Here you go." Candace placed Kayla's food in front of her.

"What's happening in your world? Besides eating the best burger in town?"

"Enjoying the summer until I move back to college." Kayla cut the huge sandwich with a knife to make handling it easier. No use mentioning her call from Cody. "But you're the one with all the excitement. Have you and Uncle Smiley set a date for your wedding?"

"As a matter of fact, we did that today. Friday before Labor Day. Right after we come back from our mission trip to Mexico." Candace turned as another customer came in. "At the pavilion behind my house."

"Not a lot of time for planning." Kayla took a bite, wiping the grease that dripped down her chin.

"My sister the wedding planner is having a fit." She laughed. "But, if Felicia can raise three strong sons, she can put together a wedding in a month. Right?" She waved and bustled to another table, grabbing a glass for a refill.

Labor Day. By then, Kayla and her roommates would be adjusted to the routine of classes during the week, coming home on weekends.

Uncle Smiley's proposal at Candace's compound had been so sweet. After years of heartbreak, these two deserved happiness. As long as they didn't get sick of each other during the mission trip.

Couples all over the diner tilted their heads toward each other to keep their conversations private. Would she and Cody be able to talk like that again? They seemed to be doing so well, until the Snowville visit.

"Everything good?" Candace brought her ticket to the table. "Come back anytime. I know from experience that cooking for one is no fun.

"You're right." Kayla had a sudden inspiration. "In fact, I think I'm going to cook for your youngest nephew tomorrow night. Not sure what he'd like."

"Something simple and summer-like. Maybe sandwiches.

Nothing too heavy." Candace pursed her lips. "He's not picky. Just add a sweet dessert, and you'll make him happy. Have fun." She hurried away again.

Dessert. She'd fix Zanna's banana pudding. That was a no-brainer. Sandwiches? Maybe a BLT. But would that be enough food to fill him up?

Kayla looked out the front window to the parking lot where the farmer's market would take place tomorrow. *Mmm.* Visions of green beans and new potatoes filled her head. Perfect. If she couldn't get through to Cody with a meal like that, they weren't meant to be friends—or more—at all.

"So how was your grandpa?"

Cody was glad Kayla sounded cheerful at the beginning of their phone call. Maybe his silent treatment hadn't completely turned her away.

"Oh, I guess he's okay. Nothing critical health-wise. But, he's not himself anymore." He opened the window shade in his room. No clouds, so there should be plenty of moonlight tonight.

"I know that must be hard. You've been worried about him lately, right?" Kayla asked.

Sounded like she was fishing. Trying to get to the bottom of his lack of communication? Grandpa Dee was not the problem.

"Yeah. But, it's just something I'll have to get used to." Not something he could fix, anyway. "So how was your day?"

"I met the teenager Rod wants to hire to help with the horses. I think she'll be good," Kayla said.

"She'll treat them better than Austin did?" Cody knew the ranch hand's careless ways had bothered her more than the cattle thefts.

"Definitely," Kayla responded. "I have seen her at barrel races. She's just trying to get some spending money during her senior year in high school. On her way to college in Russellville and then to veterinarian school."

"Perfect." Cody breathed a sigh of relief. This would make Kayla's move to Fayetteville so much easier for her.

"I missed you at supper." Kayla's voice was instantly quieter.

"I missed you too." Did she understand how much?

"Are you ready to take a chance tomorrow night that I can cook more than grilled hot dogs?"

"Sure, if you want to go to all that trouble." Alone at her house? Well, they did need to talk.

"It won't be that fancy. Just good summertime food," Kayla said. "Come on, you like living dangerously, right?"

"Of course." He grinned. She did know him pretty well. Give him a challenge, and he was not likely to back down.

"Good. So, what time works? I'll be here all day, so I'm flexible."

"Let me go home and clean up after work first. I can be there about six o'clock." He checked his laundry hamper. Better get some jeans washed tonight too.

"And since you're off work the next day, there's no big rush. Maybe we could swim afterward."

Swim? Could he be alone with her in a swimsuit? Oh, boy.

"Yeah. We'll just play that by ear." He caught his reflection in the mirror over his dresser. *Cody, Cody, Cody.*

"Okay, well, then ..."

Should he tell her about his welding school plans now? No. He'd need something to talk about tomorrow during supper. And during swimming.

"Can't wait." That was only partly untrue. "Good night, Miss Kayla." He'd try to lighten the mood with his western accent.

"Good night, Marshal, sir." The mischievous sparkle in her eyes somehow traveled through the phone. It would be good to see her again. Very good.

"Oh." He almost forgot. "Don't forget to watch the news."

He turned on the small set in his room just in time to see a "No comment" from Quinton Heston.

"This was the response we received when we told Mr. Heston about the video that has been shared with us." Tara faced the camera. "We are sharing it with local law enforcement first. Tune in tomorrow. This little piece of evidence may be all that is needed to connect our local casino owner with several cattle thefts in the area."

> Wow! Who has a video?

Kayla was quick on the draw with her text tonight.

> I don't know. I guess we'll have to tune in tomorrow!

Well, it wasn't what he needed to say to her, but at least it was a start.

Kayla adjusted the market basket she carried on her arm. This vendor had the perfect new potatoes and fresh green beans she needed. At another table she'd spotted big, ripe tomatoes.

With fresh veggies stowed in her truck, Kayla headed to the grocery store. An advertisement for the rodeo she was obligated to attend played on her radio. Thankfully, this was for Saturday only. Fulfilling her role as Arkansas Teen Rodeo queen had been wonderful, but time with her favorite bull-rider made her happier these days.

"Hey! Kayla Grace!" Junior flagged her down in the store's parking lot.

"What's up?" She gave him a quick, hug.

"Joy's coming to our place for supper tonight. Dad and I are cooking for her and Candace." He leaned to one side, trying to look past her into the store.

"That's exciting." She laughed. Uncle Smiley had never cultivated his cooking skills as far back as she could remember.

"He sent me for a graham cracker crust. Mom's lemon icebox pie recipe calls for it." He held the door open for her.

"Yeah." Had he never shopped before?

"So, how do you do that? Do I need to buy a box of graham crackers? What else do you put in it?" The panic in Junior's voice was funnier than any of his rodeo clown routines.

"Calm down." She touched his arm. "They have them premade on the bakery aisle. Follow me." She grabbed a shopping cart and led the way.

Cody rolled across Kayla's driveway with the bouquet of flowers balanced carefully in his lap. He shouldn't have complained aloud about arriving for dinner empty-handed. Mom had convinced him to allow her the pleasure of sending something for Kayla's table. Probably a good thing to make two ladies happy at once. Besides, it hadn't cost him anything.

"*Aww,*" Kayla exclaimed as she opened the door. "How pretty!"

"Mom's picky about these daisies. They're some kind of fancy variety or something. She's been babying them in this heat." Cody bumped over the threshold. "I hope you like them."

"I usually see white ones. These are so pretty." She took the bright orange and yellow flowers to her kitchen sink. "I know Mom stored her vases around her somewhere." Several cabinet doors were opened before she found what she was looking for. In no time, the daisies sat in the center of the round table a few feet away from the kitchen island.

"Everything's almost ready. You can turn the television on if you'd like." She took two long steps back to the kitchen.

"Hey, look at this." Cody pointed to the screen over the fireplace.

Kayla walked over to join him. The video on the screen showed a familiar scene in one of the booths at Amy Lou's Diner.

"So, it won't be that hard," Quinton Heston was speaking quietly. "Since the Caldwell land butts up against ours, we won't even need a truck. Get Shane here to show you how to cut the wire and rewrap it on a moveable post. It's not rocket science. I'll give you half of what we agreed on, and the rest when I have a few cows on my side of that fence."

The video ended as the camera was covered with something. Maybe stuffed in a pocket?

"Amazing." Cody spun around to face her. "That was clearly Heston. Who do you think made the video?"

"Could be Austin. I knew he didn't come up with that whole scheme on his own." Kayla's eyes were still glued to the screen. "Well, Heston will have to be pretty clever to wiggle out of this."

"Speaking of clever. What have you come up with for our supper?" He moved back toward the dining area.

"Do you like BLTs?" She waved her arm over the table.

"Of course!" The table left him gaping. He had stepped into the pages of a magazine. A blue gingham table-cloth was the backdrop for bright red plates, with navy cloth napkins holding the silverware. He couldn't imagine a better centerpiece than Mom's flowers.

A plate full of sandwiches and a big pot of green beans with potatoes made his mouth water. An architect? Maybe she needed to be a chef with a television cooking program.

Kayla sat across from him.

"Will you say the blessing?" She asked when the napkin was safely on her lap.

He reached across the table to take her hands in his.

"Father, this meal looks and smells amazing. Thank You for the heart of the beautiful person who prepared it. You have been so good to both of us, and we appreciate Your daily blessings. In Jesus' name, Amen."

He released her hands, and their eyes met.

"Thanks. You do that very well." She placed her napkin in her lap.

"You do this," he waved his hand over the table, "very well."

"I didn't get a lot of practice. Mom was a little too 'take charge.'" She blushed. "But when my school vacations didn't jibe with my cousins', I got some one-on-one time in Zanna's kitchen."

Did she guess that Bacon, Lettuce, and Tomato was his favorite sandwich ever? The toasted bread, just the right amount of mayo, perfectly crisp bacon. Admittedly, vegetables were not always his favorite dish on the table. These beans, though. Tender, rich in flavor. And the potatoes were cooked to just the right doneness. He needed to look up some synonyms for amazing.

From the smile on her face when he looked at her, she understood without a word from him. But he'd offer a couple anyway.

"Incredible. Maybe instead of being an architect, you should open a restaurant." Did that say what he wanted?

"Probably not. Cooking for the masses is a different ballgame. After a few more suppers, you will probably reach the end of my expertise."

"I look forward to testing that." He guided another green bean to his mouth. "But first, let me finish this meal."

"Save room for banana pudding." She laughed.

"No problem." He winked at her.

She brought dessert to the table before he'd had a chance to move his plate out of the way. If all of this was intended to soften him after his childish behavior, he was tempted to do the same thing again and again.

"Wonderful meal. Now, you can go watch television while I clean up." He rolled away from the table with dishes in hand.

"That's okay. I know where things go. It'll be faster if we do it together." Kayla took the plates from him.

Happy chatter continued as they worked. He could easily bring up welding school now, but what about the bigger issue?

Kayla hung a dishtowel up to dry, then turned around to place a kiss on his forehead.

He pulled her into his lap.

"Thanks for inviting me over." He ran his finger down her nose and kissed her. She leaned into him.

This. This is why they needed to talk. Any more idle time would be dangerous.

"*Uh* ..." He gently pushed her back a few inches. How to start? "We need to talk." That was right to the point.

"Is something wrong?" She straightened.

"No. We just need to talk. Instead of ... Instead of *this*."

"*Oh*." She stood up, her cheeks bright red. "You know I'm not like that."

"No. It's not you. It's me. Oh, boy. I've messed this up. I don't trust myself alone with you for very long."

"That's so sweet. I love that you want to respect me. Like, I matter to you." She squatted in front of him for a quick peck on the cheek. "So, we talked about swimming. It's plenty hot enough, still."

"*Uh* ..." He pictured her in a swimsuit. "It might be nice out on the patio, but do you mind if we don't swim?"

"Not a bit. I'd be glad to talk to you. Anytime, anywhere." She walked to the refrigerator. "How 'bout I get us each a glass of lemonade? I'll meet you outside."

Cody pushed the back door open and shook his head as the still warm breeze hit his face. He would have liked nothing better than to hold her in his lap, with the possible exception of swimming with her. Would she think there was something wrong with him for bringing things to a halt?

"The sky is pretty out here." Kayla handed him a lemonade.

"God likes to show off about this time every day." Cody followed her to the wicker loveseat, moving to be next to her.

"This is nice." Kayla leaned her head on his shoulder. "After classes start, we'll only get to do this once or twice a week."

"And there may be times we'll have to study on weekends." Cody pulled her closer.

"We? I thought you had your job duties pretty well down by now." She sat up, turning to face him.

"That's why I'm going to see about getting a certification so I can move up. I found out welders make more than paint-prep techs, and it's a lot more fun."

"Welding? Can't you just learn that on the job?"

"There's a lot to learn, if you want to do it right. Certified welders can get jobs in all kinds of places. Building boats, cars, buildings, even bridges." Was he still trying to talk himself into this?

"Where is the school?"

She seemed interested. Why had he waited so long to talk to her about this?

"Ozark. That's another reason I might want to move to our family's cabin. By the time I work all day and then go to school, it's going to be a long trip home every night." Would this take them back to their earlier argument?

"That's so exciting!" Kayla clasped his right hand in hers. "I still can't believe you stayed home to help me with my ranch problems. Of course, if you need to move somewhere to go to school, you should do that."

"That's such a relief." He put his arm behind her and re-settled her into his shoulder.

"Is that what you couldn't tell me on the way home from Snowville? Why would I be upset about you going to school after you encouraged me to do the same thing?" She sat up again. "Silly boy."

One kiss. He'd allow himself that. He pressed his lips to hers, but pulled back before it deepened.

"That's only part of it. The truth is, I was feeling left out. I know it's dumb, but with you and Junior and Joy talking about remodeling a gym, applying for grants, all that stuff, I thought my idea of being a welder sounded lame." He sat back against the wicker seat.

"What? I think that's the coolest thing ever." Kayla shook her head. "I can't imagine how much skill it takes to light up a piece of metal and use it to hold huge things together. Even if I get my degree, I'll just be dreaming and drawing. You will be making things happen."

He allowed himself one more kiss.

If only that was everything. This next topic was so much harder. Might as well start. He cleared his throat, and moved to where he could look into her face.

"I have to be honest with you. If we plan to have any kind of future together, there's something you need to know."

Her eyes moved back and forth across his face, but she didn't say a word.

"Since I was only sixteen when I was injured, I didn't think too far past the idea that I might not ever ride a bull again." He stopped. How to say this?

"Sure. That was a very scary time." Kayla squeezed his hand.

"My next goal was to walk. When that didn't happen, it was a huge adjustment."

She nodded, waiting.

"But I didn't think about the rest of my life, especially when I find the right girl and get married." He shook his head. "Boy, this is tough.

"Physically, the doctors say my paralysis starts at my thighs. The doctor says that feeling and function might keep coming back a little at a time."

"Cody ..." She sat up, pulling away.

"Let me finish. The thing is, I know you want to have kids someday. You would make a fabulous mom. But I'm not sure I'll be able to be a good dad. Or even to be a father at all."

He took a deep breath and closed his eyes. He wasn't sure he wanted to see how she was reacting to this.

His arm was still around her shoulder. Would her next move be to stand up and walk away? He stopped talking, allowing the crickets and tree frogs to continue the conversation.

"I wish you would have talked with me sooner," Kayla finally said. She sat up straighter.

Her chin quivered when she faced him. Were those tears in her eyes?

"I guess I need to go." Cody moved away, holding her hand until they were too far apart. "Thanks for the delicious supper. We'll talk soon."

She nodded, walking a step or two closer before stopping.

He didn't turn to look as he approached his truck. What was the proper way to leave after dropping such a bombshell? Would she think he wanted to end everything that was building between them? He started the process of loading himself into his truck.

Okay, God. You take over from here. It's between You and Kayla now.

Chapter Twenty-Four

Kayla turned toward the church aisle after Uncle Smiley's 'Amen' ended the Wednesday night prayer service. With both Cody and her covered in prayer for their upcoming studies, she should be prepared. Moving into her apartment a few days before classes started made perfect sense. So, why was she blinking back tears tonight?

They had only had one text conversation since Cody had shared his doubts with her. Stilted and formal, nothing like the relationship she thought they had been building.

"Everything loaded?" Cody followed her to the double entrance doors.

She struggled to find their old way of speaking to each other. "Probably not. But I'll be back next Friday night. By that time, I'll have a list of things that the others promised to bring but didn't."

"You're sure you want to drive up there at night?" Uncle Smiley opened the doors leading to the parking lot.

"Yes, sir." She hugged him. "It won't be nearly so hot on the freeway. I can unload boxes tonight and spend tomorrow putting things away. Maddie has been there this whole week. The other two move in tomorrow. I didn't want to arrive in the middle of the chaos."

"Good plan. Avoid as much chaos as possible." Cody rolled a little closer.

"Okay. Well. Know these two things." Uncle Smiley checked the tarp straps on the load of boxes in the bed of the truck. "I am only a phone call away, even while on the mission trip. And two—your mom and dad would be extremely proud of you for continuing your education. God loves you, Kayla Grace."

"I know." She hugged Uncle Smiley again. He patted Cody's shoulder as he walked away.

"I'll miss you this Saturday and Sunday." Cody held her fingers.

"I won't stay up there forever, I promise." Maybe being apart this weekend would give them both time to think. Were they still moving from friendship to love? Could she allow herself to get closer to someone who might not be able to share her dream of a large, happy family?

"I'll call you." She placed one hand on each side of his face and kissed him quickly, then climbed into her truck. Best not to look in the rearview mirror. Too late. She caught a glimpse of him watching her as she pulled out of the church's lot.

Why was this so hard? They had agreed that finishing their education was a good thing. She would see him again in a little over a week. What would their next conversation be like? Had his confession to her been his way of telling her to move on?

The emotions of the past several weeks spilled down her cheeks. No matter how strong the memories of Mom and Dad were, she was an orphan. Even with all the support she received from Uncle Smiley and her grandparents, she was by herself now. If she had a serious relationship with Cody, she could end up in a virtually empty house.

Maybe by the time she reached her new apartment, she could hold her head high and face the future. For the next few miles, she would drive with a lead weight in her chest. Alone.

"Dangerous drought conditions continue as burn bans are still in effect for almost all counties in Arkansas." Cody watched the late news in the living room.

"We might need to take some stock to the auction this weekend," Dad spoke up from the couch.

"Why now? I thought we were going to keep our numbers the same for a bit." Mom looked up from her novel.

"I don't know how long we'll be able to support them." Dad drummed his fingers on the couch cushions. "If this drought keeps up, hay is going to be scarce.

"Probably a good move." Cody moved closer. "I'll help all I can."

"Thanks, son. O.D. will be here too. I'd call your oldest brother, but I'm afraid he'll be on call with the fire department." Dad pulled out his phone to make a note.

"Hopefully people have enough sense not to start fires with the burn ban going." Unless someone still had leftover fireworks.

"We can hope." Mom smiled at him.

"I guess I'll turn in for the night." Cody took his popcorn bowl to the kitchen. "Just a few more days working full time. Next week, I start my welding classes."

"Those will be some long days." Dad replaced his phone in his pocket.

"Yes, sir. But I'm excited. More interesting work, and eventually more pay."

"We're proud you are taking on something new." Mom stood and walked over to give him a hug. "Say an extra prayer for Grandpa Dee. His nurse asked me not to come by tonight. They were trying to settle him down a little earlier. He's agitated and having trouble sleeping."

"I'll be glad to pray." He squeezed her hand. "We'll let God work this whole thing out."

"Exactly right." She smiled. "Good night."

Cody stared at the ceiling in his room. Grandpa Dee had been on his mind this evening, but so had Kayla. After weeks of talking about nothing else, the idea of moving to her new apartment didn't seem to sit well with her when she drove away. He could sympathize. Change was never easy, and she'd had more than her fair share lately. What if her relocation was the first of many moves that would pull them further apart? Had his doubts about his physical condition been the breaking point for her?

You know my heart, Lord. We all need a measure of Your peace to go to sleep tonight. For Grandpa Dee, for Kayla, and even for me. Close our eyes and comfort our hearts. Amen.

Kayla used the remote to turn on the giant screen that dominated one wall of their apartment. For the first time since she'd arrived Wednesday night, she had the whole apartment to herself. Maddie had been so excited when her parents helped her pick out this humongous television. Evidently, this would be the gathering place for their friends. The big set was vital.

Kayla would not be sad if most of those gatherings happened while she was back home in Crossroads.

"As you can see from the map, burn bans are still in effect for a large part of the state." The news and weather reports hadn't changed in the last few days. No rain in sight, a huge risk for dangerous fires.

"Unfortunately, we have a new map to show you," the news anchor said. "Since any grass or brush fire can easily get out of hand, we will show you the major hot spots that our rural fire departments are dealing with. The Forest Service is doing their best to stay on top of these outbreaks."

Kayla moved closer to the television. She used her finger to try to pinpoint a red spot on the Arkansas map. West of Interstate 49, and north of Interstate 40. This was a small fire, but how long would it stay small? Was there a possibility it could get close to Coach and Zanna's property?

She glanced at the clock on the other side of the living room. Her purchase. Even with modern technology, she needed a good old-fashioned clock now and then. Two-thirty. Not long before Cody got off work. That didn't matter much when they were so far apart.

The news anchor returned from a sports report and abruptly displayed the fire map again.

"We have received an update from the Forest Service. This fire," he pointed at the map, where the red spot had grown, "has escalated. Local fire departments are responding and will be doing everything possible to control it. We will let you know each time we hear something new."

Kayla stepped back to get a broad view of the map. Escalating? In this dry weather? What exactly did that mean? How fast was the fire traveling, and in which direction? Should she call Coach and Zanna?

Cody. She'd try him first. Maybe he'd tell her there was nothing to worry about.

He was still working. She sent a quick text.

Call when you can. Important.

She switched to other channels on the television. Was anyone else displaying that fire map?

"What's up?" Hearing his voice made her heart stop racing.

"Are you off work? Will you get in trouble for calling me?" This was so foolish.

"It's fine. I'm just sweeping up. What's wrong?" No surprise he knew she was worried.

"There's a forest fire. I can't tell from the television how close it is to Coach and Zanna. I think I need to go to check on them." She paced from the kitchen to the front door and back.

"A fire? Probably not a good idea to just drive over there.

Roads could be blocked. You might get in the way of emergency responders."

Her eyes widened.

"Let me call John K. I think he just got back from Forest Service training. Maybe he knows what we should do next."

What *we* should do. She liked the sound of that.

"Okay, I'll stay here until I hear from you." It wouldn't be easy. The urge to jump in her truck and start driving was about to get the best of her.

Maddie opened the front door, arms full of bags. "Hey." Maddie placed her groceries on the kitchen counter.

"Need some help?" Kayla walked closer.

"Sure. I got some snacks for the weekend. I think we'll start a Friday night movie tradition." Maddie opened the refrigerator, making room. "I'm so glad you're here."

"I may not be staying all weekend after all." Kayla placed a box of cookies in the kitchen cabinet.

"What?" Maddie closed the refrigerator and faced her. "I know you will want to leave on weekends sometimes, but I thought this first one ..."

"Sorry. It's an emergency. There's a fire ..." Her phone rang. "I'll take this call in my room."

She closed the door.

"You're right. I think we probably need to go to your grandparents' house." Cody's voice was calm.

"Oh, Cody." Her hand popped up to cover her mouth.

"Everything's going to be okay," he said. "But we don't have a lot of time to talk. The volunteer fire department John K. worked for has something I can bring to help."

"What can you bring? I don't understand." If he was trying to ease her mind, it wasn't working.

"Listen. I will explain everything when I see you. I'll meet you at their house. Be careful driving. I'll see you in an hour or so."

"Maddie, I have to leave." She rushed past her roommate and grabbed her backpack.

"What's happening?" Maddie touched her arm.

"There's a big fire getting close to my grandparents' house. Cody has a plan to keep them safe, so I'm headed down there." Kayla waved on her way out the door.

"I don't know how you can help. But, be careful."

If Maddie said more, Kayla didn't hear. What was she driving into? How close was the fire to Coach and Zanna's place?

Lord, help me keep my thoughts together so that I can help in some way. Keep us all safe. Amen.

Faith's number popped up on the display screen in her truck before she reached the freeway. She pulled into a parking lot and stopped before answering.

"Hi." She tried to control her pounding heart.

"Are you driving?" Faith asked.

"Not at the moment." She wouldn't sit here long, though.

"John K. said you and Cody are on the way to your grandparents' house." Was Faith going to try to talk her out of this?

"Yeah." Nothing she could say would stop her.

"I just want to let you know that John K.'s department is headed out to help with the forest fire. It's not close to their place yet."

"Thanks. But I still want to be there. They may have to stay at my house in Crossroads." Her mind raced with ideas.

"Maybe. We'll talk again when you get there. No roads are closed yet, but that could change. The Forestry people are sending big plows to make a perimeter to stop the fire," Faith said. "I'll let you go. The people with the training and the equipment will take care of this. The best we can do is pray for their safety."

"Thanks, Lainie. I'll call you after I check on Coach and Zanna." She turned out of the parking lot, driving a little slower toward the entrance ramp.

"Lord," she prayed, eyes wide open. "Take care of John K. and the other firefighters. Be with Cody as he drives up to help. I'm so thankful for him, Lord. Be with me too. I am trying to stay calm. Thank You for being here with me. Amen."

"Are you sure y'all want to come?" Cody started his truck. "John K.'s fire department is on the way Everything may be stabilized when I get there."

"I get that. But you have two things you'd like to tow—your UTV, and the water tank from Big River County." Dad stood outside his truck window. "I can pull one behind my truck."

"Okay. Thanks," Cody said. "You remember how to get to the Pruitt's place, right?"

"It's in the GPS," Mom yelled from her side of their truck.

"Chief MacDonald is meeting me at the volunteer fire station. Tell Kayla I'm on the way." Did he remember where this fire department was? Hopefully not too far from their cabin.

Dad backed up to the trailer he stored his UTV on, and Mom jumped out to help with the tow hitch. Cody turned his truck toward the volunteer fire station. Would Kayla be surprised to see such a large Billings response?

He rolled his windows down and allowed the wind to blow through his cab. It would be nice to feel a hint of rain in the air.

John K. had said that keeping the perimeter of the Pruitt's land wet would help until the fire department could get there. Kayla's grandpa could use the water hose near their house, but Cody was most concerned about the overlook nearby. He'd need his UTV to check out that part of the land and then use the portable tank to keep everything wet.

Kayla's family had done a good job of keeping the brush and grass mowed, but there were still a lot of tall trees. If the fire jumped through the treetops, it could move very quickly.

Chief MacDonald waved as Cody turned into the parking lot

next to the volunteer fire station. Good thing the GPS brought him straight here.

"Back in over here, and I'll hook you up."

Good. He wouldn't have to get out of his truck. He made a big circle in the driveway and threw the transmission into reverse. The water tank appeared to be full. Hopefully, using it would be self-explanatory.

"Our department hasn't been called out yet," the chief said after hooking up the trailer. "Folks around here are obeying the burn ban pretty well."

"If you need this thing, just call me. You have my number, right?" Cody held up his phone. "I'll bring it right back down or meet you somewhere."

"Good man." The chief slapped the side of the truck. "Hope your folks are okay."

"Thanks again." Cody headed to the main road. 'His folks.' He hadn't known the Pruitts very long, but Kayla's family already qualified as part of his.

He should have asked the chief if he knew anything else about the location of this fire. No matter. Better to keep moving.

I'm on my way, Kayla.

"Thanks for doing that, sweetie." Zanna wiped her hand across her forehead as Kayla tossed a bag of trash into the dumpster.

"A hot day for your first birthday party rental." Kayla stood with her hands on her hips.

"We're hoping for rain." Zanna waved at a car driving away. "This family wanted a campfire so they could have s'mores at their party. I found a recipe that made them happy. Chocolate, graham crackers, marshmallow, but no fire. We could have switched to the barn if it rained. I'm excited that they paid to have their party here. New idea for me, but I like it!"

Kayla blinked. Where was Coach? Was he oblivious to the

danger too? Down the hill, she spotted him with a water hose, dousing his vegetable garden. After a deep breath, she looked at a fire map on her phone. Obviously, Zanna had been too busy to notice this.

Gravel crunched under truck tires as a pickup pulling a trailer stopped next to Coach's large garage. Not Cody, his parents.

"Who's that?" Zanna walked toward the truck.

"Cody's parents." Kayla followed her. "It looks like they brought Cody's utility vehicle. He said he wanted to use it to make sure your property stays safe."

"That is so sweet." Zanna waved at Cody's dad. "Those are some good neighbors."

Coach walked up behind Zanna.

"Welcome," he greeted the Billings.

"Where is Cody?" Kayla checked her phone for a message.

"On his way." Cody's dad stepped out of his truck. "He went by the volunteer fire station to bring their portable water tank."

"He's a firefighter too?" Coach shook Dave Billings' hand.

"No, sir. Our oldest son suggested it." Cody's mom spoke up. "The Forestry service is having a tussle with that fire west of here."

Kayla hugged each of them. How would she ever thank them for doing this for her family?

"I saw something about that fire on the news." Coach walked closer to Zanna." I figured our chief would let us know if it's getting close to us"

"He probably will." Cody's dad turned his head, scanning the property. "If you've got another water hose, I'll help you make sure everything close to your house stays damp."

"Thanks. I'll show you." Coach led the way to an outdoor faucet.

Kayla jogged to meet Cody's truck as it lumbered down the driveway.

"How's everybody doing?" Cody waved while unloading his chair.

"They're peachy." She stood close to his door. "Are we overreacting?"

"No. I don't think so. John K. said the Forestry guys would be using a big plow to create a barrier ahead of the fire. I'll feel better once that happens."

"Do you know how wonderful you are?" She whispered.

"I've heard something like that. But it doesn't hurt to be reminded."

"What's the plan, Marshal Cody?" His dad walked closer.

"I think we can get a better view of what's happening at the end of this road." Cody pointed.

"I got a text from the nursing home." Cody's mom stood behind them. "I think we're going to have to go back. Is it okay if we leave your UTV here?"

Cody turned toward Kayla.

"Of course," Kayla answered. No need to check with Coach or Zanna.

"Do I need to come too?" Cody reached for Kayla's hand.

"No, son. You take care of things here, first. There's really nothing any of us can do for Grandpa Dee right now." His mom hugged him.

"He'd be here directing this whole operation if he could." His dad agreed.

Cody nodded silently.

"We'll update Coach and Zanna, then drive up the road. Okay, Kayla?"

She squeezed his hand, nodding.

"Wait." Her mind was processing this excursion. "Can you show me how to drive this thing?" She pointed at the UTV. "Unless you want to pull the water tank behind it."

"Really?" His eyes were wide.

"Yeah. You're not the only one who has been raised driving

every vehicle on the ranch. I think with one short lesson, I'll be good." She walked closer, examining the hand controls.

"Okay. I'll get it off the trailer, then." He winked at her.

Chapter Twenty-Five

Cody followed the Forestry Service truck as it passed him, headed for the overlook at the end of the road. Kayla bounced along beside him, just off the pavement. Rodeo queen, ranch detective, future architect, and now all-terrain utility vehicle driver. Amazing.

He continued past Kayla's family's private road. The public parking spot might have a less spectacular view, but it faced west, toward the fire.

Just to the right of Kayla, who had parked next to the Forestry truck, he pulled in and began unloading.

"You can see the column of smoke right over there." The man in green coveralls pointed across the valley.

"Great view from here, right?" Cody approached them.

"Fantastic." The man scanned the mountain, his binoculars in place. "My maps show a road that our plows could use, but I wanted to make sure it was the best one."

He lowered his binoculars.

Kayla pointed. "I think the best way runs right along that creek."

Cody nodded as the man followed her finger. "How long would it take for the fire to reach us up here?"

"Not long if we don't get this barrier plowed quickly. Where is your land, young man?" the forestry man turned toward him.

"The Pruitt place, just back there a ways." Cody's cheeks warmed as he pointed over his shoulder. His land? Well, today it was.

"My advice is to keep the perimeter as wet as possible and take a quick look in this direction now and then. Be safe." He pulled a portable radio out of his pocket and ran toward his truck.

"I'm glad they're here." Kayla stood next to the UTV.

"Me too. I wonder where John K. is." He peered at the smoke, searching for anything that resembled flames.

"Doing what he loves, I guess." Kayla wrapped her arm around his shoulders.

"Yep. There was a time he couldn't handle it. He has showed a lot of guts." Cody turned toward her.

"Maybe we should pray." Kayla reached for his hand.

Cody swallowed. At this moment, his thoughts were so mixed up. Could he form complete sentences?

"I'll do it." She must have read his scrambled mind.

He closed his eyes, clasping her hand in his.

"Heavenly Father, from where we stand, this fire is scary. You are so much bigger, and You can see it better. Please take care of the firefighters, and the people who live in the path of the flames. Thank You so much for sending Cody and his mom and dad to help. Be with Cody's grandpa tonight. Let him know You are with him every moment. We love You so much. Amen."

He opened his eyes, and she crouched beside him.

"Amen." He smiled at her.

Thanks, Lord. That was all he could add to her prayer. He knew God understood.

"So, are we riding this thing or is it just here for decoration?" She straightened to her full height, then slid into the driver's seat of the UTV.

"Let's go." Cody went back to his truck. "I need to see how

far the water will reach while I'm pulling this thing behind my truck. Unless the fire jumps the new barrier they're carving, we'll probably be safe."

They headed to the Pruitt's private road. Kayla jumped off the UTV to open the gate, then drove closer to the edge of the cliff.

"There's more brush, the closer we get to the fencerow." She shouted in his direction as he parked the truck.

Cody called over the engine noise. "You ride with me, to help me spray it."

"Coach hired someone to mow when one of my cousins can't be here. I guess they only mow what can be seen from the parking area." She climbed into his truck.

He stopped, and Kayla peered across the fence. "I hope the fire doesn't get this close."

"Me too. We'll use Dumbo to water down the mowed part, at least."

"Dumbo?" She laughed. "Who are you calling Dumbo?"

"Chief MacDonald said that's the name of the water tank." Would they have enough daylight left to finish this job?

"I think you'd better come up with a nicer name. He has an important job to do tonight." She held on with both hands. "Let's go."

They developed a routine of sorts, with Cody driving the truck, and Kayla jumping down to stand beside the water tank, spraying as far as possible with the hose.

"Climb in. I think that does it for tonight." He waited, with the engine running.

"Should we go take another look at the fire before we go to Coach and Zanna's house?" She eased into the seat beside him.

"Let's see if we can spot anything from our ... I mean ... *your* overlook." His cheeks blazed. Had she picked up on that?

"Sure. If we can't see the fire from here, that means everything is okay, right?" Her eyes met his.

If only he could guarantee that for her.

"I hope so." That was an honest response.

They parked where they could almost see around the western edge of the mountain. Nothing was in view on the ground, but the sky had a reddish glow. How much of that was the normal sunset? Cody took a deep breath. If the fire was close, they should be able to smell smoke. At least he hoped that was true.

"It's so peaceful here." Kayla leaned into his shoulder.

"Maybe it will stay that way." All he could smell right now was damp grass. They had done all they could do to protect the place.

"You're not driving home tonight." Kayla was not asking a question.

"John K. is supposed to send me a text if he hears the fire has jumped the barrier." He hadn't thought that far ahead. He didn't want to leave if there was still danger.

"Zanna has plenty of room. I'll feel so much safer if you're here." Kayla sat upright, staring at their clasped hands.

"Well, that settles it."

He sent his Dad a text.

How's Grandpa Dee?

The answer came quickly.

No change.

I'm staying at the Pruitts' tonight.

Good plan. We'll talk in the morning.

Night, then.

Good night.

"Can you get the UTV back to Coach's place?"

"You bet." She moved toward the door, but he stopped her, leaning over to give her a quick kiss.

"I'll follow you. Two sets of headlights will show up better on this dark road."

"Wouldn't have it any other way." She kissed him again, then climbed out of the truck.

"Do you have everything you need?" Kayla leaned against the wall outside the guest-room.

"I think so." He rolled inside. "My phone is charging next to the bed. The notification should wake me if John K. has anything to report."

Kayla closed her eyes. Hopefully, they would have a peaceful night without any jarring messages.

"Okay. Sleep well." She walked away from the door.

What a day. She stared at the bottom of the bunk above her bed. Zanna and Coach had been so calm when she arrived. How could they go about their normal business with a forest fire just a few miles away?

A long deep breath relaxed her body. The pit she'd been carrying in her belly lifted as soon as Cody arrived tonight. Having him nearby brought as much reassurance as the man from the Forestry Service, if not a bit more.

Only a few feet away on the other side of the wall, was he worrying about the fire? Did he know she was still awake, thinking about him?

His tender kiss, and the way he held her hand as they prayed together must mean something. They were more than a mystery-solving team, more than amateur firefighters. Were they meant to be together permanently? She had dreamed he might ask her to marry him. But now that he'd confessed his worry about his limitations, was he trying to break off their relationship?

Tears washed her cheeks. Could she abandon her dream of a large family to spend her life with Cody?

She rolled over with her back to the bright moonlight streaming through the bedroom window. Since there was no smoke blocking the moon, did that mean everything was okay? Was Cody's phone notification loud enough to wake them in time to evacuate if necessary?

Lord, my mind is a confused mess right now. You helped me bring Cody peace earlier. Please let me find enough to get some sleep now. Amen.

Cody's eyes popped open as a loud beeping noise blared into his ear.

Grandpa Dee is very close to leaving us.

From Mom, not John K.

"Cody?" Kayla shouted in alarm from the room next door.

"Not a fire alert." He reached to the floor to find his blue jeans. "I'll be over to your room in just a minute."

He answered Mom.

On my way.

Oh, Grandpa Dee. Don't be in a big hurry, okay? I'd like to say goodbye.

What about the fire? Would the local firefighters be able to protect Kayla's grandparents' place? What about "their" favorite spot on the bluff? The thought of looking down on a landscape of charred trees turned his stomach. That was out of his control. He'd have to trust God to take over from here.

Fire is contained. See you at home.

John K.'s message was timed perfectly. All three brothers would be under the same roof soon, drawing strength from each other.

Cody knocked on Kayla's door. She opened it fully dressed, except for boots, running a hairbrush through long, soft waves. He blinked to keep his composure. All of that auburn hair hanging on her shoulders was beyond beautiful.

"It's my grandpa. I've got to go right home," he whispered.

"Oh, Cody." Kayla reached for his hand. "Of course."

"I also got a message from John K. The fire is contained." He reached up with his free hand to touch her cheek. "I'll take Dumbo back to the Big River fire station on my way."

"Thanks so much for bringing it up here." Kayla pressed his palm into her cheek. "You made us feel so safe."

"Hey, I couldn't stand doing nothing." He reached into her hair, enjoying its silky softness for a moment.

"And I'll bring your UTV when I come home." She leaned down to kiss his forehead.

"No rush on that. I don't think I'll be using it for a while. Walk me to the truck?"

"You bet." She pulled on her boots and led the way to the front door. "I guess Coach and Zanna are still sleeping."

"I haven't done a lot of that." Should he tell her how hard it was to have only one wall separating them?

"Same." She walked beside him to the bottom of the ramp. "Do you need me to come with you now?"

"No." He was firm on that. They didn't know how long it would be before Grandpa Dee officially went Home. "I'll keep you posted on what's happening. We both need to start our classes this week if at all possible."

"I guess so." She stood next to the water tank. "Good thing we left this hooked up to your truck."

"Yeah." He pulled her face down to touch his. "I'll miss you so much."

"Be strong, Marshal Cody, sir." She fought back tears.

"I'll do my best, Miss Kayla." Had anyone else in his life always known exactly what to say at the best possible time? That was easy to answer. She was the only one.

His lips met hers, lingering longer than they should. Time to leave.

"I'll text you. See you soon." This would not get easier. He loaded his chair after she moved out of the way.

"Bye!"

His rear-view mirror captured her waving as he drove away. Leaving her felt so wrong.

Curvy roads led to the busy freeway. Taking the next exit, he was back under the tree tops. The next few days were guaranteed to be tough for all of them. Grandpa Dee would probably say something like, 'No one promised you it would be easy.' How he would miss that man.

Zanna met Kayla at the door.

"Bad news from home?" She held the screen door open.

"Cody's Mom asked him to come home." Kayla nodded. "But he also got a text from his firefighter brother. The fire is contained."

"I am so grateful for those folks. Now, a little rain would be appreciated too." Zanna placed three plates on the kitchen table. "Sit down, honey. It's early, but we might as well have breakfast."

"I won't argue." Kayla settled into a ladder-back chair. "I didn't sleep much. Now that I know we're safe, I'm starved."

"We'll take care of that little problem right away. Do you want to start with coffee?" She checked the water level in the coffee maker.

"Fix me up. Cody drinks his coffee black, but I need to ease into this. Put some cream and sugar in mine, please."

"I'll fix yours just like mine. We'll make a coffee drinker of you yet."

Zanna placed a mug of light brown coffee in front of her. She inhaled the rich aroma.

"I'm so glad you and your young man came to help us." Zanna said from the stove. "Coach and I live in our own world up here, and we're sometimes out of touch with what's going on."

"That's a good thing, right?" Kayla took a deep breath.

"A very good thing." Zanna patted her shoulder. "Like your mom and dad had, and like you will have some day."

Kayla blinked back a tear. Her dream about that future had begun to include Cody. Now, she didn't know if he would be in the picture.

"Why so quiet?" Zanna placed a plate of pancakes on the table. "Are you missing them?"

She meant Mom and Dad. Kayla was growing accustomed to that empty spot, but this was a new burden.

"Honestly, I was thinking about Cody." She fiddled with her fork instead of diving in to her favorite breakfast.

"You've been doing a lot of that, right?" Zanna moved the butter dish closer.

"Yes. He's amazing. So sweet and thoughtful. So strong." That would be a surprising statement to those who couldn't see past his limitations. "But he told me something that has me worried. I don't know if we can have a future together."

"Why, Honey?" Zanna stopped eating too.

"Cody has come so far since his accident. He's able to do so many things now." She paused. How to say this? "But he's worried that he may not be able to father children if he ever gets married."

"I see." Zanna waited.

"I don't know what I think about that. I love him, Zanna. I really do. But I always wanted a house full of kids. My visits up here with my cousins were fantastic. I wouldn't want to raise an only child."

Zanna stood and looked out the window. "You know, your

mom didn't want that either." She refilled her coffee cup and sat across from Kayla.

It was Kayla's turn to wait. She had never heard this story.

"There were two babies before you." Zanna stared into her coffee cup. "Neither made it to full-term. Each time, your mom and dad were so excited—and then so devastated. You were their rainbow baby."

"That must have been terrible" Kayla placed a pat of butter on her pancakes.

"Your mom didn't have an easy time when you were born. The doctor advised she shouldn't try again." Zanna reached across the table to touch Kayla's hand. "She wanted to foster or adopt but your dad couldn't stand the heartbreak that might come if things fell through. If someone took a child away, he would have been crushed all over again."

Tears flowed freely down Kayla's cheeks. She had never talked to her parents about this, but then, she'd had less than nineteen years with them.

"We had a talk just like this one morning, your mom and I." Zanna stood again. "She was trying to convince Dub at that point. It was starting to come between them."

"But they stayed together." Kayla couldn't imagine them separately.

"Yes. She loved him so much," Zanna said "She gave up the idea of more kids, and became the best mom to you, instead."

No wonder Mom spent so much time volunteering as a Sunday School teacher or a 4-H leader. Dad would go off to be by himself, and Mom thrived on chaos. So different. But they made it work.

"Thanks." Kayla hugged Zanna in front of the stove. "Love never fails."

Chapter Twenty-Six

The ceiling fan above Cody's head wobbled and squeaked.

"Hang in there," he whispered. "I don't want to share my bed with you." Oh good, now he was talking to inanimate objects.

Leaving his bedroom, he found John K. sitting at the kitchen island with a cup of coffee.

"That won't help you sleep." He pointed at the steaming mug.

"I've given up on that. Want some?" John K. stood to restart the coffee maker.

"Sure." He stopped at the kitchen table. "Everyone else down for the count?"

"Mom is with Grandpa Dee at the nursing home. Dad's snoring." John K. held his hand to his ear.

Cody grinned. "Hey, I didn't get a chance to thank you for the inside information about the fire."

"No problem." John K. placed Cody's coffee on the table. "If we don't get some rain, we'll be dealing with that same threat all over again."

"I think we convinced Kayla's grandparents to pay closer attention to the fire alerts. That helps Kayla sleep better." Cody sighed. Spending the night in the same house with Kayla had been tough, but tonight, with more miles between them, things weren't much better.

"I keep going back to the last time I talked to Grandpa Dee." John K. sat beside Cody. "He didn't know who I was, but in a lot of ways, he was still the same as he's always been. Does that make sense?"

"Yeah." Cody sipped his coffee. "I think he knew we belonged, even if our names and relationships had slipped away. He was comfortable with us. When I was his roommate, he asked if I was married."

"Really?" John K. added some sugar, "Why?"

"He said I should always pay attention to my wife. He said something like 'making a good woman happy is more important than anything else you do in your life.'"

"Yeah. I guess that was a lesson he learned from Grandma." John K. stared into his cup. "I spent time with them when I was small. He always seemed to be rushing off somewhere."

"More than once, he made me promise when I found the right girl, I would let her know how I felt about her." Cody wrapped his fingers around the warm cup. "I tried to tell him there was no one special. He just kept saying, 'There will be.' Then he'd say, 'Don't waste a minute. You don't know how many minutes you'll have.'"

"Good advice, little brother." John K. patted his shoulder. "You and I both know about life sending unexpected things our way."

"True." Cody sat silently. Did Kayla know how much he cared? Had he scared her off with talk of his physical condition? He couldn't imagine his future without Kayla. He'd have to find a way to tell her. She might decide having kids was more important than being with him. At least they would know now. Coffee wasn't the only thing keeping him awake tonight.

Kayla left the website she'd been viewing and closed her laptop. Before this past weekend, she hadn't given too much thought to the importance of landscaping around a new building. There was more to this than curb appeal. Imagine if Coach hadn't kept the area around their house mowed. The threat of a fire would have been so much scarier.

On Tuesday, she walked out of her first class and headed across campus for the next one. A notification caught her attention, and she looked down to read Cody's message.

Grandpa Dee passed away early this morning.

Oh, no. Everyone had been expecting this, but that didn't make it easier. The heartbreak was here to stay. She could testify to that.

She sat on a bench. He answered her phone call immediately.

"Hello." He sounded exhausted.

"I'm so sorry, Cody." She really was.

"Aunt Candace got home from Mexico this morning. They're going to make arrangements this afternoon. I'll let you know."

"I can be home in less than three hours." She reviewed her schedule in her head. No tests or papers due, so early in the semester.

"I know. But you might as well continue classes. I plan to work tomorrow. I'll call you tonight"

She remembered that feeling of wanting to continue all the normal things. If she'd learned anything, it was to let a grieving person have their space.

"Okay. I'm here. Call or text anytime. Really."

"Thanks." He was gone.

Lord, hold Cody in Your arms at this moment. I know he's strong, but he needs Your comfort. Help me to listen for ways I can help him. Thanks for always being there. Amen.

Another message popped up, this one from Faith.

Did you hear about John K.'s grandpa?

Yes. Just talked to Cody.

Can I call?

Kayla checked the time. Ten minutes before her next class.

Sure.

"Hey. John K. says it might be a few days before the memorial service," Faith said when Kayla answered the phone. "They're making sure his grandpa has the proper military honors."

"That's great. Cody said his military service was very important to him." Kayla knew helping plan the service would be good for everyone. "I promised Cody I'd wait to hear from him before I come down. Are you going today?"

"No. John K. said I should keep my regular routine until the services are scheduled," Faith said. "I plan to be at Dad and Candace's wedding Friday night, so I'll see you then. Should we ride together?"

"You think they'll still get married this weekend?" Kayla blinked. Wouldn't everything change for Candace now? Maybe not. After all they had expected to say *goodbye* to Grandpa Dee soon.

"Wait." She suddenly remembered Cody's UTV. "I have to pull Cody's all-terrain vehicle home from Coach and Zanna's, so I'll bring my truck home."

Old Main's clock chimed to denote a new hour. Five minutes until her next class started.

"I'd better go. I'll talk to you later tonight." Kayla stood up from the bench.

"Take care, Gracie." Faith used her childhood nickname. Another attempt at continuing their normal activities?

She pulled out an old-school notebook and a pencil for algebra class. This subject didn't hold her attention nearly as well as the earlier one.

A message appeared on her phone as she took her seat. No words, just a heart emoji. Was Cody trying to tell her he loved her? She couldn't think of anyone she'd rather spend time with. He'd been such a big help navigating through the loss of her parents. But love? That simple word made everything different. Would she ever hear that word coming from his mouth?

The professor outlined their next assignment. She glanced down at the page she'd been taking notes on. Covered in hearts, instead of algebraic formulas. *Uh-oh*. Hopefully, the upcoming chapter would be self-explanatory, because her notes would obviously be of no assistance.

"Hey." Cody was happy Kayla answered her phone so quickly.

"How are you?"

I'd be better if you were here. No. She had offered to join him. Be strong, Cody.

"I'm okay. None of us have slept much. I'll need to give it a good try tonight if I intend to be productive at work tomorrow," he said.

"I have a feeling your boss would allow you some time off if you need it."

Her motherly tone was firmly in place today.

"Yeah, probably. Honestly, I've done enough sitting around talking to my family about Grandpa Dee to last another day or two," he said.

"I get that. Have you heard about arrangements yet?" She was good at keeping the conversation moving.

"Yeah. We heard back from Veteran's Affairs. Everything is a go for Saturday afternoon. He only wanted graveside services. Mom said he was never a fan of drawn-out indoor ceremonies." He could understand. Weekly worship actually felt good but sitting with a room full of people trying not to be sad grated on him.

"Is Uncle Smiley doing the service?"

"No. Grandpa Dee was a member of another congregation across town. The same preacher who did my grandma's funeral will handle it." Cody had never met this guy, but Mom said Grandpa Dee had planned most of his service years ago.

"So, is your Aunt Candace still getting married Friday night?"

"Yes. Mom said she knew Grandpa Dee would love the family having two celebrations in a row."

"You don't sound convinced," Kayla said.

"No, it's fine. Like I said, I'm just a bit worn out." He sighed. "Hey, I can't wait to see you Friday."

"I feel the same way," she said. "I hope you get some sleep tonight."

"I'll do my best." He smiled. Talking to her relaxed him.

"Good night," she said.

"Night."

Cody settled into his bed. Maybe he could sleep now. Kayla had given him confidence once again. More and more, he pictured his future with her by his side.

After a brief prayer, and a few quiet deep breaths, his eyes snapped open.

He knew how he felt about Kayla. But what if she had a completely different picture of her future? She seemed to accept his wheelchair-bound life. In fact, her plans to be an architect were rooted in creating accessible buildings for others in a similar situation. What if she couldn't accept the fact that they might not have kids together?

What was that verse from the Bible that Grandpa Dee liked

to quote? 'Don't worry about tomorrow. Tomorrow has enough worries of its own.' Something like that. He took a deep breath. Maybe Dad would have some insight on the big question in his mind. Time for another fishing trip.

Chapter Twenty-Seven

"What's up?" Faith asked as Kayla answered the phone.

"One more day of classes over with," Kayla said.

"Are they that bad?"

"No." Kayla opened the refrigerator. She'd probably need to go to the grocery store if she planned to cook for her roommates tonight. "It's just hard to concentrate. I want to be with Cody and his family right now."

"Exactly." Faith agreed. "Tomorrow's Thursday, we'll be home Friday evening. Maybe we'll survive."

"I guess. Right now, I'm trying to figure out what to cook for supper." They did have some frozen veggies. She opened a cabinet and found a box of rice. "I'm thinking I could go get a rotisserie chicken and make some fried rice. You want to come over?"

"Will there be enough?" Faith asked.

"Yeah. Maddie has dinner plans tonight, so there will be three of us. My recipe works better for four." Kayla grabbed her purse.

"You convinced me. How 'bout I bring the chicken?" Faith asked.

"Perfect. I'll cook the rice and throw it all together when you get here."

Paige and Lydia dropped their backpacks on a chair as they entered the apartment.

"Hey!" Paige retrieved a soda from the refrigerator.

"How about chicken fried rice for supper?" Kayla plugged in the rice cooker.

"Perfect." Lydia headed toward the bathroom. "I'm going to take a shower."

"What would we do without you?" Paige laughed. "It's like having one of our moms for a roommate."

She apparently had these girls fooled. A few things she'd learned from Zanna that would work in a pinch. Luckily, her turn to cook didn't come up very often. Kayla fumbled with the measuring cup as she poured rice into it. Did she act like a mother? That wasn't totally terrible. Would she ever get the chance to cook for her own family?

Cooking would help this evening pass, but what about tomorrow? Friday seemed weeks away right now. As soon as the supper dishes were done, she'd call Cody. She was supposed to be supporting him, but hearing his voice would do wonders for her too.

"No. I'm pretty sure I can do this all on my own." Cody waved off Dad's help with the boat launching process. "Have you ever seen a remote-control toy this big?"

He loosened the chain holding his boat and backed the trailer farther into the water.

Dad paced back and forth. Cody smiled. He was pretty nervous himself. This must be hard to watch.

He rolled to the back of his truck and used his controller to get the trolling motor in place. Now, to make good use of his old gaming skills.

"Just one more minute." He returned to his truck. After unloading his chair again, he hurried back to the edge of the water and used the remote to maneuver the boat to the best loading spot.

"Amazing!" Dad clapped his hands. "You don't need me here at all."

"Not true. I'm counting on you to catch supper." Cody teased as he rolled onto the boat.

"I hope you have a backup plan." Dad laughed.

Their fishing reels buzzed and whirred as he waited for the perfect time to bring up the subject weighing him down.

"Dad." He moistened his lips. "I need to ask you about something important."

"I thought you might have more than my incredible fishing skills in mind tonight." Dad laughed.

"Yeah. Well, it's like this." Cody cleared his throat. "Grandpa Dee got me to thinking a few weeks ago."

"He was good at that," Dad said quietly. "Made me think just about every time I talked to him."

"I've made an important decision." Might as well just spit it out. "I've been praying about this. I've decided Kayla is the person I want to spend the rest of my life with."

"Sounds like a very good idea to me. She's a keeper, that one." Dad slapped his shoulder.

"There's just one thing. What if she doesn't want me?" This was so hard to talk about.

"I can't imagine why not. Even to a non-romantic guy like me, she seems to think pretty highly of you, son."

"But ..." Out with it. "What if she wants a family?"

"Of course, she wants a family. She'd be joining a pretty good one, right?" Dad said.

"No, I mean, what if she wants us to have kids. I mean, I never ..." Oh, boy. He was stuck now. "I was so worried about walking again that I never talked to the doctor about this. I was just sixteen, and it seemed too early ..."

"Well, I did ask." Dad reeled his fishing line back in. "I knew you'd need to know someday."

Thank You Lord, for Dad. "What was his answer?"

"You know your paralysis starts at the thighs." Dad was the king of maintaining composure. "And if you keep up with your strengthening exercises, it could move down a little bit each year."

"I remember that." Cody nodded. Hope for the future.

"When you find the right girl, your body will let you know it's ready." Dad still didn't flinch.

Cody couldn't hold back the heat rising in his cheeks. His body had been letting him know. Another reason he was avoiding swimming with Kayla.

"So, we could have kids of our own? "

"There are never any guarantees for any of us." Dad searched his tackle box for a lure. "But I don't think that should keep you and Kayla from being very happy together."

Cody baited his hook and made a cast out into the water.

"I don't know. She might not want to take that chance. What if I ask her, and she says *no*?" He didn't think he'd survive that.

"You will never know if you don't ask. What did Grandpa Dee say to influence you?"

"He just kept talking about life being short, and making sure you told others how you feel." Cody blinked back tears.

"Very good advice. I couldn't say it better, son." Dad threw out his bait.

Only trivial matters interrupted the silence as they relaxed.

The sound of someone's boat motor finally intruded. Did he have the answer he needed now? This might require one more good night's sleep.

"Okay. If you're not going to catch our supper, I guess we'd better head back home." Cody secured his pole and started their own motor. "Hopefully, I can get this boat back on the trailer the same way it came off."

"These patio lights come in white or multi-color." Kayla took a box from the shelf and showed it to Faith.

"I think white Edison bulbs." Faith tapped her bottom lip. "Agreed?"

"Yes. It's a wedding, not a party." Kayla scanned the shelves. "But it's a big pavilion. We'll need two strings."

"John K.'s mom seemed pretty stressed over this when she called last night." Faith added another box of lights to their cart. "Normally, she'd be enjoying planning and decorating for her sister's wedding."

"The bride and the wedding planner don't normally lose their dad the same week as the wedding." Kayla secured her purse in the seat of the cart.

"I told her this was the perfect job for us. Since we're just sitting around missing our men."

"You didn't say that!" Kayla's cheeks flamed.

"No, not in so many words." Faith laughed. "But it's true."

"I'm glad I get done with classes at ten tomorrow. I'll be rushing to get down to Coach and Zanna's to pick up Cody's UTV and get back on the road." Kayla stopped at the end of the aisle. "Is there anything else we can find at this store?"

"Let's see." Faith pulled her list out of her bag. "Tablecloths, votive candles, fake flowers ... Hey, Paris is not too far off the path. We could run by that wedding rental place ..."

"Lainie!" Kayla used her sternest voice. "We have to get this done now. Tonight. Use your head."

"Yeah. If I didn't have you and Hope to rein me in, I'd be wandering around in the clouds when it comes to this stuff." Faith laughed. "So, I guess, the hobby and craft store here in town?"

"Sometimes I wonder if you should be a pre-med student." Kayla grumbled on her way to the cash register.

"Thanks for coming with me, Mom." Cody navigated past her into the brightly lit store.

"You don't know how happy this makes me," she said. "I needed a break so badly."

"This is important. Kayla is so fashion conscious. How will we know what she wants?" Cody stopped between two long cases of rings.

"You know her better than anyone. We'll figure it out, I promise. Now, keep in mind what you want to spend. The salesperson will steer you toward something more expensive." Mom walked toward a gleaming display on the right.

"Hi." The young lady behind the counter walked toward them. "How may I help?

"Well, I'm, I mean, we're getting engaged," Cody fumbled.

The salesgirl's brow furrowed.

"I'm his mom." Mom laughed. "Here for moral support only."

"Got it." The clerk smiled. "Well, the best advice I can give is to see what catches your eye first. Folks tend to always come back to that one."

Cody spotted a rectangular-shaped stone, sparkling on a thin band against a velvet-covered backdrop. Rectangular? Weren't diamonds round?

"How about this?" Mom pointed at a ring with a diamond in the center and a smaller blue stone on each side. "I've heard a lot of folks are going with color instead of the traditional white diamond."

"She does like blue." He just wasn't sure. There were so many shapes and sizes. This was hopeless.

"I saw you over here a moment ago." The salesgirl walked to Cody's right. "What caught your eye first?"

"That one. But I want a diamond. This must be something else." He pointed.

"*Ooh*. Great choice. It *is* a diamond. It's an emerald cut, so shaped like a traditional emerald ring." She unlocked and opened the case. "It's also one of the very modern rose-cut diamonds. See?" She picked the ring up and pointed. "Instead of being pointed on the bottom, it's flat. That makes the top of the stone sparkle even more. And it has just the slightest blue tint."

Cody held the ring in front of him, watching the light bounce around on the top of the stone. Unexpectedly perfect. Much like the two of them. A rodeo queen and an out-of-shape bull rider. Somehow managing to shine.

Mom spoke, breaking the spell. "Can this one be stacked with a wedding band?"

"See why I brought you?" Cody winked at his mom.

"Definitely. The right style will stack flush against this band." The salesgirl turned to another case.

"Thanks. We'll wait to choose the bands." Cody said. "If she goes for this engagement idea, we'll do that together."

Cody pulled out his debit card.

"That's the one." Tiny beads of sweat formed above his eyebrows.

Two shiny gift bags perched on the truck seat next to Mom.

"I love that necklace you found too." Mom peeked into the larger bag.

"She loves turquoise. Isn't there something about something new, and something blue at a wedding? This would work for either." He started the truck.

"Such a thoughtful boy. I guess we'll keep you." Mom patted her shoulder.

"Okay, you and Dad know about this. Not a word to my brothers, though."

"Cross my heart." She even made the silly gesture.

"Because ... I don't know." Why was he fumbling for words today? "I'm not sure when I'm going to ask her. The timing might be wrong. We're both in school. I'm living at home. I might need to quit my job and welding school and move to Fayetteville. I mean ..."

"Son." Mom patted his arm. "The two of you can work out those details. What's important is that you let her know she's the one. Love finds a way."

"Isn't a guy supposed to have consent from her father first?" His mind was still going ninety miles an hour. "I need to talk to Smiley Caldwell."

"Okay. Do you mind dropping me at home first?" Mom unfastened her seat belt, moved over, and pecked him on the cheek.

He laughed out loud. Wow, did that feel good.

Now to convince Smiley. Would he be okay with the third Billings brother coming into the family?

Chapter Twenty-Eight

Kayla used the light blue bandana in her back pocket to dab the sweat on her forehead.

"I wish I could have helped more." Coach tugged on the padlock Kayla had placed on the trailer hitch. "Cody's blessed to have such a good friend."

"I've been hauling things around as long as I've been driving." She fastened the last connections. "You can give me a thumbs up if you see the lights working." She hopped into the truck, watching for his signal as she put her foot on the brake then tested the turn signals.

"All set," Coach shouted from the back of the trailer.

"Give our love to your Uncle Smiley and the rest of the crew." Zanna touched her hand as she stood next to the truck window. "We were invited to the wedding tonight, but we're actually hosting one here tomorrow, and I have some last-minute things to do."

"Really?" Kayla looked down the hill at Zanna's garden. "You're having a wedding here? I'm sure it will be beautiful. Send me pictures."

"Ellen will take care of that, I'm sure." Zanna laughed. "I'll be too busy supplying ice water. It's gonna be another scorcher."

"Okay. I'll text when I get home. Love y'all!" She headed up the driveway, turning at the newly painted "Shoe Tree Road" sign.

Before she reached the busy highway, a text popped up on her phone. She stopped behind the gas station at the corner.

Call before you get on the freeway if possible.

Cody had perfect timing.

"Hey," she said when he answered.

"I'm off work early this afternoon. If you don't mind, I need a favor," he said.

Her mind raced. Boxes behind the seat held artificial flowers, plastic plates and utensils, and tons of miscellaneous for the wedding tonight. Could she make room if he needed her to bring something else?

"Sure." That was the only answer, regardless.

"You could bring the UTV by our cabin, instead of taking it all the way home," he said. "Dad wants to use it up there this week, getting ready for deer season."

"I've never been to your cabin." Could she put an address in the GPS?

"Are you still at your grandparents' house?" he asked.

"Yes." Close enough.

"I'll send you a pin. Just get off at the very next exit off the freeway. It's not too far down that road," Cody said.

"Is there a shoe tree at the corner where I turn?" She laughed.

"Nope. But there is a shiny mailbox that says 'Billings.'" He laughed too.

"Sounds easy enough. How long should it take me?" She started the truck.

"Oh, about thirty minutes, I guess. You might beat me there."

"I'll wait." She'd only have a minute to change at home before meeting Faith and Hope at Candace's in time to decorate. "See you soon."

"Not soon enough."

She had half-way expected a "love you" at the end of that conversation. Best not to expect too much.

Busy Labor Day weekend traffic already crowded the interstate. Trucks pulling boats and campers with bicycles on board passed her on both sides. She checked the rear-view mirrors to be sure the little vehicle behind her was riding well. They should give this thing a name. Even the fire department's water tank was called Dumbo.

What a funny thought. What gave her any right to pick a name for Cody's UTV? She flipped the turn signal up and left the freeway, following his directions to his family's cabin. Yes. It definitely needed a name. She'd chew on that for the next few miles.

Had she even seen pictures of this place? John K. had lived here for a while. It had required extensive remodeling after a freak explosion. That was the limit of what she knew about the Billings' cabin. She wouldn't have much time to explore. Not today. Glass candle holders clinked together behind her seat. Too many things going on.

A gleaming new mailbox identified the road leading to the cabin. She turned between some small pine trees into a large, paved parking lot. The broad porch of the wood-sided building was accessible by a ramp that turned in the middle to provide just the right slope.

She should have known the family would make sure Cody could use the cabin. Shifting into 'Park,' she killed the engine and stepped out of the truck. Happy bird songs greeted her, and a flowerbed at the other end of the porch told her that Cody's mom enjoyed spending time here too.

She took a deep breath of the pine scented air. What a peaceful and inviting place. Why had he asked her to come here?

A loud horn startled her, and Cody's truck stopped next to hers.

"Where do you want this thing?" She pointed at the trailer behind her truck.

"Hello to you too!" He leaned out the window.

"I'm sorry." What happened to that peaceful deep breath she had just taken in?

"Understandable. It's a busy weekend."

Was he blushing? What was that about?

"How's everybody at your house?" She had almost forgotten they were preparing for a funeral.

"They're fine. It'll be good to see Grandpa Dee get some overdue recognition." He eased himself into his chair. "Come this way, and I'll show you where we're headed."

The blacktop continued around the side of the house to a canopy sitting a few feet from a small shed.

"I brought a big heavy chain to attach the trailer to the canopy, and another one to hold the UTV to the trailer." He pointed. "If you want to hook it to my truck, I'll back it in."

"I'm pretty sure I can handle it." That would save time. "Let's give it a try. Oh, and by the way, the UTV needs a name. Let's call it Gideon." The bible story had been in her head since she exited the freeway.

"Gideon?"

"The hero who doubted himself and did so much more than expected." Like someone else she knew.

"Okay. Rodeo queen, ranch detective, and bible scholar. Let's get Gideon taken care of, then."

With only hand signals, they moved around until the trailer was safely under the canopy.

"Excellent work."

Cody met her as she stepped down beside her truck door.

"My pleasure." She performed a mock curtsy.

"Hey. I need to tell you something." His voice dropped.

She moved closer. He caught both of her hands, pulling her forward.

"I love you, Kayla Caldwell." His eyes captured hers. He pulled her onto his lap.

She reached behind his head, pulling him closer for a kiss.

"And I love you." Why now? When they were in such a huge hurry? "We're much too busy today." She laughed.

"A typical day for the Billings brood." He grinned.

"Busy is good. The next time you see me, I will look more like a wedding guest."

"I like this look just as much." He captured her lips for another kiss. "See you soon."

"Not soon enough." She ran behind her truck to be sure the trailer was completely unhooked before driving away.

Cody followed Kayla's truck along the winding road toward their houses. He could have volunteered to take the lead, since this was her first visit to the Billings' cabin. No. That would have cast doubt on her abilities. Today, her superhero powers were shining.

The beautiful ring waited in his room at home. No ordinary proposal would do for her. He'd been going over the details all day. Tomorrow was dedicated to Grandpa Dee's memorial. They would both need to attend worship services on Sunday. So, the Labor Day holiday would be theirs. A special day for them, forever.

He slapped the steering wheel of his truck. He hadn't talked to her uncle. The uncle who was about to be married. How was he going to pull this off?

The quandary was still not solved when Kayla pulled into her driveway. He honked his horn and drove past.

Junior's truck and Smiley's were both in the other Caldwell driveway when he pulled in.

Let's make this happen.

"Hello, young man." Smiley greeted Cody as he navigated the short ramp to their back deck. "Come in. I'll tell Junior you're here."

"Actually, I need to talk to you." Cody stopped just inside the door. "Can I have just a minute?"

"Hey, it's Cody!" Junior came out of his room in stocking feet.

"Let's step outside." Smiley opened the door to the patio.

"Catch you later." Cody waved at Junior. He should have known his buddy would be in on this secret.

"How are you doing?" A pretty lame way to start this conversation but it would do.

"Believe me, I'm happy about what's happening tonight, but the butterflies in my stomach are trying to set NASCAR records." Smiley leaned against the post holding up their porch roof.

Cody took a deep breath. How could he calm someone down? His own heart was about to pound out of his chest.

"I'll try to make this quick. It's like this. Over the past few weeks, Kayla and I have been spending a lot of time together."

"I've noticed that." Smiley nodded.

"I think we grew closer because we've both been through some pretty tough times." Cody cleared his throat. "I know we're both too young to have life figured out, but whatever comes next, I want her at my side for all of it."

Smiley nodded again.

Okay, Billings. Out with it. "Sir, I'd like your permission to ask Kayla to marry me." He took a huge breath.

Smiley had been a rodeo announcer, and now he was a preacher. Was he really at a loss for words? Cody waited.

"Son, you have summed up exactly what I feel about your Aunt Candace." Smiley's eyes filled with tears. "If I've learned one lesson after my sweet Catherine passed away, it's this. Life on earth is short. God didn't intend for us to be alone. So, when you find the perfect person, you should do what's right in

His eyes. If she helps you live life to His glory, you should go for it."

Cody let out the breath he'd been holding.

"Thanks for understanding. I want you to know, I'll do everything I can to make Kayla happy. I've encouraged her to continue with architecture school so, we may wait a while for the wedding. Besides, I want to live on my own first. I can't be a provider if I'm still letting my parents provide for me." His words came out in a rush.

"Wisdom beyond your years." Smiley shook Cody's hand. "On behalf of my brother and his wife, I give you the family's blessing. You and your older brothers have all chosen very wisely."

"Y'all raised some pretty awesome girls, sir." Cody nodded. "And then there's Junior."

"Then, there's Junior." Smiley laughed. "Nobody's perfect."

"Okay. I'd better let you go." Cody headed toward his truck. "I'll see you at Aunt Candace's house. And tomorrow and Sunday, too, I guess."

"I've arranged for someone else to take the pulpit Sunday. Candace and I will head for out for a honeymoon whenever she's ready after the service tomorrow." Smiley opened his kitchen door. "It's like the Proverb says, we may try to do the planning, but God directs our steps. May as well sit back and let that happen, right?"

"Yes, sir." Cody turned his chair toward the ramp. "He's much better at it than we are."

Cody's phone rang before he was completely parked in his own driveway.

"What?" He never used formality when Junior called.

"Was that what I think it was? Asking for someone's hand?" Junior's voice was an octave higher than normal.

"Can you possibly keep that big mouth of yours shut for a couple of days?" Cody massaged his forehead with his fingers. He had no time for a headache right now.

"Sure, buddy. Sure," Junior replied. "But it won't be easy."

"Nothing worthwhile is." Cody smiled. More of Grandpa Dee's wisdom. "I'll see you in just a bit, and we'll talk more after the service tomorrow."

"Okay, dude. Hey, congratulations."

Cody headed for his bathroom. Time for one of the fastest showers on record.

Kayla tossed another handful of birdseed as Uncle Smiley and Candace passed in front of her on the way to his truck.

"What a beautiful wedding." She sighed.

"Pretty special, all right." Cody emptied his own bag on the ground. "You and your cousins did an amazing job decorating the pavilion."

"Thanks. Your Mom had some of it planned. We just had to hustle to pull it all off today."

At the bottom of the hill, the moon reflected off the perfectly still water. Cody was still facing her when she turned back. She reached down to squeeze his hand.

"You know what? I'm exhausted," she said. "But I promised Hope and Faith I'd help clean up."

"Then, let's get after it." He headed down the hill. "I don't think I'll have any trouble sleeping tonight, either."

She hurried to follow him. Uncle Smiley was extremely happy, but how must Candace be feeling? Her father was being buried tomorrow. Probably not how she had pictured her wedding night. Like Zanna said, though, love finds a way.

Kayla blinked back tears. Life had been coming at these two families at a blinding pace. There might be time to dwell on things later, but for now, they could only look to the future.

Cody turned in circles in the pavilion. He seemed overly happy tonight too. Maybe the Billingses had been dealing with Grandpa Dee's illness for so long, they were ready for celebrations instead. Could she help him put this event behind? What was next for them?

Instead of turning circles like Cody, she gathered up a paper tablecloth and stuffed it into a trash bag.

Thanks Lord, for the example these folks are showing me. Celebration does feel much better than sadness.

Chapter Twenty-Nine

Kayla reached for Hope's hand on her left, and Faith's on her right, as the strains of "Taps" filled the hot stillness under the funeral canopy. Two uniformed men saluted, then began the task of folding the flag that covered the casket.

In the row ahead of them, Cody's mom leaned against his dad's shoulder, and Candace's head inclined the opposite way, toward Uncle Smiley. The minister standing to the left waited for the soldiers to present the flag to Felecia and Candace before leading a final prayer.

Next to Uncle Smiley, the three Billings brothers sat straight and tall.

"That was impressive," Hope whispered to Kayla. Well-wishers filed between the casket and the family members, shaking hands and offering hugs.

"I was so proud of the remarks our three guys made today," Faith said from her other side.

Kayla nodded. *Our three guys.* She liked the sound of that.

"I don't know about y'all, but I've been hearing about Grandpa Dee from my hubby since day one." Hope reached for her purse.

"He was the greatest." Faith dabbed her eyes with a tissue.

"He had a big influence on all of them." Kayla stood and watched for the end of the reception line. She found her sunglasses in her bag and prepared to leave the shady protection the canopy offered.

"Hey," Cody reached for her hand. "Thanks for being here."

"You knew I would be. You showed up for me at my parents' services." She squeezed his hand.

"I don't know if I was looking forward to this or looking forward to it being over," he whispered.

"Hey, man." Junior stepped around Kayla to hug Cody. "How're you holding up?"

"Oh, not bad. Having friends around helps, buddy." Cody patted Junior's back.

"Yeah." Junior responded. "Back at 'ya, buddy."

"Hey, can you hang around a minute?" Cody asked Junior.

"Yeah. No problem." Junior moved down the line, shaking hands.

"You want to come over to see what kind of food the neighbors brought?" Cody's thumb made circles in Kayla's palm.

"Do you need me there?" She still wasn't fond of funeral dinners.

"Honestly? I'm fine. I'll probably just take a nap this afternoon." He took a deep breath.

"I'll go on home. I have some studying to do before my Tuesday classes." Quiet, alone time might be just what they both needed right now.

"Okay." He caught her eye, and silently mouthed two wonderful words. "Love you."

"Love you too." Her heart pounded as she responded.

She hugged his brothers, then Uncle Smiley. Next was Candace.

"I guess I can officially call you Aunt Candace like everyone else." She squeezed Candace's shoulders. "I know about losing a dad. I'll be praying for you."

"Thanks, sweetheart." Candace looked her in the eyes. "Your uncle came along at just the right time for me."

"He's pretty good at that," Kayla had to agree.

After hugging Cody's mom and dad, she walked across the dry grass to her truck. Now, both of the Billings-Caldwell events were behind them. Instead of dreading the silence of her big, empty house, she looked forward to some peace.

Cody and Junior were huddled with O.D. and John K. next to Cody's truck. Junior was nodding and making big hand motions, to the delight of the three brothers. What outrageous story was he telling? Yes, the Caldwell girls had found some pretty great guys. And then, there was Junior.

"This is going to taste so good." Cody served Kayla at the pizza restaurant.

"Too many casseroles?" Kayla laughed.

"You know it. Don't get me wrong, we're blessed by so many good cooks. I'm just ready for normal again."

"The new preacher was pretty great tonight," Kayla said.

"Yeah. I hope your uncle and my aunt are enjoying their honeymoon."

"Did you know they took off on a motorcycle? Caldwells really do their own thing." She sprinkled parmesan on her pizza. "Are you glad tomorrow's a holiday?"

"Sure. This school and work thing makes for long days." But first, something very important was happening. He went over his plans in his head. What if she wouldn't go along with it? Might as well dive in. "So, what do you have planned for tomorrow?"

"Not a thing." She picked up a large slice. "I've been putting off cleaning out some closets at my house."

"Sounds like fun." He took a bite of his own pizza.

"The opposite. After all this time, I haven't gone through

Mom and Dad's stuff. I've managed to stay out of their room. Nancy goes in to clean it ..."

This conversation was headed in a bad direction.

"Well, I have an idea. It would involve getting up early, though." It wasn't easy to sound casual about this. "Want to go fishing?"

"Are you serious?" Her voice brightened.

"Yeah. Since it's so hot, we'd need to get out there around sun-up. The water is nice and smooth, and ..."

"The fish are biting?" She wiped her mouth with a napkin.

"Yeah. Yeah." Would they be biting? He couldn't care less.

"Sure. That sounds great."

He used his napkin to wipe his sweaty palms. Maybe this crazy plan could work.

"Great. I'll come get you around 6:15." He hoped his math worked. Could they be on the lake by sunrise at 6:45?

"I'll be ready at 6:00. I think I even have some frozen sausage biscuits I can warm up to take with us. Then, we can have fish for lunch."

"Sure." He'd need to take some live bait to keep up the ruse for a few minutes longer. The main star of the show would be that emerald-cut diamond.

"I'm excited. I haven't been fishing in forever."

"I thought you might like it. I think it's just what I need after the insanity of the last few weeks." Cody took a big bite of pizza.

"You're a smart man, Mr. Marshal, sir."

Oh, how he loved that silly Western accent of hers.

Kayla unzipped the light jacket she'd worn as Cody stopped his truck on the boat ramp.

"You might want to stand on the shore while I launch." He unlocked her door.

"You won't shove off without me?" She remembered helping

her dad with this process. Did Cody intend to do it all by himself?

"Not a chance."

She walked to a safe location and watched as he backed part way into the water, unloaded his wheelchair to unhook the boat, and reloaded. This was no easy feat.

The boat floated a few feet out as Cody parked the truck and then came back in his wheelchair. She gasped as the boat turned around and pushed itself onto the bank.

"Mademoiselle." He gestured for her to board the boat, then followed in his chair.

"I didn't know you had such an intelligent boat. Is it going to need a name too?"

"Mercy." He laughed. "This is getting out of hand. I guess you can name her if you want to."

"Mercy. Yes, that sounds perfect." She settled in a seat behind the captain's spot, and watched him look to the left, the right, and even back to the launching ramp before motoring into the water. "You're right, it is peaceful out here."

"I may be getting old before my time. The calm out here really grabs me these days."

The sky in front of them lightened to gray, and then showed tinges of pink and purple as the sun climbed into the sky. The birds along the shoreline started their daily vocal warmups.

"Is this the right spot?" Kayla looked around in amazement. This was definitely one of the prettiest spots she could imagine, whether there were fish around or not.

"This is it." He touched his blue-jean pocket.

"Which fishing rod should I use?" She looked at the selection attached to the inside of the boat.

"I'll help. But first, could you come over here? I have something to show you."

Were his hands shaking? She must be seeing things in the dim light.

"Kayla." He cleared his throat and pulled a velvety box out of his pocket.

Her hand flew to her mouth as she stood directly in front of him.

"I've learned a lot over the past several months. The most important lesson is that we can't waste a minute of the time God has given us on this earth." He opened the box, and a beautiful diamond caught the first glint of morning sun from the east. "I've been trying to prove to everyone that I can do things on my own. I almost missed the fact that I don't *want* to do that. God did not intend for us to live this life alone. There's no one else I want to have by my side." He held tightly to her hand. "Kayla Grace Caldwell, would you do me the honor of being my wife for as long as God allows?"

"Oh, of course I will!" She leaned over to kiss him, lost her balance, and landed in his lap.

"Here, let's see if this fits before I drop it." He slid the rectangular diamond on her left ring finger. She welcomed his kiss but was distracted by the sight of two canoes several feet to her left.

"What are they doing here?" She laughed, pointing at three familiar men in the boats.

"Paparazzi." He lowered his voice. "But listen. I don't want to say this too loud because sound carries out here. I don't want to get married until at least after you finish this year of your classes, and I get my welding certification. We might move into the cabin until we can get a place of our own."

"Fine!" She laughed. "I'll need some time to plan, anyway. And I'm in love with that cabin."

"And one more thing."

He whispered the next words in her ear. "What about the whole house full of kids issue? If that's a deal breaker ..."

"Marshal Cody Billings." She sat back and looked directly into his big brown eyes.

"What?"

"Hush. I already said *Yes*, and you're *not* talking me out of it."

He raised both of his hands with thumbs up.

"What are you doing?" Had he really done that?

"They were instructed to wait for the signal before sharing any pictures."

She giggled uncontrollably. This was certainly not the reaction most people had to a marriage proposal. But this man was not 'most people.' He was the one she'd waited for. The one God had selected just for her. She relaxed into his arms to cheers from his brothers, and of course, Junior.

Thank you, Lord. Your plan is perfect, and it never fails. Amen.

The following June.

Cody used his right hand to navigate his power chair up the long hill, with Kayla in his lap, his left arm holding her firmly in place.

"Wait." She reached down to gather her huge skirt into her lap.

He readjusted his grip. This dress was nothing like the outfit she'd been wearing for the rehearsal.

"Thanks again for this necklace." She touched the turquoise stone at her neck. "It's perfect with my bracelet. I had Mom and Dad and you all close to my heart all day."

"You're welcome." He pressed his lips against hers, his right hand leaving the wheelchair controls to dive into her pinned up hair.

"Happy?" She asked as he allowed her to take a breath.

"Couldn't be happier." He smiled, fighting back tears. "Hold on!" He reached down to his right, moving them up the hill as they were pelted with birdseed.

"You hold on too." She tightened her grip around his neck.

"Your chariot, Mrs. Billings." He stopped next to his truck.

"Wait! I'm still holding the bouquet. I'm supposed to throw it!"

Kayla stood next to him as a mob of young girls huffed and puffed up the hill. She lofted the flowers high in the air.

Junior dove in to intercept the bundle before the closest squealing teen could grab it.

"What? Can you believe that?" Kayla laughed.

"Of course. Wouldn't expect any less." Cody waved at his buddy. "Okay. Now can we leave?" He helped her tuck her skirt in before closing the door.

"I should let you drive. I don't know where we're going." He settled in after securing his chair.

"It's not far. Turn left at the end of Shoe Tree Road."

He drove toward the end of the road, catching a glimpse of Junior with flowers raised in victory.

"What are you dragging?" Kayla leaned out to look back.

"I think it's shoes!" He laughed.

"No problem. Stop at the end of the road."

She jumped out and ran to the back of the truck.

"The mural your mom painted on the back of the new sign needs christening." Kayla dropped the skirt of her wedding dress as she untied the bundle of shoes, draping them over the sign. She gathered up the billowy fabric again as she climbed back into the truck.

"Okay, now what?"

"Keep driving. The gate is unlatched."

The late summer sun reflected off a new addition to "their" overlook.

"What's this?" Cody stopped the truck.

"You said if you had a proper tent, you might never leave. Ever heard of 'glamping?' There's electricity, a portable air conditioner, and even a fancy port-a-potty over there." She pointed to the edge of the clearing.

"You're amazing, Mrs. Billings." He laughed. He'd never seen a platform tent with a ramp before.

"Wait 'til you see the inside. Fully furnished studio. Bed, dining set, refrigerator, and camp stove included." Kayla climbed out of the truck after he parked.

"Ranch detective, firefighter, budding architect, and honeymoon planner." He shook his head.

"Come on, I want to show you the inside before it gets dark." She led the way up the ramp.

"There can't be a better view than the one I have right here." He caught up to her and pulled her back into his lap. "I love you Kayla Grace Caldwell Billings."

"So glad to hear that, Marshal Cody, sir." She grinned.

He reached up to pull the string that dropped the tent flaps.

"Kayla," he whispered.

"What?"

"Stop talking." He covered her mouth with his.

You're amazing, God. My steps couldn't have been directed any better.

The End

Acknowledgments

"I can do all things through Christ who strengthens me." Philippians 4:13 NKJV

Thanks to our son Chris. I can still get free legal advice until he officially passes the bar and "hangs up his shingle."

Apologies to our grandson, Austin. I used your first name and your appearance as a misguided character in this book. I know you would have behaved better than this guy.

Elena Hill, whose brainstorming about day-to-day life on the farm got me thinking about modern-day cattle rustlers.

Cody Burkham, Executive Vice President of the Arkansas Cattleman's Association, who actually responded to the "contact us" button on the Association's website. Thanks for your patience with my totally off-the-wall questions. You were a tremendous help.

Tyler Rollins and Micah Stafford, who helped me understand what Cody's life would be like, and even helped me find him a job. Micah, I still fully intend to come to a Rolling Razorbacks game when the season starts again!

Jerome Davis, for the inspirational articles I read about his life following his life-changing accident.

Michael at Walking Eagle Fishing, whose innovative boat inspired Cody's graduation present and then his employment. Someday, I hope to take a fishing trip to your beautiful backyard.

Tonya Ashley and her fire-fighting son and husband for their expertise in Arkansas rural fire department response to brushfires.

Brannon McMinn and his mom, Stacy. I continue to be inspired by your posts about thriving after a terrible bull-riding accident. We never got to meet in person because you have such a busy life. That is a blessing in itself. Please know that my prayers for you and your family continue.

The help I received from my God-sent critique partner Julane Hiebert was immeasurable for this third book in the series. You told me it would be the most difficult, and it was. Thanks for helping me weed through all the stories I wanted to tell to concentrate on what was most important.

Everyone at Scrivening Press, especially my content editor, Amy Anguish. You have more patience than the law allows, and I love the way you buy into my vision for the community and people of Crossroads.

My best friend and business manager, my husband James, had to be incredibly patient with my poor deadline management. Yes, sweetheart, now that I've turned in the manuscript, we can be married again.

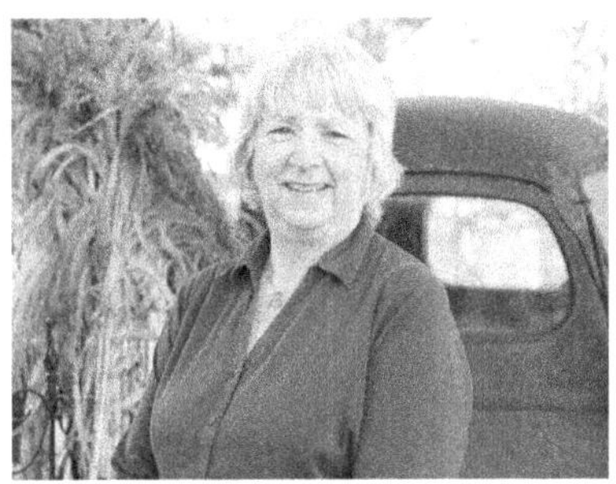

Jenny McLeod Carlisle had a happy childhood in a small midwestern town. She and her younger sister had the love and support of their hard-working mother, as well as a church family and lots of friends and neighbors. Only five years old when divorce took away her favorite reading buddy, Jenny included her Daddy in her life by making him her first pen pal.

When her mom's second marriage took them to Arkansas, she quickly acclimated to a smaller high school. New friends introduced her to a wonderful young man who became her prom date, and then her husband. Instead of finishing college, Jenny and James built a family that included three children with two working parents.

Jenny pursued her dream of becoming a fiction author by joining writers' support groups. She attended conferences and entered contests while learning all she could about writing a marketable book. She is a past president of American Fiction Christian Writers-Arkansas Chapter.

Her inspirational articles appeared in Gospel Tidings, a national publication of the Churches of Christ. She was a columnist for Ouachita Life magazine for over ten years. Two self-published non-fiction books share memories of the past and encouragement for the future.

Scrivenings Press published the first two books in the Crossroads Series, *Hope Takes the Reins* and *Faith Moves Mountains* in 2022 and 2023. A collection of Christmas novellas called *A Gift for All Time* includes her story, "Rejoicing with Joy."

Now retired from the State of Arkansas, Jenny and her husband love to travel together, especially for adventures that include their three married children and eight grandchildren. On Saturdays in the fall, you can find them either in the stadium or in front of the television cheering for the Arkansas Razorbacks. On Sunday, they worship with the Church of Christ.

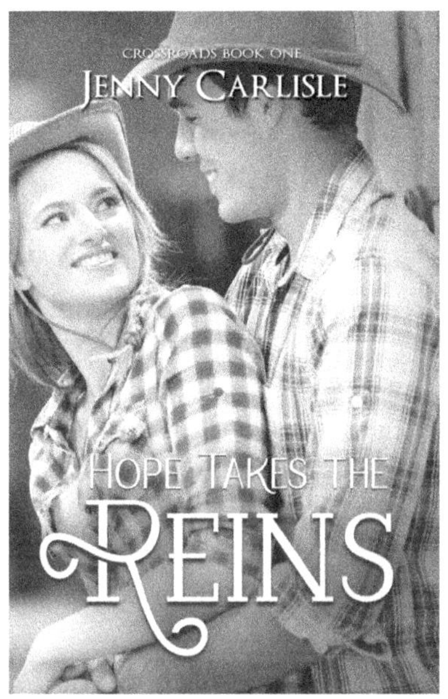

Hope Takes the Reins

Crossroads Series—Book One

O.D. Billings has lived in the shadow of his brothers all his life. Even his name brings him down, so he has used only initials for years. Now, his older brother has returned home from the army, rejecting the role his family expects him to assume in their pickup truck dealership, and the younger brother is intent on risking his life on the back of a bucking bull. O.D.'s fans at the rodeo love his confident swagger during tie-down roping competitions, but every trail he heads down on his own seems to wind up going nowhere.

Hope Caldwell's world is still reeling after her mom's recent death from cancer. She thrives on keeping the family's rodeo business going. Getting back to normal seems impossible when she overhears her uncle's plans to sell out. How can she continue without the only way of life she has known for all of her nineteen years? Can she rely on the help of a big-talking cowboy? Or does he have too many problems of his own?

Get your copy here:

scrivenings.link/hopetakesthereins

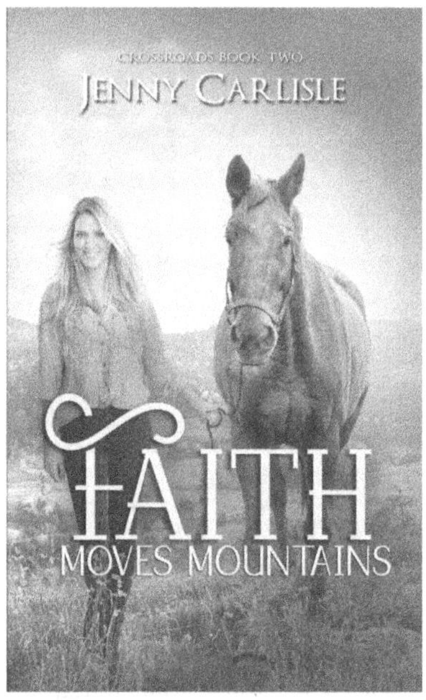

Faith Moves Mountains by Jenny Carlisle

Book Two in the Crossroads Series

John Kennedy (John K.) Billings has spent his whole life living up to his hero inspired name. Now, back from a traumatic incident in the military, he finds himself running from the fact that he is only human, with real-life struggles to overcome.

Faith Caldwell feels free to pursue her own dreams now that her family's regularly scheduled rodeo has ended. After helping care for her cancer-stricken mother she is determined to bring big city medical expertise to small-town Arkansas. While trying to prove she can fulfill her dream on her own, a new admirer seems determined to pull her down.

Both enjoy the idea of seeing more of the world, but find their hearts are still tied to the mountains of Arkansas, and the people who live there.

Can these lifelong neighbors help each other face their weaknesses while following God's plan for their lives?

Get your copy here:

https://scrivenings.link/faithmovesmountains

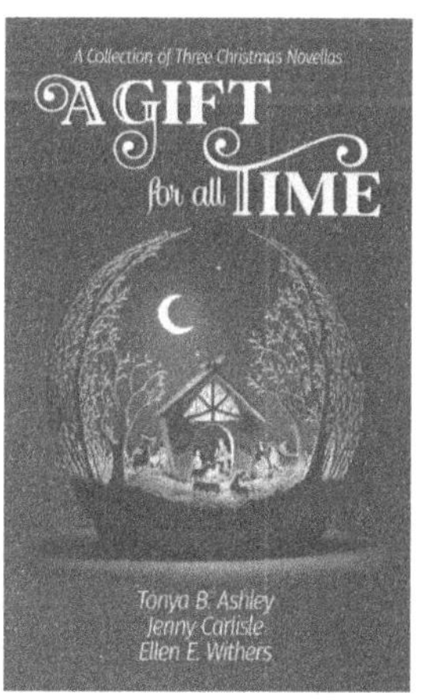

A Collection of Three Christmas Novellas

Includes "Rejoicing with Joy" by Jenny Carlisle

Joy Fredericks is trying to keep her Christmas spirit alive while her tiny hometown is emptying rapidly. Without the traditions that put

Snowville, Arkansas, on the map, will she soon be the only one left who cares?

Former rodeo clown Junior Caldwell brings a spark of hope, but with obstacles at every turn, can they focus on the reason for the celebration, that tiny baby who changed everything?

https://scrivenings.link/agiftforalltime